No Villain Need Be

As Dell Shannon:

CASE PENDING
THE ACES OF SPADES
EXTRA KILL
KNAVE OF HEARTS
DEATH OF A BUSYBODY
DOUBLE BLUFF
ROOT OF ALL EVIL
MARK OF MURDER
THE DEATH-BRINGERS
DEATH BY INCHES
COFFIN CORNER
WITH A VENGEANCE
CHANCE TO KILL
RAIN WITH VIOLENCE
KILL WITH KINDNESS

SCHOOLED TO KILL
CRIME ON THEIR HANDS
UNEXPECTED DEATH
WHIM TO KILL
THE RINGER
MURDER WITH LOVE
WITH INTENT TO KILL
NO HOLIDAY FOR CRIME
SPRING OF VIOLENCE
CRIME FILE
DEUCES WILD
STREETS OF DEATH
APPEARANCES OF DEATH
COLD TRAIL
FELONY AT RANDOM

As Elizabeth Linington:

NO VILLAIN NEED BE
PERCHANCE OF DEATH
THE PROUD MAN
THE LONG WATCH
MONSIEUR JANVIER
THE KINGBREAKER
POLICEMAN'S LOT

ELIZABETH I (*Ency. Brit.*)
GREENMASK!
NO EVIL ANGEL
DATE WITH DEATH
SOMETHING WRONG
PRACTISE TO DECEIVE
CRIME BY CHANCE

As Egan O'Neill:

THE ANGLOPHILE

As Lesley Egan:

A CASE FOR APPEAL
THE BORROWED ALIBI
AGAINST THE EVIDENCE
RUN TO EVIL
MY NAME IS DEATH
DETECTIVE'S DUE
A SERIOUS INVESTIGATION
THE WINE OF VIOLENCE

IN THE DEATH OF A MAN
MALICIOUS MISCHIEF
PAPER CHASE
SCENES OF CRIME
THE BLIND SEARCH
A DREAM APART
LOOK BACK ON DEATH

No Villain Need Be

ELIZABETH LININGTON

DOUBLEDAY & COMPANY, INC.

GARDEN CITY, NEW YORK

All of the characters in this book
are fictitious, and any resemblance
to actual persons, living or dead,
is purely coincidental.

For my old friends

Arthur Bridge,
Barbara and Paul

In tragic life, God wot,
No villain need be! Passions spin the plot;
We are betrayed by what is false within.

Modern Love, George Meredith

No Villain Need Be

ONE

Maddox came into the kitchen knotting his tie; they were late, and he'd only have time for coffee. Sue, still in her robe, was pouring it. "I must say," she observed, getting half-and-half from the refrigerator, "it'd be more convenient if we had the same day off. As it is, if I do find a possible house, you'll have to go look at it too—"

"It'd be even more convenient," said Maddox caustically, "if we knew what size house we wanted."

"Oh, well, I suppose we do," said Sue. "We'll never argue Mother around, Ivor."

"Want to bet?"

"I know, you're her fair-haired boy, but I don't think you can persuade her now. Our timing was all wrong. We had the bright idea of all of us living together just after she'd been talking about finding a part-time job because of the dividends being down and inflation, and she got the notion we were offering charity or something—"

"And I never thought I'd see the day I was annoyed at your mother. It's really the only answer, after all."

"Try to tell her."

"Oh, I haven't given up yet." Maddox swallowed coffee hastily. "You go look at some four-bedroom places. Damn, I'll be late." He got up and bent to kiss her. "Good luck."

"Have fun chasing the burglars," said Sue.

Heading uptown in the little blue Maserati, Maddox reflected that they were spending a good part of their time on burglars these days, and with very little result. In the nature of things, there was seldom any good solid lead to the burglars; they spent a lot of time on legwork which didn't often pay off, and nine times out of ten when they did nail some X for a job, the court accepted a plea bargain and let him off with nine months in the slammer, or even probation.

Of course there were other things on hand than the burglars, though they'd like to catch up to the team of daylight burglars who had been cleaning out whole households while everybody was at work. There was nine-year-old Harold Frost, abducted, sexually attacked and strangled last month; and now there was ten-year-old Freddy Noonan, reported missing last Friday afternoon and found in the street on Saturday morning, strangled. That looked like the same X, and one they'd like to drop on right quick. There was also the heister, by the description the same one, who had held up a pharmacy, an all-night dairy store and a bar in the last two weeks. None of the witnesses had picked a mug shot, and there weren't any leads on that; but witnesses weren't always reliable, and it was back to legwork, chasing down men with likely pedigrees and checking alibis. And the thankless job being what it was, doubtless new cases would go down today and tomorrow, and on and on.

He caught the light at Wilcox and Fountain and glanced across the street at his destination rather fondly. The Hollywood precinct had had a present from the city fathers a couple of months ago: a brand-new precinct station. They had known it was in the works, but the city had taken its own time finishing it; the move had finally been made a couple of months ago, in October. They hadn't had to move so much as a typewriter; everything in the building was new—the old Social Services Building, given a new face and completely remodeled inside. It occupied the whole block on Fountain Avenue, between Wilcox and Cole, a long one-story building painted creamy beige, with a flat roof. There were two strips of well-kept green lawn in front, and red brick planters against the building filled with bright yellow daisies, and a handsome pair of double doors up two low steps. It had given them nearly double the space they'd had at the old Wilcox Street precinct house, and had boosted morale considerably; sometimes cops felt that the city fathers consistently overlooked them. In the early morning sun of this crisp January day, the building was handsome and gleaming, with the bold black lettering above the double front doors: **Los Angeles Police Department, 6501 Fountain Avenue.**

The new building didn't have a jail; that had been left behind at Wilcox Street.

He turned left on Cole and into the big parking lot behind the station. Heading for the back door, he caught up with Rodriguez just going in.

"Any bets on what went down overnight?" asked Rodriguez.

"More heists. All the burglars seem to operate in daylight now. What I'm interested in seeing," said Maddox, "is the autopsy on the Noonan boy. If he was sodomized, you know it was the same joker who killed the Frost kid."

"I'd take a bet." They went into the big rectangular detective office. D'Arcy was already there, lounging at his desk, talking on the phone. Feinman was typing a report; Sergeant George Ellis was reading one. At the end of the room Sergeant Daisy Hoffman was just uncovering her typewriter, and Joe Rowan came in just after Maddox and Rodriguez.

Ellis, the senior sergeant, was concentrating on the counterfeiters who'd been scattering phony twenties all over town for the last month; he was talking more to Secret Service men than his own men lately. The night-watch report had been left on Maddox's desk, and he sat down, loosened his tie, lit a cigarette and scanned it rapidly.

There had been a fatal accident off Mulholland Drive just as the night watch had come on: a Mrs. Louise Sexton. Donaldson had clipped a note to the initial report: "Dick and I both think something funny about this one—can't put a finger on it, but see what you think." Maddox skimmed the report: three-year-old Chrysler apparently out of control, over the embankment, totaled at the bottom of the hill, the woman thrown out with apparent fatal injuries. The car would be hauled in for examination; eventually there'd be an autopsy report. The husband, Herbert Sexton, address on Pyramid Drive, would be in sometime this afternoon to make a statement.

There had also been a heist at a pharmacy on Fairfax. No description: the heister had been wearing a ski mask. There had also been a brawl in a bar on Santa Monica Boulevard that had left a man dead of a knifing. The knife wielder had got away but the bartender knew him, Manfred Guttierez; he lived on Poinsettia. Brougham and Donaldson had gone to look, but the apartment was empty. They'd got a make on his car from the computers and put out an A.P.B.

Under the night-watch report on his desk was another one, evidently sent up after change of shift last night. He slid it out of the manila envelope, and it was the autopsy report on Freddy Noonan. "What did I say?" said Maddox to Rodriguez. "Here it is —the Noonan boy was sodomized and manually strangled. That's the same joker, César, it's got to be, and it's an educated guess he's just hit town from somewhere else. We haven't had that kind of homicide in a while."

"What does that say?" countered Rodriguez, taking the report. "Any of the little nuts can graduate into big nuts overnight. He might have been right here for years, started out as a flasher, gone on to bribing kids with candy to get his nasty little kicks and just now gone in for the bigger kick."

"True," said Maddox, rubbing his chin, "but two within—what is it?—twenty days—I don't know, César."

D'Arcy came over and perched one hip on Maddox's desk. "You'll be happy to know," he said, "that the D.A.'s office has decided to charge Hogan with involuntary manslaughter instead of Murder Two."

Both Maddox and Rodriguez uttered various rude words. "For God's sake," said Rodriguez, "how unrealistic can those legal eagles get? But it's par for the course, all right." Alfred Hogan, last month, with nearly a fifth of whiskey inside, had beaten his wife to death. On the lesser charge, he would be back on the streets in a year or less, and quite likely to kill somebody else the next time he got drunk.

Maddox handed D'Arcy the report on Guttierez. "Suppose you go see if he's come home yet. Ken doesn't seem to have checked for him in Records—we might ask if he's there. I suppose we'll see some photographs of this accident sometime—I wonder if they've brought the car in yet, a hell of a job—and somebody'll have to talk to the husband. I wonder what struck Ken funny about it." The phone buzzed on his desk and he picked it up, looking at the autopsy report again. "Sergeant Maddox."

"I've got a new one for you," said Patrolman Gonzales. "Homicide. It looks a little offbeat."

"Where?" asked Maddox resignedly.

"Kingsley Drive. You'd better bring one of the girls. I've got a kid here pretty shook up, little girl."

"It's my wife's day off. O.K., we'll be along." Maddox went over to get Daisy, hunched over her typewriter. He called the lab and passed on the address. D'Arcy and Rodriguez went out to look for Guttierez; that was a simple thing, a matter of picking him up, and then they could get back to the legwork on the heisters. Maddox and Daisy went out to the parking lot and started for the new homicide in Maddox's car. Trim blonde Daisy Hoffman didn't look like the grandmother she was; she'd be useful at soothing any shaken-up youngster.

At the address on Kingsley, which was an old frame duplex on a quiet block of older homes, Gonzales was leaning against the hood of the black-and-white waiting for them. They could see somebody else, somebody small, in the back seat. There weren't any curious neighbors out at all; this would be a neighborhood of working people, most of them away all day. Gonzales came forward as Maddox and Daisy got out of the car.

"The kid's aunt is on the way," he said. "From La Crescenta. I don't know what to make of this one. It was the kid called in. When she woke up, she says, Mama wasn't there. She thought maybe she'd gone next door—the other side of the duplex—but the door was locked and nobody answered. So she called her aunt, and the aunt told her to call us. When I got here I checked the back, and it was open, so I went in—" An ambulance siren came screaming nearer. "One of them is still alive— That's for her. I—"

"Damn paramedics trampling all over evidence," said Maddox, annoyed. "Which side?" Gonzales indicated the left side of the duplex, and Maddox went around to the back. There was a screen door, a solid wooden door half open. He used his pen to hook the screen open, shoved the door wider, went in. The kitchen, small and square, was very neat and clean, no dishes visible; the refrigerator hummed. At one end a door led into a living room, long and narrow, furnished with a pleasant miscellany of old pieces; it too was neat except for one of the end tables beside the couch, which had been knocked over and spilled a milk-glass lamp, an ashtray, a vase. A scatter rug in the doorway at the end of that room was a crumpled heap. Maddox edged through that door to a narrow little hall; through a door opposite was the front bedroom.

They were both in there: two women looking to be in the mid-thirties, one dark and one blonde. The blonde was dead, obviously beaten and possibly raped; she was naked, and clothes were scattered around the room, a brassiere torn in half, a pair of ripped panties, a navy-blue dress, slip. The other woman was dressed in a housecoat and bedroom slippers; she was unconscious, breathing hoarsely, lying half across the double bed, half on the floor.

The ambulance attendants came in and Maddox said automatically, "Don't touch anything." They got her on a stretcher and he followed them out.

There was another car behind the Maserati, an old Ford with one front door open and Daisy standing beside it. He went up there.

"What's happened?" The woman in the car, who held the little girl tightly on her lap, looked frightened and bewildered. "I can't imagine where Ruth would be—she'd never leave Emily alone— Doesn't Lisa know anything? I just can't— I got here as soon as I could—"

"Just a minute." Maddox raised an arm at the ambulance attendants. "Would you take a look and see if you know this woman, Mrs.—"

"Carradine. Rose Carradine." She relinquished the child to Daisy and hurried after Maddox; the attendants were waiting by the open doors of the ambulance. "Oh, my God, it's Ruth! What happened to her? I can't imagine what— Where was she?"

"Your sister?" Maddox nodded at the attendants and steered her back toward the car. "What's her name?"

"Ruth Butler. But what—where—"

"I know you want to find out how she is, Mrs. Carradine, but we don't know what happened here and we'll have some questions for you. There's another woman in there, dead."

"Oh, my God—not Lisa?" she asked, horrified.

"I don't know. Lisa who?"

"Lisa Martin. She owns this place."

"Is she blonde, around thirty-five, thin?"

"Yes— Oh, it is Lisa— My God, what happened?"

The mobile lab truck pulled up, turned into the drive, and Rowan and Dabney got out of it. There wasn't any need to tell them what do do; Maddox waved them in and looked at Mrs. Carradine speculatively. She was probably a little older than her sister, dark hair going gray, a little too plump, motherly-looking, dressed in a neat cotton dress and cardigan; she was upset and shocked, but under control. He looked at the little girl beside her. Maybe about ten? He didn't know much about children. She was a thin, leggy child with a good deal of curly blonde hair and big blue eyes. She looked shaken up all right, but like her aunt, in control of herself and not crying.

"Did either your sister or Mrs. Martin have a car?"

"Yes, of course. Ruth has an old Chevy, but it's in the garage for a new transmission, she was worried about the bill. Lisa's got a Datsun."

"Um." Maddox went up the drive; there was a single garage at the rear, detached, and the door wasn't locked. He looked in. The Datsun was sitting there. He went back down the drive. "Look," he said gently, "I'll have some questions for both of you, if Emily feels up to it." Emily inclined her head stiffly.

"That's Mama in the ambulance, wasn't it? Is she going to be all right?"

"We certainly hope so. Now if you wouldn't mind, Mrs. Carradine, Mrs. Hoffman will ride back with you, show you where to come, and we'll talk at the office. Then you can check with the hospital and see how your sister is."

"Yes. All right. But I just can't imagine—" She got into the car obediently.

On the way back to the station, Maddox reflected that one annoying thing about this job, to which you had to adjust the best you could, was that you were continually forced to quit one case in the middle and transfer attention to another. Now he wanted to get back to Freddy Noonan's parents again, to the legwork on that; there was also the heister, and the daylight burglars. But crime was no respecter of detectives' routines; crime was always very untidy.

He led them into the parking lot and took them in the back way, settled them in two chairs beside Daisy's desk, perched on the edge of the desk and smiled at Emily. "Can you tell us about the beginning of this? From what Patrolman Gonzales said, you're the one called the police."

She nodded again. "Aunt Rose said to. He was very nice. I never met a policeman before, but Mama says they're mostly nice.

He said he's got a little girl just my size too. But I don't know what happened to Mama— I don't know your name."

"Sergeant Maddox. When did you first find your mother was gone?"

"When I woke up. The alarm didn't go off so I didn't wake up till way late. We always get up at seven so I can be ready for school and Mama can do the dishes and make the beds before she goes to work—"

"She works at the Bank of America," said Mrs. Carradine. "So does Lisa—it's how they got to know each other—Lisa owns the house, and they took to each other, and the other side was vacant — Ruth's lived there nearly five years—"

"And it was nearly eight o'clock and Mama wasn't anywhere, and her bed was all made up. I went next door to see if she was at Aunt Lisa's, but the door was locked, and I didn't know what to do, so I called Aunt Rose on the phone."

"You kept your head just fine, dear," said Mrs. Carradine. "But for the life of me I can't imagine—"

"When did you see your mother last, Emily?" asked Daisy.

"Oh, last night when I went to bed. At eight-thirty. She came into my room like always and heard my prayers and kissed me good night and turned off the light. And I guess I went to sleep pretty soon."

"Did you hear anything in the night? Screams or loud noises?"

Emily shook her head. "I don't think so. I could've, and maybe just thought it was dreams."

"She's a heavy sleeper," said Mrs. Carradine. "I've never known Ruth to leave her alone at night—" Suddenly she said sharply, "Oh! Oh, but I just thought—that could be it! It could be!"

"What?" asked Maddox.

"Why, if some robber broke in on Lisa's side! You see, two women alone—Lisa was divorced, and Ruth lost Emily's father six years ago, he was killed in an accident—and you know how the crime rate's up, terrible things going on all over, and they were both nervous. They never went out much, both sort of home-bodies, you could say, and that was one reason. Lisa had the best kind of locks in that place, but things can happen— They both kept all the doors locked tight all the time—but just in case, they had a code, you see."

"A code?"

"Yes—in case either of them needed help. They'd knock three times on the wall between. And I just suddenly thought, if somebody broke in on Lisa's side and she knocked for Ruth to come—"

"Um," said Maddox. Nobody had broken in the front door, but the lab men might turn up something at the back. "It's an idea." But if there'd been a fight in there, it was funny the little girl hadn't heard any screams or thuds. Had the neighbors? City people tended to be curiously apathetic about things like that: the don't-want-to-get-involved syndrome. They would be asked. "Has your sister any men friends? Or did Mrs. Martin?"

Mrs. Carradine shook her head decisively. "It was a terrible blow to her, losing Bob. And it takes all her time, working and looking after Emily—she wouldn't be interested in another man. Lisa wasn't either, she was studying hard for a promotion at the bank." She groped for a handkerchief and blew her nose. "Oh, dear, I can't take it in—she was such a nice woman, they were such good friends—the awful things that go on, to think of Lisa getting murdered! Please, I would like to find out about Ruth, if— and I'll take Emily home with me, of course."

"That's fine. Just leave us your address," said Maddox. He left Daisy to type up the initial report and drove back to the duplex on Kingsley.

He found Rowan and Dabney dusting for prints. It was one of the motions they went through, and now and then it paid off, but considering the time it took, it was another annoyance that it so seldom turned up a lead.

"What's the word?" he asked.

"Well, nobody broke in here," said Rowan. "Good dead-bolt locks on both back and front doors. I picked up two pretty good latents on the knob of the back door, but they may be hers, of course. I'll go down to the morgue and get hers before we look at them. The morgue wagon's just left. You can see there was a struggle of some kind in here."

"Yes." They were in the bedroom, and there had been a fight here all right, but possibly not a prolonged one. The curtain rod was pulled halfway down; the table beside the bed was knocked over; the bed had been made up, but the spread was pulled off half onto the floor. There didn't seem to be any blood around. Maddox stood looking at the room, and gradually a graphic little scene formed in his mind. "She let him in?" he said to himself. "Somebody she knew, if only casually, and wouldn't hesitate to let in. And then he—um—made the unwelcome advances, and she jumped up and knocked on the wall for Ruth to come and help her. And all that says is—"

"Who's Ruth?" asked Dabney.

Maddox told them absently. "All that says, he must have been big and powerful, if he got hold of her and knocked her out before she could scream. We'll ask the neighbors if they heard anything. And he went out the back door and left it open. Well, we'll just hope that Ruth will make it and tell us something about him." He looked around the little house, but there was nothing to contradict what Mrs. Carradine had told them. It was a modest, decently furnished house lived in by a woman living a humdrum, respectable life—closet neat, kitchen clean, furniture dusted. Probably Mrs. Butler's side looked much the same.

He went back to the office and called the hospital. Ruth Butler had sustained a beating and had a depressed skull fracture. She was in surgery now; there was every expectation that she would recover, but it would probably be some time before the police could interview her.

However, that was something.

———◆———

D'Arcy and Rodriguez had turned up a petty pedigree for Manfred Guttierez: one count of B. and E., one of shoplifting. He hadn't shown at the apartment on Poinsettia or the garage on La Brea, where he worked. It was to be hoped the A.P.B. would turn him up eventually. It would only add up to involuntary manslaughter.

About that time Maddox came back and filled them in on the new homicide. "Wait and see if those latents do us any good. Meanwhile, the Noonan boy—we'll have to talk to the parents again, but what the hell they could tell us—he was supposedly on his way home from school."

"Like the other one, Harold Frost." Rodriguez sat back in his chair, fingering his neat moustache thoughtfully; his eyes strayed around the room with absent approval. The city fathers, once they decided to be generous, had done the job thoroughly. There was smart and practical dark gray vinyl flooring, large metal desks, brand-new standard typewriters, efficient fluorescent strip lighting; the big room was airy and bright. The view out the tall windows was uninspiring, just the parking lot outside, but in comparison with the tired old Wilcox Street station, it was elegance. "And the parents said—just like the Noonans—that he'd been warned about strangers, he'd never have got into a strange car or anything like that. But it occurred to me at the time, Ivor, parents are apt to stress the warning about strangers to little girls, but not so much to little boys, because the nutty strangers are more apt to go for little girls."

"Which is so," agreed D'Arcy thoughtfully. "But—look, say he pulled a car over, called to the kid and asked directions, say even if the kid came over to the car, could he have yanked him in by force without anybody noticing? The Frost kid would have been walking up La Brea, a main drag—"

"And eventually turning onto Waring, not such a main drag," said Maddox. "It's probably not much use going at it from that end—it's back to legwork, taking a look at every nut with a sex hangup in our books, hauling them in to lean on. But I've still got a gut feeling that he's new in town."

"Gut feelings provide no leads," said D'Arcy. He uncoiled his lanky seventy-six inches and stood up. "Let's go have lunch."

◆

Sue looked around the living room of this latest house the real estate agent had brought her to and said, "Well, the bedrooms are rather small. And the yard—"

"Prices these days, you know, Mrs. Maddox," said Mr. Parrott, and cast his eyes expressively upwards. "Unless you can afford to go over a hundred thousand—"

Sue felt even more annoyed at her mother than she had been. Timing! she thought. Margaret Carstairs had been twenty years younger than Sue's father; he had left her a comfortable estate invested in sound stocks. But lately the dividends hadn't been keeping up with inflation. And after the little Welsh corgi Gor had

died at the age of sixteen, a couple of months ago, she'd been a little lonely, talked about a part-time job; she was only fifty-one, she
said, and ought to be able to find something to help out the dividends. And so, when the Maddoxes had decided they had better
buy a house before prices went up any more, and suggested they
all go in together, she had taken it as charity. Old people, she said
briskly (not that she felt all that old), ought not to live with young
people, it wasn't fair to either.

The thing was ridiculous, thought Sue, because they all did get
along so well. Her mother thought Ivor was a paragon, and he was
fond of her. And she owned the house on Janiel Terrace, and
while much of Hollywood was run-down these days and not the
most desirable place to live, the house would be worth at least
fifty thousand, and if she put that toward the new place it would
lower the payments so much. And if Sue ever did succeed in starting a baby, it would be so convenient—the really silly thing about
it was that she knew her mother would adore living with a family
again, she was just being stubborn.

"You did like the house in Toluca Lake," said Mr. Parrott.

"Well, yes," said Sue. They had agreed, not Hollywood; there
were quieter, nicer areas around, in easy driving distance. She'd
looked at houses in Burbank, Glendale, North Hollywood. "Only
three bedrooms, of course." Suddenly she decided to be reckless
and pin all faith on Ivor's persuasiveness and her mother's weak-
ness for him. Somehow they would bring her round. "I think I'd
rather have four." Just in case. They had said two children. If she
could ever get started. "That place in Burbank—how much was
it?"

He shuffled papers in his briefcase. "Ninety-nine thousand."

"I'd like to look at it again," said Sue.

Mr. Parrott sighed.

———◆———

D'Arcy and Rodriguez went out to see the Noonans, and Maddox went back to the office after lunch. There was a new manila
envelope on his desk. Feinman was the only one in. "Where've
you been?" asked Maddox.

"George roped me in to chase up a suspect. That damned counterfeiting ring—it's the Secret Service's job, not local police, they're fouling up all our routine."

"Well, you can switch back to the local scene for a while. I'm told we've got somebody coming in to make a statement." Maddox opened the envelope and a lot of glossy 8 x 10's slid out of it. "Well, helpful." They were the shots taken last night of the accident off Mulholland, the accident Brougham and Donaldson thought was a funny one. He looked at them interestedly.

The descriptions inked on the backs pinpointed the location. Off Mulholland Drive just south of Pacific View. He thought that was one of the straighter stretches of Mulholland, not particularly steep or curving. The embankment still steep, a long drop down the hill, but a good wide road. The shots had been taken at eight-forty, after dark, but the floodlights had lit up the scene eerily. Feinman came over and Maddox passed them on to him one by one.

"I see what Ken means, in a way." The bank was steep, but unless Louise Sexton had been drunk, or suddenly taken ill or fainted, there wasn't any reason for her to have gone over the edge. The car, upside down, was a good three hundred feet down the side of the hill, but Louise Sexton wasn't. Her body was plainly visible not sixty feet down, sprawled head first down the steep slope. There was just low brush on those slopes, no trees.

"Some people never fasten seat belts," said Feinman. He brushed a hand over his dark hair; his long saturnine face looked faintly cynical.

Maddox massaged his jaw, which was beginning to show faint blue stubble even at this hour. "I guess we've all seen enough accidents where people would have been killed if they had had the damned things fastened—but enough of the other kind too. And a good many citizens just refuse to use'em because they're damned annoyed at the government trying to tell them what to do, and amen to that. But it is—or was—a four-door sedan, Joe."

"A Chrysler, I make out. So?"

"And it was cold last night. The address is Pyramid Drive. I take it she was coming from or going to. Coming from likeliest, the hill is on the right side of Mulholland. How come there were any windows open? Front windows?"

"Oh. I see what you mean," said Feinman. "That is a little funny."

Maddox found a magnifying glass in his desk and peered through it at all the shots showing the body. "She was wearing a coat all right, but it doesn't look like a very heavy one. How the hell was she thrown out of the car just after it went over? Out of a front window—the only way she could have gone—"

Feinman said mildly, "People. There's this old friend of my wife's. She never drives with the driver's window up. Raining like hell, cold, whatever, it's open. She says she gets claustrophobia, it isn't open."

"Yes," said Maddox, "but she must be an exception. Well, we haven't heard chapter and verse on this yet. But—"

"Excuse me," said an incisive voice. They both turned. "The desk sergeant said to come in here. About the accident last night— Mrs. Sexton. My name is Richard Troy. My wife, Thelma. Mr. and Mrs. Ray Gibson."

"Yes, sir?" They were two exceedingly handsome couples. The girls in the middle or late twenties, both dark, both good-looking, though both had evidently been crying and looked rather ravaged. Troy was tall, dark and rugged, Gibson stockier and sandy, both sharply dressed in conservative business suits.

"Thelma and Amy are Mrs. Sexton's daughters," said Troy. "We thought we had better make a statement to the police."

"Yes, sir?"

Thelma blurted out, "Because he's going to tell you a pack of lies—that man! We don't know what happened, but Mother just couldn't have had an accident like that—she lived in the house thirty years, she could drive Mulholland practically blindfolded! That man—he must have had something to do with it— Oh, we tried to tell her, but she just wouldn't listen! She said we were being jealous and silly, but we weren't! Daddy died ten years ago, and of course she missed him, of course she was lonely—they used to go out a lot—but we never thought *Mother* would do such a thing, fall for a—a—a con man! Whatever you want to call him— anybody could see he was just interested in the money. I don't mean Mother hadn't kept herself up, she did, she was a nice-looking woman, but she wasn't young, she was fifty-seven—she just fell for his line like a teen-ager—"

"Thelma, let's calm down and tell it in order," said her husband.

"That's water under the bridge," said Amy Gibson in a soft voice. "Simmer down, Thel. The point is what he tried to feed us last night—after we found out about the accident. Mother telling him she was going out to dinner and a play with us. How he found out afterward she'd had a couple of drinks before she left. So surprised, he was, when we didn't know anything about the dinner or play—she must have lied for some reason. Which is simply silly. Mother liked a drink before dinner, but she never drove after she'd had even one. She was still absolutely crazy about the man, and convinced he was about her. She didn't like to drive at night anyway. I don't know what happened, but I know Mother never started down that road after she'd been drinking, and ran the car over the side. She knew that road, as Thel says. She'd driven for forty years and never had a ticket even for overtime parking. There's something very queer about that accident, and you'd better look into it."

Maddox and Feinman regarded the quartet interestedly. Maddox put his finger accurately on the one suggestive word. "Money?" he said. "Your mother was well off?"

"You could say so," said Amy Gibson. "Daddy left her about three million. And real estate. And so far as we know, when she married that man, she made a will leaving most of it to him outright. You couldn't talk to her—it was just as if she was hypnotized. We always thought Mother had good sense, but—"

"I beg your pardon." It was a soft, pleasant voice, hesitant and refined. "The sergeant directed me here. I'm Herbert Sexton—about the sad accident to my dear wife last night."

TWO

There didn't seem to be any point to getting a free-for-all started, to disturb Ellis huddling with the Secret Service men at the other end of the room. Maddox beckoned Daisy with a lift of his chin, suggested smoothly that the Troys and Gibsons should tell their story to Sergeant Hoffman. He and Feinman, in the interests of privacy, shepherded Sexton toward one of the interrogation rooms down the hall. The Troys and Gibsons looked very gratified, the last look he had at them, and he realized they thought the detectives were going to start grilling Sexton at once and possibly fetch out the rubber hoses.

Sexton looked at the bare little room somewhat distastefully, but sat on one of the straight wooden chairs. "It's very unfortunate," he said, "that the girls should have resented me—their mother's remarriage—so violently. Of course I couldn't take their father's place—to Louise or to them. But to grudge both of us some happiness— I've been very sorry about it. It distressed Louise." He was not exactly a handsome man, but there was something very attractive about him. He was tall, well built, with a thick crest of gray hair and a pleasantly rugged face. He was well dressed in a dark suit, white shirt and discreet tie.

"Yes, sir," said Maddox. "We'd like a little more information about your wife's accident, Mr. Sexton. According to Mrs. Gibson and Mrs. Troy, it was unusual for Mrs. Sexton to drive after having had a drink. Apparently she gave you the excuse of a date with her daughter—er, Thelma?—which turned out to be a lie—"

Sexton stared indignantly. "Is that what Thelma told the officers last night? I wasn't exactly thinking straight then, the shock— I don't know what the Troys did tell the police, and we were all upset, probably Thelma just didn't understand me. On the phone, that is." He got out a cigarette, sat turning it in his long fingers until Maddox proffered a lighter. "Thank you. I'll tell you just what did happen. I got home about five o'clock. I'd been playing golf. Louise had been expecting an old friend in the afternoon, Leona Walters, but as it turned out, she had an emergency dental appointment and didn't come. When I came in, Louise said, 'Well, you took your time coming home,' and then she laughed and said of course I couldn't know she'd been home alone all day." He hesitated. "She wasn't much of a reader, didn't enjoy being alone, you see. She wasn't one for TV either. We talked a few minutes, and then she said if I didn't mind getting myself a meal, she thought she'd go and ask Thelma to go out to dinner with her and take in the play at the West Ebell Theater. She said Richard was working late at the office—he's a lawyer, you know— I suppose she'd talked to Thelma on the phone earlier. I said I didn't mind at all, and she went upstairs to change her dress. A little later on I went up too, I'd decided to shower and get into a robe before fixing a steak. In fact, I was in the bathroom when Louise left, she—"

"Did you share a room, Mr. Sexton?"

"Why, yes, the master bedroom with its own bath. She called good-bye, and I said to have a good time. It wasn't until I came out to the bedroom that I saw she'd been having a drink as she got dressed. That was unusual, I'd have expected her to wait till they got to the restaurant—and it looked as if it'd been a double too."

"Of what?" asked Feinman.

"Oh, whiskey sours, she always drank whiskey sours. I never knew her to have more than two. But I didn't think much about it—"

"What time was it when she left?"

"The nearest I could get would be about a quarter past six. I had a drink myself, and cooked the steak. I didn't expect her home early—I was reading. And then about nine o'clock Thelma called asking for her, and I said I thought they were together. Of course we were both terribly alarmed then, and Thelma and Richard started for the house—" Sexton shut his eyes and was silent for a moment. "Only as they came up Mulholland, they came right on the accident—one of your patrol cars had spotted the Chrysler, there was an ambulance and police all over—a terrible sight for

Thelma. One of the patrolmen came up for me— I had to identify her, you know."

"Yes, sir. She seemed quite competent when she left the house?"

"Certainly." He sounded a little indignant. "I was surprised to find she'd had a drink, but I suppose we all do impulsive things now and then, Sergeant."

"Do you know whether she habitually kept the driver's window up or down?" asked Feinman.

Sexton looked surprised. "Why? I suppose it would depend on the weather, I can't really say. When we were out together, I always drove my car."

"You understand there'll have to be an autopsy, and an inquest."

He nodded; he pinched his forehead in two fingers, tiredly. "It seems such a waste. She was still such an active, vibrant woman— enjoying life. We'd both been sorry about the girls' attitude— heaven knows I'd tried to be friendly." He smiled faintly. "Oh, I know all about their suspicion that I was after Louise's money. The absurd part of that is, although some of my assets are tied up pending the outcome of a timber deal in Oregon, I daresay I was worth slightly more than she was. Which is off the subject." He stubbed out his cigarette in the glass ashtray. "What about the inquest? And funeral arrangements? I suppose I should leave that to the girls, though either way they'd have some fault to find, I can guess that."

"The inquest will probably be next week," said Maddox. "You'll be notified, and also as to when the body can be released."

"I see. Thank you. Is that all you need from me?"

"For the moment, thanks."

Sexton stood up abruptly. "Terrible thing," he said. "So sudden. I don't think I've taken it in yet. Well—" Maddox held the door for him and he went out, unexpectedly turned and offered a formal handshake. "Thank you," he said, and headed down the corridor the way he'd come in.

They went back to the detective office. Daisy was alone at her desk. "Is there anything in what Thelma said?" asked Maddox.

"Sexton seems perfectly straightforward, a nice fellow. I read those girls as pretty vindictive, without much reason."

"If you want a female opinion, they were more concerned about Mother's money than Mother," said Daisy. "We don't know that it wasn't just another accident. Tempest in a teapot, if you ask me. The Sextons had been married two years—they met each other on a trip to Hawaii, by the way—and he moved into her house. Apparently he never said much about his background, or maybe he just didn't to the girls. Said to be in land and timber in Oregon, he's originally from Eugene. They had to admit that Mother seemed perfectly happy."

"There's nothing in it," said Maddox. "So it was a chilly night. She'd had that hefty drink, she was feeling warm and rolled down the window. And sometimes a familiar road is the most dangerous to drive, you think you know it so well you're not paying attention. Wait and see what the autopsy report says."

It was getting on to end of shift. Ten minutes later a middle-aged couple came in, and Maddox had to rack his brain for the name—last Monday, the latest daylight burglary—Mr. and Mrs. Clyde Pollock.

"You told us to come in when we made up a list of what was missing," said Pollock. He was a big, heavy man going bald, a pharmacist at a Thrifty drugstore. "My God, it'd be easier to list what was left! I don't know what they expect people to *do*. The taxes— I don't like Marcia working, but if we're going to have enough to eat and pay the house taxes, there's no choice. We've lived in that neighborhood twenty-five years, used to know a lot of the neighbors, but quite a few of them had to sell out, find some place cheaper—houses nearest to us mostly rented now, people coming and going."

Mrs. Pollock just looked tired and defeated. She was a thin dark woman in shabby clothes. "If Mrs. Robinson had still lived next door, she'd have gone asking questions, see a moving van at our place and men carrying things out. But—"

That had been the M.O. on all the team burglaries, eighteen of them in the last two months. The working-class neighborhood where neighbors were away all day or incurious about anonymous neighbors. The moving van pulled up in front, the house cleaned out. God knew where it was all getting fenced, and they wouldn't have got many valuable individual pieces, but the sheer volume was evidently paying off. Like many other things, secondhand furniture was at a premium these days, a good deal of it of better quality than new, and dealers might not ask many questions. A flyer had gone out to all secondhand dealers in the county three weeks ago, but nothing had come of it yet and possibly nothing ever would.

"Well, for what it's worth, there you are," said Pollock, slapping two handwritten pages on the desk. "All the furniture, the TV, portable radio, refrigerator, even the rugs, by God. We've got a stove and nowhere to sit and eat. Been staying with my brother, but they really haven't got room. I expect I'll have to go into debt for new furniture and just hope the insurance pays off most of it."

"It's been rough on all of you," said Maddox sympathetically. "And rough for us to work—no leads on it at all."

"Oh, we can't blame the police," said Pollock surprisingly. "Crime rate the way it is, you can't be everywhere at once. It's just I don't know what the government expects people to *do*. Always slapping more taxes on the working stiffs to hand out the welfare to the bums—turning everybody into poor people. Property taxes go any higher, we'll be better off to let the damn city take the house and go on welfare too." They trailed out dismally.

"That bunch of bastards," said Feinman. "And we'll never catch up, you know that."

"Don't be defeatist," said Maddox.

It was five minutes to end of shift. D'Arcy and Rodriguez came in looking glum. "Do any good?" asked Maddox. They just looked at him.

◆

They'd gone back to see the Noonans again, to tell them about the autopsy report. "It's the same fiend killed that other boy!" said Mrs. Noonan fiercely at once. She had been crying again; her husband, sitting beside her on the shabby couch in the small living room, was also red-eyed, more subdued. "Oh, they called us to say we could have Freddy's body—reason Al's home, we've been out making the arrangements. Some maniac, it is, snatching children off the street—"

"Well, not quite, Mrs. Noonan," said Rodriguez. "He must have got the boys to come up to him some way—maybe asking about an address, something like that."

"Freddy'd never have gone up to a stranger, we told you that! I don't know about this other boy, but Freddy was real shy. He always had been. Never had but a couple of real close friends. He liked to read, he was always awful good in school, you know."

"But he was a real boy too," said Freddy's father, as if anxious they shouldn't put Freddy down as a sissy. "He went out for Little League, he was crazy about baseball. But like Mary says, he knew about not going up to strangers."

The Noonans couldn't tell them anything, which they'd known. They had some empty facts to string together, but what this one came down to was the computer and the legwork.

They sat in D'Arcy's Dodge and looked at the facts: The Frost boy had been missing presumably on his way home from school on a Friday last month. They'd started looking right away because he was a juvenile. He'd been found just after dawn the next day, lying up against the curb at the corner of Rosewood and Vista, roughly the same area he'd disappeared from, by a bus driver on his way to work. The autopsy said he'd been dead since about eight the previous night. His pants and shoes were missing. Freddy Noonan hadn't come home from school last Friday, been reported missing at six o'clock. He'd turned up in the street, on Lucerne Boulevard just south of Melrose, at dawn the next day, spotted by the driver of a refuse truck just starting collections. His pants were gone. The autopsy said he'd been dead since around midnight. Neither boy had been fed, apparently.

They had, of course, talked to the teachers at the school, some of the other boys. Both the Frost boy and Freddy had been quiet students, posing no problems. They'd gone to the same public elementary school, but there had been a year's age difference; they'd been in different grades and hadn't known each other.

D'Arcy started the Dodge and they drove the routes both boys would have walked going home from school. The quietest block was along Waring Avenue, and that was still a street in downtown Hollywood, with cars and people coming and going.

"I don't know," said D'Arcy doubtfully. "The average person sees an adult dragging a kid into a car, the kid trying to get away, does he take it for granted it's a family squabble?"

"Even if he doesn't," said Rodriguez cynically, "he looks the other way. Don't want to get involved."

"A *kid*," said D'Arcy.

"As Ivor says, not many brothers' keepers around. You know if we drop on him, it'll be the long way round."

"Likely," agreed D'Arcy. They had a list, and it was a long one. The computers had made the job easier in some ways; programmed efficiently, a computer downtown had produced for them a list of all the men in records with pedigrees of molesting male juveniles, and their present whereabouts if known. They would find most of those men, with luck and persistence, to bring in for questioning; but a lot of men like that were loners, and it was on the cards that not many would have firm alibis, which would leave it all up in the air. And if the man they wanted didn't happen to be on the list, all the legwork would go for nothing. This might be the first time he'd gone in for sodomy and murder, or he might have just hit town from a thousand miles away and be in somebody else's records.

It was possible they'd never find out either way. But they had to work it into the ground.

"And," said Rodriguez as they turned into the parking lot, "pray he doesn't get the urge again soon."

------◆------

Thursday was supposed to be Maddox's day off; it was Sue who only had time for coffee, hunting clean stockings and misplacing car keys before kissing him hastily and running out of the little house on the rear of the lot on Gregory Avenue. Maddox had intended, sometime today, to tackle Margaret Carstairs; he had approved Sue's reckless gamble on a four-bedroom house—they'd persuade her yet. But the best-laid plans of off-duty cops have a way of dissolving.

Overnight one of their street snitches had phoned in a warning: a massive gang rumble set for Fairfax High School this morning. The watch commander had briefed the morning patrol and the squads were out in force. It got under way about nine o'clock, but they were right on it and not much damage was done. Only when they shook the kids down—"Kids!" said Patrolman Carmichael, nursing a knife slash along his cheekbone. "That big bastard outweighed me by twenty pounds!"—inevitably they found a lot of them holding the dope, from several decks of H to angel dust. A dozen of them were over eighteen and no longer minors; in any case, they had to be questioned. The holders were formally arrested. Maddox got called in to help out at eleven o'clock.

It was a nuisance, and almost certainly a waste of time. Even if the arrests stuck, the holders would probably get probation. At twelve-thirty, a sullen pimply punk Maddox and Feinman were talking to reluctantly parted with the name of the dude he'd bought a deck from, and they both recognized it; Everett Evans had served two two-to-fives (read six months and parole) for dealing, and was just off his latest parole. They checked with his recent P.A. officer and got an address over on Martel Avenue. They took Feinman's Chevy to ferry him back.

At the light on the corner of Hollywood Boulevard and Highland, Maddox said, "I grew up in this town, Joe. And I'm not exactly senile yet. But it's changed one hell of a lot just since I was idiot enough to join the force."

"Yeah," said Feinman. "Say it again." They looked along the boulevard, where once there had been clean pleasant shops, bright restaurants, department stores, well-maintained store fronts, clean sidewalks. The boulevard looked sleazy and dirty, miscellaneous refuse collected in the gutters just since street-cleaning day last week. Where a good many of the larger stores had been, and the little family movie-houses dating from the thirties, now the daylight neon screamed silently, ADULT FILMS, X-RATED TOPLESS, 24-HOUR TOPLESS BOTTOMLESS! And down the side streets, though not as many as before the crackdown on them last year, were still the dreary massage parlors. Some of the people on the street were ordinary-looking people, decently enough dressed; but there were also quite a lot of teen-agers in freakish clothes wandering around aimlessly. There had been a drastic rise in teen-age prostitution the last six months, largely concentrated in Hollywood; it was beginning to look as if that was an organized thing.

"Sodom and Gomorrah," said Maddox.

"And it may end the same way," said Feinman. "Maybe I'd have done better to study for the rabbinate, like my mother wanted."

They picked up Evans with no trouble; he hadn't been expecting them. He did some cussing about dirty little snitches; they applied for the warrant and booked him into the Wilcox Street jail. With luck, he'd be one dealer out of their hair for another six months; but there was always enough dope floating around. These days heroin was old-fashioned; the going thing was cocaine, and the latest fad, angel dust—phencycladine, PCP—which could create mental zombies much quicker than heroin or acid.

They went out for a belated lunch. When they got back, there were still a dozen juveniles to talk to and everybody was busy except Sue, who was on the phone. A man came in behind them and stood looking around the big office with curious eyes. "Say," he said to Maddox, "you've got quite a setup here. The desk sergeant said to come in here and see one of the detectives. My name's Harkness, Earl Harkness."

"What can we do for you, Mr. Harkness?"

Harkness scratched his ear. He was about forty-five, with thinning brown hair and a bulldog face with a pushed-in nose. "Might be the other way round," he said. "Only it sounds like such a damn-fool thing, and I don't want to waste your time."

"We're just here to serve the citizens," said Maddox. "Sit down and tell me about it." He led Harkness over to his desk, Feinman ambling after. Sue put down the phone and stood up.

"Another burglary," she said tersely. "One of you want to come along?"

◆

It was an address down on Alexandria Avenue, in the heart of old Hollywood, a narrow street lined with old houses. Along some of the old streets, here and there the old houses had made way for occasional jerry-built apartments, but on this block there was only one of those, at the corner, painted bright orange. The black-and-white was sitting in front of one of the oldest and smallest houses, a little square frame house once painted white but now peeling and flaking to a dispirited gray. Patrolman Rinehart was talking to an angular woman on the sidewalk, and there was somebody else in the front seat of the squad.

As Sue and Feinman came up, they saw that there was an incongruous brown bag of groceries on the sidewalk, just where a broken cement walk led to the house. There was a box of crackers on top, part of a plastic bag of string beans visible under that. Rinehart turned to them with relief.

"This is the damnedest thing I ever saw," he said. "I mean, we see a lot of damned things, and even the eight years since I've been riding a squad, worse and worse things, but this—! My God. Haven't you front-office dicks got any line on these bastards yet?"

"If it's the boys with the moving van, nary a one," said Feinman.

"Oh, it was them. It was them all right. This poor damned old lady— I mean, the gall!" said Rinehart.

"What happened?" asked Sue.

The angular woman had moved up to listen. "How could I be expected to know what was going on?" she asked sharply, as if they'd accused her of something. "Sure I saw it there, that van, I just thought the old lady'd sold out or died or something. I don't know her— I got no time to run in and out talking to neighbors. Only reason I'm off work today, I got a cold. When I saw the police car I come out, see what's going on, but I don't know anything about it."

Rinehart turned a shoulder on her and led them over to the squad car. "You feeling better, Mrs. Eady?" he asked gently. "These are the detectives—Mrs. Maddox and Mr. Feinman. It's Mrs. Constance Eady."

"I guess so," she said thinly. She was a very little old lady, sitting sideways in the front seat. She had once been a very pretty girl, the bones of her face delicate and fine, but that was a long time back. She had thin white hair, frizzed in an old-fashioned style; she wore metal-framed glasses, one temple held in place with adhesive tape. Her blue cotton housedress was clean, if faded; the old black coat over it was threadbare, and her black oxfords were shabby, with run-over heels. Her thin old hands were shaking a little, folded in her lap.

"She'd been up to the market on Fountain," said Rinehart. "Came back as they were cleaning out the house, and they held a gun on her till they finished."

"Oh, my God," said Feinman tiredly. "Now I've heard everything."

"I couldn't do anything," she said in a reedy voice, breathless. "I just had to watch. My glasses don't do much for me these days,

I never even saw the van, saw it was right outside my house, till I was turning in—then there was that man with the gun, he made me come inside—just had to stand and watch. I dropped my groceries when I saw the gun, and probably the eggs broke—" Her eyes filled with sudden tears. "I hadn't bought any in a long while, so expensive now, but they were on sale and I got a whole half dozen. I just had to watch. They took everything. Things I had all my life. Mother's walnut curio cabinet—and Bert's rolltop desk—the same bed we got when we were married, that's sixty years ago in August and Bert gone for twelve years. Things—things nobody could afford to buy now even if you could get them. Mother's silverware, and the silver tea service. I had to sell all Grandma's silver last year to pay the taxes, it's hard to save on Social Security." She was gasping a little. "We bought the house in nineteen thirty-four for twenty-two hundred dollars. Bert did a lot, fixing it up—and the yard too—he could fix anything went wrong. But since he's been gone—workmen seem to charge so high now. This was a nice street then, nice friendly people around."

"Mrs. Eady." Sue bent to touch the shaking old hands. "Is there some relative we can call? Any of your children—family?"

"Oh, no," she said. "No. Bert and I never had a family. There's nobody left. I'm eighty-seven, and the only real good friend I've got still alive is Bessie Adams, and she's in a rest home." And suddenly, without warning, Mrs. Eady slumped forward and Sue caught her slight weight.

Rinehart ran around the squad, leaned in to grab the mike and called for an ambulance. "Heart?" said Sue. Feinman lifted the old lady out and laid her flat on the sidewalk, feeling her pulse, lifting an eyelid.

"Don't think so, her pulse is pretty good. I think she just passed out, delayed shock, and no wonder."

It was another chilly day for southern California, down in the upper forties; Sue put her own coat over the old lady and knelt by her until the ambulance came.

The angular woman just stood by, watching avidly. When the ambulance was gone and all the excitement over, she marched back to the house next door, went inside and slammed the door. "My God, people!" said Rinehart. "I'd better get back on tour." He slammed the door of the squad feelingly and took off.

Sue and Feinman went up to the open door of the little house. It had probably been built in the early twenties, and it had been neglected for a long time, perhaps since before Bert had died. The steps to the porch were broken. Inside the front door was a little living room starkly bare: all that was left were two cheap religious pictures on the walls. The walls were dirty and much in need of paint. They went from there into a square kitchen, where only an ancient gas stove was left. On the tiny service porch beyond that, an old gas hot-water tank stood mutely, its pipe unhooked, rusted holes in its sides.

"She'd been heating water on the stove," said Sue, horrified. "I wonder for how long."

There were two small bedrooms, both bare. The closet in the front bedroom held a scanty collection of old clothes.

"What do you suppose the taxes run?" asked Feinman. "Two, three hundred?"

"Now? It's still Hollywood, whatever the house looks like. What are yours?" Feinman lived in Burbank.

He winced. "Up to eleven hundred last year."

Sue thought about her mother's property taxes. "I'll bet not under five or six hundred, even for this place. It'd cost her more than that to move, and where could she go? She said she's just got Social Security. I don't see how she's been living on it. Probably not getting enough to eat. But why on earth would these—these *devils* pick a place like this? I know most of the places they've cleaned out have been just ordinary houses, but nobody could expect to find any loot here!"

Feinman sniffed. "Don't know. It doesn't look as if they'd singled out any particular house before. Just picked the kind of neighborhoods where most people work, and neighbors mind their own business anyway. But didn't she say a walnut curio cabinet, Mother's silver, and so on? Sound like antiques to me. Maybe valuable. It just occurs to me that maybe this time they did pick a particular place. Maybe somebody knew or suspected what loot was here."

"At least maybe we'll get a description of them—at least somebody saw them this time, Joe. Maybe she can give us some description, if she's going to be all right."

Feinman sniffed again. "Don't hold your breath. Her glasses

don't help her much these days. She never noticed the van until she was on top of it."

"Oh, Lord," said Sue. "And if she is going to be all right, will you tell me what on earth she's going to do? There isn't a bed or a chair left!"

"Social Services," said Feinman.

"And don't hold your breath," said Sue. "You know the red tape. It'd probably take them a month to get her on their lists. And I'll bet she doesn't have a dime of insurance."

"Unlikely," agreed Feinman.

"There are rest homes where they take people just for the Social Security."

"Damn few. And they're not very good ones. It's damn depressing, all right. We'd better get back and write a report."

Outside it had grown overcast and dark, though it was just past four. The paper had said possible rain; for a change they were having a wet winter. Sue shivered in her lightweight coat. She thought suddenly of her mother. Maybe Mrs. Eady, thirty years ago, had been brisk and strong and enjoying life too. At least this could never happen to Mother, thought Sue, she's got me and Ivor —and immediately she thought, How do you know? How could anyone know? She might be killed in an accident and Ivor shot by some hood. *In the midst of life—*

Back at the office, she let Feinman do the report and called the hospital. After a wait, a cool-sounding nurse told her that Mrs. Eady was in stable condition; she'd be kept for observation overnight and probably released in the morning. And could the police provide any information about possible medical insurance? There had not been a Social Security card in her handbag, and without an identifying number—

"Oh—" Just in time Sue remembered she was a lady. She referred the nurse to the local Social Security office and hung up.

Her spouse, across the room, seemed to be enjoying a joke with Joe Rowan.

———◆———

"I don't want to waste your time," Earl Harkness had said again. "But the more I thought about it, the more I thought I'd better come in. It sounds crazy, but then a lot of things seem a little crazy these days."

"You are so right. What's it about?" asked Maddox.

"Well, I'm a security guard at Paramount Studios. I'm on night shift. And this last six weeks my wife's been back east—her sister had an operation, she went back there to take care of her awhile. Both the girls are married, so I've been on my own, see? I can't say I'm much of a hand at cooking, and a lot of the time I've been dropping in at this place on Melrose—called the Melwin Grill, it's just down from the intersection at Windsor. It's a nice quiet clean place, handy to the studio. I've been hitting it say at five, six o'clock, sit around and have a few beers, read the paper, get talking with somebody—maybe four, five days a week. And then have dinner there and go on to work."

"So?"

"So," said Harkness, "this is really weird, Sergeant, but I think this guy is looking for a hit man to knock off his wife."

Maddox sat up. "Who and why?"

"His name's Erhardt, if he gave it to me straight. I first got talking to him maybe a month ago, he was sitting next to me over a beer. Seemed like an ordinary guy, nice enough fellow—we ended up having dinner together. They've got a pretty damn good cook there. He's a fellow maybe thirty-five. Told me he was separated from his wife, living alone, so I wasn't surprised to run into him there a lot of times I dropped in."

"Front name?"

"Oh, Jim. He's a photographer, he's got a photographic studio on Santa Monica—that's kosher, I looked it up. But it's just been casual conversation, you know what I mean, wonder how the Dodgers'll do next season, they sure got a great pitcher in that Rog Brent, and they say we're due for a lot more rain, and the trouble he's had with his new Chevy, and taxes, and politics. We agree mostly on politics," said Harkness, "which is funny because I'm pretty conservative most ways. And a guy wanting his wife knocked off— The weird thing is, he doesn't know me—just come out with that to a bare acquaintance— Well, come to the point, we were talking last Monday, and he said he supposed in my line of work I ran into a lot of tough characters, and I said not specially—unless you want to count these so-called stars. I tell you no lie," said Harkness earnestly, "up to three years back I was a guard at Lockheed, but I never heard the gutter talk from those guys you hear from these damned snotty TV people—females worse than the men sometimes. Anyway, he went on to say he'd pay a little bonus to anybody could introduce him to some tough hombre who'd do a job for him. I thought he was kidding, and then when I thought twice I thought maybe not.

"Well, yesterday I was there again and so was he. And he brought his beer over to my booth and says he has it pretty straight that some of these big TV and movie people are hooked up with the Mafia, isn't that so? I said I didn't know, and he came right out and said he's got five hundred bucks for anybody can put him in touch with a hit man, and up to two thousand for the contract. I said, for real, and he says, in spades. Who, I says, and he says that bitch making all the trouble for him. Suing him for back alimony, when his business is practically bankrupt, and she doesn't know it but he kept up the premiums on the life insurance he took out on her, she's worth ten grand cold."

"What did you say?" Maddox was interested.

"Hell, I didn't know what to say!" said Harkness frankly. "Me with top security clearance and not even a parking ticket on my record. I said he had to be kidding, and he didn't say anything, so I waited a minute and started talking about the latest damn-fool thing Congress is up to. But the more I thought about it, damn it, the guy meant it. I thought I ought to tell you about it."

"As if we needed anything else to do," said Maddox resignedly.

"What can you do about it? Anything? I mean, if he's really serious about it, I suppose sooner or later he'd find some hood to oblige him."

Maddox smiled wryly, thinking of that vista down the boulevard: this dirty town. There were people around who would slash their own mother's throat for a week of fixes. The wolves prowled in any big city. But this was a tiresome complication, coming up right now; it would be tiresome at any time. They had to do something about it, but there were some finicky laws about entrapment, and if they didn't stick to the letter of the law, the court would throw the evidence out.

"So, I tell you what we do, Mr. Harkness. You encourage

Erhardt to talk about it some more. You tell him you might be able to introduce him to somebody to do the job for him."

"But—"

"You set up a meeting. Wherever he specifies—let him arrange it. Then you come and tell us. And we provide the hit man."

"A cop," said Harkness.

"A cop. The trick is, Erhardt has to do all the talking—the cop can't lead him on, or technically it's entrapment. Erhardt has to spell it out—so much offered for the hit, who's to get wasted, and so forth. Hopefully we'll get it all down on tape. That's evidence, and we could charge him with conspiracy to commit homicide. He might get a one-to-three."

"And be out in six months," said Harkness. "At least his ex-wife would know about it. I don't know a thing about the woman, but nobody deserves to get murdered."

"Well, if you think you can put on a convincing act, I've told you what to do."

"I'll do it," said Harkness seriously. "I'm a long way from being a real cop, Sergeant, but I guess you could say I'm on the same side. I'll go out of my way some to preserve law and order. I'll let you know how it goes."

Maddox watched him out with mixed feelings. A thing like this would come up just now. The juveniles were cleared away; he hadn't heard the latest from D'Arcy and Rodriguez on the sex killings. Ellis was still out with the Secret Service men. Across the room, Sue was on the phone. It was nearly end of shift.

He called the hospital and asked about Ruth Butler. She was in stable condition, but it was impossible to say when she might be conscious, able to be questioned.

Maddox ambled over to Rowan's desk and told him about Harkness. Rowan uttered rude words. "A thing like that, cluttering up the routine."

Sue came over and asked what the joke was. "No joke really—" But Maddox began to laugh. "Oh, indeedy, that is a thought!" He looked at Sue and laughed harder, and explained. "When I think of you, all gussied up to the vulgar nines, playing private hooker, all to nail that pompous old pimp—"

"I'll never forget *that* job," said Sue. "It was the first time you looked at me and saw something besides good old reliable **Car**stairs the female cop. What about it?"

"Cops," said Maddox, "aren't hired for their acting ability. Who the hell could we get to look like a real-life hit man and act it?"

"I had the thought on a case a while ago," said Sue, "that none of you does look like a great big tough cop. Let alone a great big tough hit man. But I've got a practical suggestion, Ivor."

"Yes?"

"Out in front, in the watch commander's office, is a two-by-three-inch photograph of every LAPD man working out of this precinct. Have a look for any of them that looks like a real tough."

"Thank you," said Maddox. "That's a very helpful idea, my love."

THREE

For once, on Friday morning, they got up when the alarm went off, and there was time for toast as well as coffee. As they came out the front door together at a quarter to eight, Maddox said abruptly, "I wish to hell you could take a couple of weeks off, locate a house definitely. Belatedly it comes to me we should have done it a year and a half ago, when we got married."

"Not quite a year and a half." Sue fished out her keys.

"Damn it, this whole area is going down the drain." Maddox looked up the drive, to the cracker box of a bastard-Spanish house across the street, its front lawn long and brown, to the Clintons' house, which sat in front of the little house he and Sue rented. The Clintons were just hanging on until he retired next year, and would sell and move out of the L.A. area, to a smaller town up north. "By two years from now, it'll be a slum, candidate for urban renewal—if the government isn't broke by then. And, by God, another reason to change your mother's mind. That old house of hers—" It was four blocks away from this one— "I don't like her alone in it, without a little dog to bark at burglars now. Now don't start crying again."

"I won't," said Sue in a wobbly voice, "only we had him since he was a month old and we loved him. She won't get another dog for a while."

"Well, after we find a house—"

"Yes. If she'll be there too, to look after a dog."

Maddox grinned at her. "And any potential offspring. I'll see you, love." He got into the Maserati; Sue went on down the block, where she rented a garage for her old Chrysler.

When she got to the office the first thing she did was to call the hospital. Another impersonal nurse told her that Mrs. Eady would be released this morning. "You tell her there'll be someone to pick her up. Tell her to wait for Mrs. Maddox." Sue put the phone down and debated with herself. You couldn't take on every unfortunate who crossed your path, but you couldn't always look the other way either. She called her mother.

"Good heavens, Sue!" said Margaret Carstairs, aghast at the little tale. "That poor old soul! It makes you feel ashamed, complaining about such little things, when someone like that— I expect you were wondering if I'd called the salvage people yet."

"Bless you, darling, yes. You said there was that old platform rocker, and a card table—"

"There's that folding bed in the garage. I'll never need it again. I've got some cot-size sheets somewhere, and a pillow. Now I can get everything into the car," said Mrs. Carstairs briskly. "Suppose you tell me the address, and I'll meet you there."

And of course in a way it was related to the job, because nobody had questioned the old woman yet. Sue drove up to the Hollywood Receiving Hospital, waited while the last red tape was filled out, and bundled old Mrs. Eady into the Chrysler.

"I'm sure I don't know why you should go to the trouble— I don't even know your name—"

Sue told her. "There are still some questions I've got to ask you. And besides, we have to help each other out when anyone's in trouble." When they got to the poor little house, on Alexandria, Mrs. Carstairs was just parking in front; Sue helped her get the furniture out of the car and they carried it in. It wasn't much, but it was something to put in the bare rooms. She looked in the cupboards while Mrs. Eady was thanking her mother; there was a fair stack of canned goods, and the burglars hadn't bothered with the kitchen utensils, the cheap tableware, the threadbare curtains.

She came back to the living room. "You've got to have the locks fixed—it isn't safe, you here alone." It hadn't been a very good lock to begin with, and the burglars had broken in rather easily.

"Oh, I couldn't afford to do that." Mrs. Eady was weeping a little. "There isn't anything left for anybody to take anyway. You're such dear, kind people to give all this to me— I don't know why you should. I was so ashamed to break down like that yesterday, it was all the walking, you see. I was so tired. I find I can't walk quite as far as I used to, and I try to arrange it so I only go to the market once a week or so. It's a long two blocks up on Fountain. And then after—after that happened, those men—well, I haven't had a phone in years, it costs so much and I don't know anybody to call. I don't know any of the people living right around here now, and I didn't like to ask to use a stranger's phone. I walked up the block to the pay phone to call the police. I was just so tired, nothing really wrong with me. I hope the Medicare will pay the hospital bill. But my, they did give me a nice breakfast there, nicest I've had in years."

"I've got some questions to ask you," said Sue gently. "But you know you can't go on this way, Mrs. Eady. I want you to let Mother drive you down to the Social Services office so you can apply for some aid. You'll qualify all right. They'll see you get a new hot-water heater, and something besides the Social Security." There was the meals-on-wheels program too, ideal for her, and some organizations had volunteer handyman services to help people maintain their homes.

Mrs. Eady, in the old platform rocker, drew herself up straighter. "Do you mean ask for charity? Oh, no. No, I couldn't do that. I get by all right, if it is a little tight. I couldn't take charity. I'd never be able to look Bert in the face when we meet again. I've got about a hundred dollars in a savings account, for emergencies."

Sue exchanged a look with her mother. "Well, you needn't decide now. What I want to ask you, can you tell me anything about those men yesterday? Give me any description of them, or the van? They've robbed a lot of other people, you know, but you're the only one who's actually seen them."

"Oh," said Mrs. Eady. She flushed a little. "Is that so? Well, my dear, I was in a state, and I told you my eyesight isn't what it was, but I'll try to remember. I can tell you, the man who pointed the gun at me was colored—pretty black. There were three others, and I don't think they were, they might've been Mexican or something. The one thing I do recall clear as day, when I first saw that big van right in front, and then there was the man with the gun and he said to go inside, and I dropped my groceries—it was just as if it got painted on my brain, I'll never forget it. That great big truck, it was painted green and on the side of it was a sign that said HERSCHEL'S FINE FURNITURE. I guess it stuck in my mind because I went to school with a girl named Bertha Herschel. But as for describing any of the men—" She shook her head. "Just that one fellow was black. And young."

Sue drew a long breath. "That's fine," she said. "Just fine, thank you, Mrs. Eady."

Her mother followed her out to the curb. "I'll stay a little while and see she gets some lunch. You know she's got to have a refrigerator, Sue. We'll just have to get her to apply for some help."

"You have a try at it." Sue, getting into the Chrysler, thought she wouldn't mind at all if she looked a lot like Margaret Carstairs twenty years from now, as everybody said she would. Margaret Carstairs didn't look her age; her neatly waved hair was still glossy dark brown, her dark blue eyes bright, and she'd kept a good figure. And, Sue thought with an inward tremor of laughter, Margaret Carstairs was just itching to have a family to mother again, somebody to look after, and just possibly it wasn't going to be so hard to persuade her after all.

"Now, Sue." The blue eyes were shrewd. "Don't think I don't know what you're thinking. I like being independent. Young people shouldn't have to share their lives—"

"I didn't say a word." Sue put the transmission in Drive. And it certainly wasn't part of her job to waste time on such a thing, but after all, Mrs. Eady had just handed them the first solid lead they'd had on the burglars. She drove down Western to a block where there were a couple of secondhand furniture stores, went in and asked about used refrigerators.

The first place had one for seventy dollars. At the second place an indifferent paunchy man puffing on a pipe and reading *True West* magazine said, "I got an old G.E. that's running for fifty. You'd have to move it."

"Damn," said Sue. "I suppose she'd think that was too much." A hundred dollars in savings— "Could you come down a little? You see—" She hadn't much hope of moving him with a hard-luck story, but you never knew. She told him the story, and he put down his pipe, closed the magazine and listened without expression. "If you could possibly—"

"Lady," he said deliberately, "that's the damnedest dirty trick I ever heard of, even in this town. I'll tell you, I'm not on the way to my first million in this business, and I don't maybe go to church every Sunday, but there's times we got to show some Christian charity. It's sure nice of the cops, try to help the old lady out. I'll tell you what. Give me ten bucks and I'll see it gets delivered to her and hooked up today."

Sue could have kissed him. It had started to rain, but she couldn't have cared less.

——————◆——————

Friday was Rodriguez' day off, but he'd volunteered to cover the Noonan inquest. There wasn't much in the night-watch report —another heist at a seven-to-eleven Jiffy market—but also waiting on Maddox's desk was the lab report on what had been picked up at Lisa Martin's place. It didn't amount to much. The two good latent prints on the back doorknob weren't hers, but they didn't show in Records either; they'd been sent to the FBI, and a kick-back should be in soon. No useful evidence other than that had showed.

Enclosed with the report was the key to the front door and a long legal envelope; the report had mentioned that briefly—her will, discovered in a steel box in the bedroom closet. It bore the name of the attorney who'd drawn it up. Mrs. Carradine had said that Lisa Martin hadn't any relatives. Maddox, passing all that on to D'Arcy and Feinman, said, "We won't find a lawyer in his office before ten, but he'd better be notified. He can take care of the funeral arrangements. Did anybody ever contact the bank where she worked?"

"I did," said D'Arcy. "Nothing. A lot of ohing and ahing, terrible thing to happen. Everybody liked both the women, they got along with everybody. And look, this list is alphabetical, and in three weeks, damn it, nearly four weeks, we've just got to the *J*'s. And a nut who might be hot for it. Clifford Jaynes, two counts of enticing boys, and he's just off P.A. No address."

"So call Welfare and Rehab and get hold of his P.A. officer. I'll be right with you. There's a witness on this heist coming in to make a statement. You stay and listen, Joe, and then you can get back to the legwork too."

"Will do," said Feinman amiably.

Five minutes later D'Arcy put down the phone. "I do not understand judges. You'd think any fool would know these nuts are always potentially dangerous, the ones who go in for kids. This Jaynes has enticed and attacked two boys, one seven, one five, two separate occasions. He got probation the first time and then a year in the joint, with parole at six months. He got fired from his job when he was picked up the second time, but the P.A. man got him another—he's a salesman at a Ford agency on La Cienega."

"So let's go talk to him," said Maddox.

It began to rain after they left, and rather quickly built up into a downpour. Feinman sat around with nothing to do, waiting for the witness. When she showed up at ten o'clock, she turned out to be about nineteen, a luscious redhead with a lot of curves and a dimple in one cheek. Her name was Marion Gunderson. Oddly enough, she was a good witness.

"Sure I'd know him again," she said. "I was scared to death at the time— I don't like working the night shift alone, but what can you do, I've got to earn a living. What you hear about these creeps high on H or coke and just as apt to shoot you whether you hand over the money or not—but I wasn't so scared I was blind. I'd recognize him. He was about medium height, he had on jeans and a black turtleneck and a black beret pulled down kind of low, but I could see his face all right. Kind of a thin face with a sharp nose, I think dark eyes, and a big mouth. But you couldn't miss the tattoo. It was on his left arm, just above his hand—I mean on the top of his arm, I saw it when he reached out to take the money. It's a big blue snake all coiled up. Ugh."

Feinman was pleased. With all the heisters running around these days, usually no leads at all, at least here was something concrete to hand the computer. He asked her to come downtown and look at mug shots, and she demurred. "I mean, is there any hurry? Could I do it this afternoon? I've got a lunch date with my agent, he might have a modeling job for me."

In view of the tattoo, Feinman let her go. He was just starting for Communications to ask about the tattoo when Sue came in and told him about the lead on the burglars.

"The first concrete thing we've got. I'd like to follow it up."

"Let's see if we can turn up the snake first." Feinman told her about that on the way. They waited while efficient hands downtown did the right things to the computer, and about ten minutes later the information was shot back at them: no fewer than five

names out of records, men with snake tattoos on left forearms.
"Snakes are popular," said Feinman, surprised. And of course the
snake might not be one of these five. But it gave them somewhere
to look. Randolph Wyatt. Jerome Simms. Andrew Sigworth.
Bruce Young. John Winters. Only two of them had pedigrees of
armed robbery, Simms and Wyatt. And going by official descriptions, only two of them corresponded to Marion Gunderson's description—Wyatt and Sigworth. They'd put out a pickup on those
three first and see what they got from them.

While he did that, Sue was looking at a city directory. "There's
only one—that's got to be it. Herschel's Fine Furniture. It's out on
Olympic."

"O.K., let's go. But I don't suppose Herschel knows anything.
A legitimate business—"

"Employees," said Sue tersely. "It's a place to start."

"And if the old lady's sure about that description, we'd better
put out an alert on that truck. Though if there are half a dozen of
them around—"

"Well, let's go and ask." Sue got into his car and the deliberate
Feinman fished out his keys and started the engine.

The address was far out on Olympic, into West Hollywood,
very much upper-middle-class. When they found the right block, it
was a short one with a drugstore on one corner, a sporting goods
store next to that, then a very wide store front with its plate-glass
windows plastered with notices saying *For Lease*. Next to that was
a jewelry store and a public parking lot.

"Damn," said Sue. "Out of business." The city directory, of
course, was last year's; the new one wasn't out yet.

"See if anybody knows anything." Feinman parked and they
tried the sporting goods store. An affable young Tarzan in a tight
T-shirt was immediately helpful.

"Oh, yeah," he said. "Herschel retired and went out of business
in August, September, about then. He'd had the store a long time
—something like thirty years, I guess. I got talking to him a few
times, having lunch at the drugstore—a nice old guy. You see,
what happened—well, it was pretty sad. He'd always figured on
leaving the business to his son, he just had one—Kenny Herschel, I
knew him too, he was one of the salesmen in the store. But he got
killed last May—drunk rammed him head-on on the freeway. So

old Herschel just closed down the business. Kenny wasn't married, there wasn't any other family."

"Do you know where Herschel lives? What's his first name?" asked Feinman.

"Oh, Julius. I think somewhere in Hollywood." He was curious, would have asked questions, but a couple of customers came in and he turned to them reluctantly. Sue and Feinman consulted the phone book in the public booth up the street.

Julius Herschel was listed at an address on Laurel Canyon Boulevard. The rain had made driving slow; it was noon, and Feinman complained that he was hungry, so they stopped at a coffee shop for lunch on the way.

The house on Laurel Canyon Boulevard was an old and sprawling one. It was pouring steadily now, the kind of soaker southern California needed. Sue tightened the strings of her plastic rain bonnet as they hurried up the front walk; there was a deep front porch. Feinman pushed the bell; they waited. Presently he pushed it again.

The door opened at the third ring, and the man facing them said, "Give me time, give me time. I've got the gout, of all damned things, and it's giving me hell— Cops?" He stared at the badge in Feinman's hand. He was a tall, bulky old man about seventy, with a gleaming bald head and a good-humored face. "Now what in hell do cops want of me?"

"Mr. Herschel? It's about your furniture business. Just a couple of questions."

"Well, come in. It's cold out, to be getting all this rain. But who's complaining, we need it." He brought them into a rather dark living room with a lot of old comfortable furniture in it. "Sit down. Now what's it all about? You a cop too?" he asked Sue. "I'll be damned."

"You closed out the business just recently," said Feinman.

"September." He told them briefly about his son, sighed and hoisted his bandaged leg to a footstool. "Suppose it's silly to keep this place—my wife died five years ago and I kind of rattle around. But we'd been here forty years, I might as well stay on."

"When you went out of business, you sold your delivery trucks? Where? That's what we're after."

"Truck," corrected Herschel. "It was strictly quality furniture, not volume. You don't have to sell the hell of a lot of sofas at nine hundred per, or breakfronts at a thousand, to turn a profit. The one van was all I ever kept."

At least that was something. "Where'd you sell it?"

Herschel regarded them curiously. "I meant to sell the going business," he said, "but I didn't get any takers. It's the hell of a time to take over a luxury business. Finally I said the hell with it, had a going-out-of-business sale and got rid of the stock. The van—"

"What is it, by the way?"

"Ford, I forget the model—I'd had it ten years. It had some mileage on it, I didn't figure on getting much for it. Intended to offer it to a used lot, but there wouldn't be much call for a thing like that. I hadn't, when I had an offer for it." He shifted his leg. "While the sale was still on, a young fellow walked in and asked if I was going to sell it. We dickered, and he gave me seven hundred for it. In cash."

"Well." Feinman considered that. "Rather funny—cash. What was his name?"

"Young colored fellow. Jim Wheeler." Herschel shot a cautious glance at them. "You're going to tell me I shouldn't have done it. I know that. But it was the day I closed the store, I had a lot to do at the last minute and I was in a hurry."

"Let me guess," said Feinman. "You signed the transfer of ownership papers and gave them to him with the pink slip instead of mailing them to the D.M.V. yourself. Taking it for granted he'd do it."

"That's right. He seemed like a nice enough young fellow. He drove it away right then. He said he was going into business for himself, reason he wanted it."

Sue laughed involuntarily. "Now that was the understatement of the year. He's certainly gone into business for himself, hasn't he, Joe?"

"Why? What's all this rigmarole about the van?" asked Herschel.

They told him, and he was still exclaiming and cussing when they ducked into the rain again and started for the station.

There, they headed for Communications again and sent a telex to the D.M.V. in Sacramento. Five minutes later the D.M.V. presented them with more information than they really wanted. There were twenty-seven James Wheelers who were registered owners of motor vehicles in the state of California. None of the registered vehicles happened to be a Ford truck, outsize. The various James Wheelers in Napa, Colfax, San Diego, Fresno and other points they could forget about, but there were twelve James Wheelers resident in the L.A. area, from Santa Monica to Sherman Oaks to Glendale.

And it was a fifty-fifty chance that the man who had bought the van wasn't named James Wheeler anyway.

◆

Maddox and D'Arcy found Clifford Jaynes at the Ford agency and brought him in for questioning. If the agency's owner had second thoughts about giving an ex-con a break, on account of that, it was just too bad. Cops did not use the word *gay;* there was nothing gay about the Freddy Noonans, the living rape victims.

Jaynes was a little, fair, plump man in the thirties; nobody would have spotted him on looks, but you seldom could. He was wary of cops, and at the same time, once he understood what the questions were about, scared enough to answer readily.

"I wouldn't do anything like that! I couldn't! When did you say —last Friday—I was at the agency all day, I couldn't have done that—"

"Have you got witnesses to say so?" asked Maddox.

"I—don't know, it's a big building, people come and go— I had a customer out on a trial drive— I didn't go to lunch until later, but I must have been back by three, I think."

"Pin it down closer," said Maddox.

"This is ridiculous," Jaynes said breathlessly. "I'm going to a psychiatrist, that was a condition of the parole, I'm perfectly all right, I'd never do a thing like that—"

They ended up back at the agency, trying to establish times, and failed. Nobody could say whether Jaynes had been there at three, three-thirty, or four. He lived alone in an apartment on Genesee Avenue; they put in a request for a search warrant and it came through just after lunch.

Both of them had looked over similar places before, but it was always depressing and ugly. A lecher was one thing; this was another. The three rooms were neat enough, clean enough; it was what was underneath that made them dirty. The piles of porno magazines in the closet, the assortment of whips and thongs in the drawers. But there wasn't any evidence to link him with the murders. Those boys had been held somewhere, if only for a few hours, but it wasn't likely that Jaynes or anyone else would have kept the missing clothes.

It was another one up in the air. He could be the boy they wanted; he might not be. He'd attacked before, if not killed. Just to be thorough, now, they went back to the station and Maddox dispatched a lab team to dust that apartment. Fingerprints, if present at all, sometimes lasted a good while; a very nice piece of evidence indeed would be a single print belonging to one of the boys.

There was still a long list of men to find, but before they started out again Dabney came in with the report on the Sexton car. "There isn't much in it," he said. "It's a mess. You can tell this and that. The windows are smashed, but they were all rolled up. That says nothing because all the doors are sprung. The transmission was in Drive. There was a full tank of gas—lucky it didn't blow."

"She came out of the car nearly at the top of the hill," said Maddox. "How the hell did the driver's door, or either front door, get sprung before the car hit? Were they locked?"

"Yep. It could have hit something right as it went over—that hill isn't a roller coaster, there are rocks and rough places."

"But," said Maddox, "I don't see that there'd be much on that hill to bounce a big heavy car like a Chrysler on the way down, especially if it'd been traveling at any speed. On the other hand, we've all seen the freak accidents."

"Anything can happen," agreed Dabney.

"See if there's anything in the autopsy report," said Maddox. About then Sue and Feinman came in and told them the news about the Herschel truck. "Well, that's a step in the right direction. It's damn funny they didn't repaint it, they might have known somebody'd notice it sooner or later."

"But nobody did until now," Feinman pointed out. "Just doing what comes naturally. Few of the punks are very bright."

"Get out an A.P.B. on it county-wide, anyway." Maddox got up and settled his tie. "Come on, D'Arcy, let's get with it. Back to the routine." But just then Rodriguez came in looking tired, slumped at his desk and lit a cigarette. "Don't tell me the inquest lasted this long?"

"Oh, no," said Rodriguez, yawning. *"Mas vale tarde que nunca* —better late than never. The coroner's clerk never showed until noon, and then I think he had lunch with the assistant D.A. waiting for him, so it never got called until an hour ago. All over in fifteen minutes. He asked me four questions and called it person or persons unknown. *Terminar.* Then I went and had lunch. What's been going on?"

They told him. "I suppose I might as well help out, the day's half shot anyway. Who's the next playful laddy we're looking for?"

"Ronald Jackson," said D'Arcy. "The address is Sherman Oaks." The rain was coming down in buckets; Rodriguez sighed and put out his cigarette.

The phone buzzed on Maddox's desk and he waved them out, picking it up. "Sergeant Maddox."

It was Sergeant Whitwell on the desk. "The hospital just called. The Butler woman's conscious. You can see her for ten minutes."

"I'm on my way." Maddox got his raincoat and hat from the rack by the door.

At the receiving hospital, a horsefaced nurse led him down the corridor to a room at the end. "Ten minutes," she warned him. "She'll be all right, but she's still weak—she was in deep shock after surgery." Outside the door Mrs. Carradine was mopping her eyes. She looked up and recognized him.

"This is silly, crying like a baby because Ruth's going to get better—but she was unconscious so long— Have you found out who did it yet?"

"We're hoping Mrs. Butler can tell us." Maddox went into the room, the nurse padding after him.

Ruth Butler lay flat and still in the narrow bed. Her dark hair was untidy on the pillow, her face drawn, but a little color showed in her cheeks. There was an intravenous feeding tube attached to one arm. He leaned over her. "Mrs. Butler?"

Her eyes opened and focused on him. "Mrs. Butler, I'm from the police. Can you tell me who did this to you?"

"Lisa?" she asked in a faint voice.

He hesitated. "She's all right."

"No. Afraid—she looked—*dead*. But—got to tell you. She said—another one coming. That night. Estimates—she was getting estimates—for the painting. We were going halves on it—needed painting inside—both places. She called—ads in the paper." She was silent, shutting her eyes again. The nurse put a hand on her wrist. "No—all right—got to tell. I put Emily to bed—was reading in the front room—when I heard Lisa knock on the wall. We both had keys—both places. I went over—went in—table knocked over, and noises— I was frightened—went into the bedroom—they were there. Lisa all—all—she looked *dead*. I couldn't scream— I tried pull him away—he just knocked me down across the bed—"

"All right, take it easy," said Maddox quietly.

"Big—a great big black man. Strong— He picked me right up—and threw me—" She shuddered and shut her eyes again.

Maddox nodded at the nurse and went out. In the corridor he felt in his pocket; he still had the key to the duplex, sent up with the lab report. He hoped somebody had remembered to call that attorney. He wondered who she'd left the duplex to. Maybe to Ruth.

It was raining so hard now, it was like driving through fog. He crept cautiously over to Kingsley Avenue, dodged through the rain and let himself into Lisa Martin's side of the duplex. After this while, there was a film of dust over everything; nothing had been picked up from where it had fallen. There was a faint sour smell: something gone bad in the refrigerator? There was gray fingerprint powder over every surface; in the bedroom, the chalk outline where the body had lain. Evidently Lisa, like Ruth, had been a reader; there were a good many books, many paperbacks, in a cheap bookcase in the living room, more in the bedroom. Incurably addicted to books himself—the second bedroom in the house on Gregory Avenue was full of them, and whatever house Sue picked had better have enough space for all his bookshelves—he bent to look at titles. A surprising miscellany it was—parapsychology, detective novels, humor, biography.

No newspapers. He went out to the kitchen; in the tiny service porch he found a neat stack of *Herald-Examiners,* and had a look at them on the kitchen table. They dated back two weeks, from last Tuesday. He separated all the classified ads. Just at a glance, under *Services* quite a few ads offered painting, redecorating. Thrifty Lisa, getting estimates on the job, might have called them all; she hadn't marked any of the phone numbers. More routine and legwork. But this was a very strong lead.

He bundled up all the classified ads and shoved them under his coat, shielding them from rain on the way back to the car.

◆

Marion Gunderson came in at three-thirty; Feinman was out, but Rowan happened to be in, and drove her downtown to Parker Center to look at mug shots. There were, of course, books and books of mug shots to look at, and she hadn't found the heister by five-thirty when he drove her uptown again. She agreed to come back tomorrow.

◆

At four o'clock Rodriguez and D'Arcy brought in Louis Johnson, who had a pedigree of approaching little boys and had once beaten one boy after attacking him. He was a gangling thin man of twenty-six with a deeply acne-scarred face. His record said borderline normal, I.Q. 85; he was on parole to an aunt and uncle in the Atwater district.

They started to ask him questions, and as soon as they mentioned Freddy Noonan, he said, "I seen about that in the paper. I can read, you know. You wanta know, I did that. I did that to him, that little kid. I like to do it to little kids."

"O.K., tell us how you did it," said D'Arcy. "How did you get him to come with you?"

"I just asked him."

"Where was this?"

"I dunno. On a street somewhere. He came along—and I—I took him— I got him behind a big billboard and I did it. I did it to him—I like doing it to little kids."

That they knew all too well, but it didn't seem to mean much here. "Then what did you do?" asked Rodriguez.

"I just left him there. I went home and Aunty Marie said have you been good and I said I always am because I don't want to go back to that place."

"What about the other little boy, Louis? Harold Frost?"

"Yes! Yes! I killed him too. I liked doing that!"

"Where'd you pick him up? How?"

"Oh—somewhere. I dunno. I did it the same way. I liked to see all the blood—"

It was a complete waste of time, but they drove him back to Atwater and talked to the aunt and uncle. Louis had never learned to drive a car, and of course the X they wanted had almost certainly been in a car. Also, the aunt and uncle were certain that Louis had been home all last Friday afternoon.

"I'll say frankly," said his uncle, and he sounded uneasy, "it's a responsibility I don't feel right about. I'm sorry for the boy, but he's right off in the head and they ought to shut him up. We can't live a decent normal life, saddled with him—I said so to that man from the parole office, and he just gave me a lot of double-talk about a home environment being better. That kid's nuts, and one of these days he might do something real bad, and he ought to be shut up before he does it—but if the authorities won't do it, what the hell can we do?"

It was a question. Considering some of what Louis had come out with, someday it might turn into a big question—why was he loose? But he wasn't the one they were after right now.

It was a quarter of six, and the rain had slackened a little. "Damnation," said D'Arcy, "take half an hour to get back to my car. Make it snappy, César, I've got a date."

Rodriguez looked at him sideways, starting the engine. He and Maddox had a theory that D'Arcy was still a bachelor because he was so self-conscious about his peculiar first name; he had everybody who knew it trained never to use it. At the same time, he was curiously given to falling—violently and temporarily—for rather unsuitable girls. So far as Rodriguez knew, the latest one was quite a nice girl, a girl named Joan Berry who worked at the phone company.

Driving through rain, he reflected that even detectives came in all shapes and sizes.

◆

Donaldson and Brougham came on night watch at eight o'clock. Usually on a rainy night, night watch was a drag; southern Californians were like cats about rain, seeing it so seldom. Sometimes it wasn't.

They looked over the A.P.B.'s out, the pick-up-and-holds. They speculated about the Herschel van. A funny one.

At eight-fifty Patrolman Nolan presented them with Manfred Guttierez: that knifing in a bar last Tuesday. Nolan had spotted the plate number, and Guttierez had been in the car. He was very drunk. Donaldson ferried him over to the jail and booked him in.

At nine-forty a frightened young couple was brought in by Patrolman Schultz. Donald Wise and Michelle Harmon. They both attended an adult-education class at Hollywood High, and as usual, had gone in Wise's car; he'd driven her home, which was Oakwood Avenue— "And we were just sitting in the car talking when this nut came out of nowhere and fired a gun at us—my God, it sounded like a bomb—hit the top of the car. I jumped out, caught a glimpse of a guy running away, but I couldn't say what size or anything, there isn't a street light right there—"

"Now that," said Brougham to Donaldson when they'd signed a statement and gone, "is all we need. Some nut copy-catting that guy in New York, taking potshots at couples in cars. My God. And no way to go looking for him. You know something, Ken, this town is getting dirtier and wilder and more unbelievable all the time. You never know what's going to happen next."

The next thing that happened was a heist. It was at a liquor store on Sunset Boulevard, and nobody would have known about it until later on except that Patrolman Percy Everard had happened to be passing at the time and heard the shots. He had hit the curb and gone in, gun out, to exchange shots with a man running out of the store. He had taken off in what Everard somewhat doubtfully identified—the rain coming down in sheets—as a Chevy or Ford sedan, white or beige or tan. He had then entered the store to find the owner, subsequently identified as Willis Mapps, just inside the door critically wounded.

"It was a mess," said Everard, who'd only been riding a squad car a year and hadn't seen quite so many messes as more experienced LAPD men. "Blood all over, bottles smashed, sure, the register was open— I called the ambulance first, those bastards were long gone—" He swallowed, collecting himself, remembering all the lessons at the Academy. "God, that poor guy—the manager, owner, whatever—he tried so hard to tell me— He was pumping blood, an artery cut somewhere, but he said to me, I was kneeling over him, the ambulance just coming up, he said, the guy had a tattoo—left arm just above the hand—a great big snake, he said—"

And Donaldson said, "A snake? There was an A.P.B. just out today—"

FOUR

That was waiting on Saturday morning; but Saturday morning was
a dead loss as far as work on their own cases went. When the day-
watch men came in, Ellis and the Secret Service men were already
—or still—there, unshaven and triumphant. They had just about
wrapped up the counterfeiting case; overnight they'd had a tip that
the ring was taking delivery of a new supply to be passed, and
where and when; they were busily plotting a raid, and Ellis com-
mandeered all the detectives to make up enough manpower.

Maddox was annoyed, but there was nothing they could do
about it.

Ellis and the government men pored over a map, handed out
walkie-talkies, assigned teams. The target was an old apartment
on the third floor of a building down on south Vermont, and the
rendezvous was supposed to be at ten-thirty, the courier landing
from New Orleans at night—if the plane wasn't late.

By nine forty-five they were all in position, two cars of Secret
Service men parked unobtrusively on the street, others with the
Hollywood men deployed on floors above and below the apartment, and the muffled communications via the walkie-talkies making Maddox feel as if he'd strayed into a bad espionage movie.

He was stationed with D'Arcy at the top of the stairs on the
floor above apartment 311, ruminating on their sex killer, on the
burglars, and the time dragged on to ten forty-five before the
walkie-talkie came whispering to life. "O.K., the agent just walked
in. Watches synchronized—ten forty-six now. Three minutes and
converge on the door."

Two minutes and forty seconds later Maddox and D'Arcy went
down the stairs and joined four Secret Service men, Ellis, Rodriguez and Rowan outside 311. The senior Secret Service man, gun
out, knocked peremptorily. They were all expecting a dead si-

lence, the necessity to kick the door in, when it was jerked open and a rough voice said, "For Godsakes, where you been?" The Secret Service men plunged in, somebody yelled *Cops,* somebody fired shots, and abruptly a wild mêlée was in progress. Ellis braced his bulk against the closed door. Within three minutes there must have been twenty rounds of ammunition fired, most of it by the counterfeiters. When the noise died down and the smoke cleared away, all the counterfeiters were in cuffs, one Secret Service man unconscious and losing blood, and Ellis swearing at the spreading bloodstain on one shoulder, breathing hard.

Maddox rode in the ambulance with both of them, waited to hear how Ellis was. "Oh, he'll live," said the young doctor at the receiving hospital cheerfully. "Torn some muscles in his shoulder, he'll be out of commission a week or so." And Maddox, commiserating with Ellis, was annoyed all over again; even with the Secret Service out of their hair, they'd still be shorthanded.

———◆———

Daisy and Sue had split up the phone numbers from the classified ads in the *Herald,* and had the phone company looking up addresses to match. They talked about old Mrs. Eady and Daisy said, "That kind dying off, aren't they? Most people these days grab the so-called free money wherever they can get it. I hope to God we can catch up to that bunch."

"All these Wheelers," said Sue. "I don't see how to use it—and it probably wasn't his real name anyway."

Marion Gunderson came in at nine o'clock, and Sue drove her downtown, envying her the red hair and dimple. At R. and I., at headquarters, the policewoman who brought out the mug-shot books had been in Sue's class at the Academy, and they were enjoying an animated gossip, forty minutes later, when Marion let out a triumphant yelp. "That's him! I knew I'd recognize him!"

Sue went to look. She'd put the finger on Randolph Wyatt, and of course, he was one of those three possibles bearing the snake tattoos that she and Feinman had put out the A.P.B.'s on. He had the right record for it: four counts of armed robbery, one as a juvenile, assault with intent, several counts of B. and E. He was twenty-nine, five-ten, a hundred and sixty, brown and blue, no marks but the tattoo.

Sue drove Marion back to Hollywood, thanked her for her help. "Any day," said Marion. "Not that I'd like to go through another holdup, no way. Oh, well, any luck and maybe I'll start to get enough modeling jobs, I won't have to stand behind a counter. Anyway, I hope you catch him." She looked at Sue curiously. "Must be a funny kind of job, being a policewoman."

"*Funny* isn't the word sometimes," said Sue. "Thanks again, and good luck."

In the detective office, Daisy told her the hospital had called; the owner of the liquor store, Willis Mapps, had just died. "So that makes it homicide," said Sue. "At least we know who."

"She made somebody?"

"Randolph Wyatt. We'd better do something about those A.P.B.'s." Sue canceled the other two and added the homicide to the one on Wyatt. Unfortunately, Sacramento had told them there was no car registered to him. It was a lot harder to spot a pedestrian, anonymous in the greater Los Angeles area, than the plate number on a fairly large item like an automobile.

The autopsy report on Lisa Martin had come in. Sue read it and said, "The Butler woman was lucky." Lisa Martin had been beaten savagely, forcibly raped and strangled. The kickback on those latents had come in from the FBI last night; the men hadn't had time to look at any reports. They weren't in the FBI files, which meant that whoever had left them had no criminal record, had never spent any time in the services or held any job demanding security clearance.

The phone company began to come through with addresses matching the phone numbers. Sue and Daisy were under strict orders not to do any follow-up on that one: leave it to the men. Daisy made a list, with a carbon, as the addresses came in, and they ranged from Vernon to Hollywood to South Pasadena.

They were just deciding to go out to lunch, at a little before twelve, when a man came in from the corridor leading out to the desk, and hesitated in the doorway. "Oh," he said. "Nothing but lady cops in, hah?"

"That's about it," said Daisy. "What can we do for you?"

"Not one damned thing," he said. "I gave your desk sergeant his big laugh of the week, maybe I do the same for you. There's nothing you can do about it, I know that, but I thought maybe you'd like to know." He advanced to Daisy's desk and sat down, got out a cigarette. He was a stocky middle-aged man in a white jump suit with the legend *Frank's Union Service* stitched in red over the breast pocket.

"About what?" asked Sue.

He shook his head. "I still don't believe it. My name's Cooper, by the way. I've got a Union station, over on Highland. There's a self-service island. You know?" They nodded. "With the machine to put the money in, you know? Well, I clear it out once a week. I suppose," he said suddenly, "I better write the company a letter about it. They ought to know. Anyway, I clear the cash out once a week, usually, and I just did this morning. I pull this stuff out, couldn't believe my eyes." He reached into his pocket and brought out some pieces of crumpled paper, put them on the desk. "Take a look."

They looked, and after a moment burst out laughing. "Yeah, it's funny," said Cooper morosely. What he had put on the desk was a handful of dollar bills, but they weren't green; they were black and white. They were Xerox copies of dollar bills, clearly and faithfully reproduced down to the Treasurer's signature and the serial numbers. "Damn it, I never knew that damned machine was color-blind!"

The same thought hit Sue and Daisy at once: everybody out rounding up the gang of counterfeiters, an elaborate intrastate organization, while some humble operator was simply using copying machines at ten cents a throw. Even if the only place he could spend it was on self-service gasoline. "Is it that funny?" asked Cooper.

"It *looks* so queer. No, not really," said Sue. And of course there wasn't anything they could do about it. Whoever had discovered that the machine was color-blind wasn't going to be getting self-service gasoline when the station was open and attendants were around. It was just to be hoped it was only a one-man operation, nothing wholesale.

Cooper had just gone away when the men began to come in, in various states. D'Arcy had a torn shirt, Rodriguez was swearing over a rip in his suit jacket, Rowan had the beginning of a black eye. They told the girls about Ellis. There was a good deal of red tape to be cleared up, but at least they'd get out of that: it was Secret Service business, the prisoners would be stashed in a Federal pen pending trial. Feinman had missed the whole thing; it was his day off.

Maddox came back just after Sue and Daisy came in from lunch, and said Ellis would be O.K., but out for at least a week. "And we're shorthanded as it is," he added bitterly. "All this damn routine legwork piling up, we have to waste half a day helping out the Feds!" He glanced at the autopsy report briefly; Sue told him about Mapps, and Marion's identification of Wyatt. "Well, some progress at least."

"No car," said Sue. "The A.P.B. might not turn him up in a month of Sundays."

"Um." Maddox felt his jaw. He'd been running a hand through his straight black hair and it fell untidily over his forehead. "Shortcuts. D'Arcy—César. This Wyatt. He hasn't been off P.A. long. Suppose you talk to his officer, find out where he's been living, if he had a job." He passed over the Xerox of Wyatt's rap sheet. "Did the phone company come through with those addresses?"

"All of them in. Nine altogether." Daisy handed over the list.

Maddox handed the carbon to Rowan. "I'll take the top half. Let's get on this at least. It's time we had some more hands around here. Get back to the sex nuts tomorrow. Well, somebody was telling me the other day that recruitment's up—maybe six months from now we'll be assigned half a dozen new detectives." He got up.

"Oh, you haven't heard about the dollar bills," said Sue.

"Later, later. If they're counterfeit, tell the Secret Service." He went out with Rowan.

Daisy and Sue looked at each other. Belatedly they realized what they should have told Mr. Cooper.

◆

These days, mere addresses or city locations didn't tell much about the color of the residents. There were some areas that were pretty solidly black. Of the five addresses of the would-be painters Maddox had to cover, two were in areas like that: Vernon and Watts. The Vernon address was closer; he stopped there first. It was a small shabby frame house.

The young woman who opened the door shied back at the badge. She was medium black, not bad-looking, modestly dressed. A baby was crying somewhere in the house. "What you *want?*" she asked.

"Someone here had an ad in the *Herald,* for painting work."

She nodded. "Len. My husband. Len hasn't done anything, he's working steady, keep outta trouble. He don't want no more trouble, he just got in with a bad crowd that time, is all."

"What's his name?"

"Len Bright. He hasn't done—"

"He's been in police trouble?"

"Just one time," she said reluctantly. "He only got a year in. For burglary. He's been straight, he don't want to mess with that stuff again. Why you askin' about Len?"

"What does your husband look like?" asked Maddox.

"What's he *look* like?" She stared. "Well, what in time—"

"How tall is he?"

"Why, a bitty taller'n me, I guess. What—"

"All right, thanks," said Maddox, and turned away. The switch here was that if those two unknown latents had anything to do with the case, anybody who had done time for a felony was automatically alibied: his prints would be on file. And Len didn't sound like Ruth Butler's great big black man.

On the way to Watts he covered three more addresses, in Inglewood, Huntington Park and Hawthorne. At the first, the painter was home, grumbling about the weather that kept him from working; he was a middle-aged white man. At the second, a plump matronly woman, also white, said her son had put the ad in, he was going to L.A.C.C. and interested in earning extra money. At the third, a thin black woman told him incuriously her husband wasn't running that ad no more, it couldn't do no good, because he'd fell off a ladder last week and busted a leg, probably couldn't go back to work for a couple of months.

It was getting on toward five o'clock and raining harder when he got down to Watts. It had drizzled all day, but now it grew to a downpour like yesterday's, and the sky was dark; he had trouble spotting addresses. The one he wanted was a single house on a small lot, and there was a dark Ford sedan sitting at the curb.

Maddox pulled up behind it, got out and ran up the walk to the porch, rang the bell; there were lights inside.

The door was jerked open by a big broad black man, who said belligerently, "You come to get some o' what you deserve, boy? You just—" He stopped abruptly and peered at Maddox, switched on a light on the porch. "Who the hell are you?"

Maddox showed him the badge. "Oh!" said the man, taken aback. He looked over his shoulder. "I thought you said you didn't call cops, Madge."

"I never called for no cops. What's the good? I'm gettin' shut of him all right, no sense call cops now."

"Well, we got one. Who you lookin' for?" he asked Maddox.

"Whoever put an ad in the *Herald* about some painting."

"Uh-huh. Whaffor?"

"In connection with a case."

"You don't say. Police business. I'm bound to say, he never been in cop trouble I know about. Madge wouldn't have married him, he had been. You better come in." He held open the screen door.

In the narrow living room, a little garishly furnished, a woman was just setting two suitcases down on the couch. She was a light-skinned Negro with rather sharp features, handsome rather than pretty. Now in the light Maddox could see that the big man was neatly dressed in slacks and sports shirt; he had the same aquiline features, was a trifle darker. "Cop looking for Scotty," he said. "I'm Lee Henderson, this is my sister Madge."

"Who's Scotty?"

"My husband," said Madge. "Scotty Coker. What you want him for?"

"Questioning. You're leaving him?"

"You're damn right I'm leaving him," she said emphatically. "I thought he was a decent man, we got married last year. He's a good enough worker, I'll say that, brings home good money—works at the Firestone plant, and takes extra jobs too. But he's got drunk on weekends and beat me up just once too often—I don't need to take that. I got away from the big bastard last Sunday night, he like to kill me—he's one mean big nigger when he's drunk. I been with Lee and Marie all week, got a divorce set up already, but I wanted the rest o' my clothes. Lee come along in case Scotty was here, but he wasn't. I don't know where he'd be."

Maddox was interested; this rang a loud bell. "Any idea where he might have gone? He's got a car?"

"Yeah, sure. He's kind of a loner, he knows guys at the plant, but nobody good enough to stay with. He's been here, there's dirty dishes in the kitchen, dirty laundry."

"Well, thanks very much." Maddox opened the door. He left them staring after him curiously.

The rain had let up a little, but it was full dark now and a slow drive in homeward-bound traffic, even on the freeway, back up into Hollywood. It was just six o'clock when he opened the back door to the station and nearly collided with Sue.

"Well, I was wondering where you'd got to. I'm just going home."

"I'll be a few minutes," said Maddox. "I've been thinking on the way back. You take tomorrow off and look at houses. Find one. Definitely. Now we've made up our minds, let's get on with it, for God's sake. You'll never find a place just looking on your day off."

Sue stared at him. "Well, I'll admit I've been thinking the same thing. But you don't decide about a big thing like a house all of a sudden. It's going to mean whopping payments, I'm afraid."

"For some strange reason banks think city employees are good risks. You go look. I'll be home in half an hour."

The detective office was empty. He went down to Communications and consulted Sacramento. Scott Coker was driving a six-year-old Ford, plate number so-and-so. Maddox put out an A.P.B. for him. Unless Rowan had come up with somebody just as likely, Scott Coker sounded on several counts like a good candidate for Ruth Butler's great big black man.

He went out again, wondering if D'Arcy and Rodriguez had got anywhere on Wyatt.

———◆———

Rodriguez had talked to the parole officer, at Welfare and Rehabilitation downtown, who had supervised Randolph Wyatt's latest parole. They'd already discovered that Wyatt didn't have a car. He'd been living at an apartment on Romaine Street, working at a service station within walking distance on Santa Monica.

They tried the apartment first. They got no answer at the door, and talked to the manageress, who lived on the premises. "I haven't seen him in a couple of weeks," she said, "but he'd dodge me. I'm not surprised, police come looking. He owes two months' back rent, I've been after him about it— If he does show up, I'll tell him to get out."

They drove up to the service station. The owner was there, Les Higgins; he looked at the badges and listened to the questions. "I swear, I'll never bother to give an ex-con a break again. This is the second one let me down. Day they're off parole, they've had it with the eight-to-five, boom, off they go. This Wyatt, he's a lazy bum anyway. Got away with as little work as he could, locked in the toilet reading *Playboy* or something. I haven't seen him since last Monday, he just didn't show. You want him again, hah? What'd he do?"

D'Arcy said, "Damnation. He could be anywhere."

"He took some loot at the liquor store," said Rodriguez, fingering his moustache. "He could have a car by now. No registration or a fake one."

"Say—" said Higgins. "I don't know if it means anything— Say, what you want him for?"

"Homicide," said Rodriguez.

"Sweet Jesus. Well, I don't know if it means anything, but he'd been saying just lately he wanted to go see his mother, she's been sick. She lives in Stockton, I think he said."

"Thanks so much," said Rodriguez. Turning the key in the ignition, he said to D'Arcy, "Always so much easier to sit inside and use the phone."

Back at the station, D'Arcy wandered out to the front hall to the coffee machine and Rodriguez got on the phone to Stockton. Wyatt hailed from Stockton originally, and his first felony arrest had been there; possibly somebody in the Stockton Police Department would remember him, at least he'd be in their files. And presumably his then home address.

The sergeant he talked to didn't remember Wyatt offhand, but after relaying the request for information, added, "Just a minute, Captain Keller just walked in. I'll ask him." There was silence, and then a heavier voice asked, "This L.A.? Asking about Randy Wyatt? I thought he was still in the joint."

"Not for six months. We've got a warrant out on him, and there's some suggestion that he might be up there. To see his mother."

"Funny thing," said Keller, "it's a decent family. Only black sheep they ever had. So far as I know, she still lives in the old family place. We'll have a look for you. What's the charge?"

"Homicide," said Rodriguez.

"So he finally got there, did he?" said Keller. "You stay put. We'll go look, and I'll get back to you."

That was at four-thirty. D'Arcy and Rodriguez sat drinking coffee and listening to the rain outside, thinking smugly of the unfortunates out on the legwork. They agreed they ought to go and visit Ellis in the hospital. "Did anybody hear whether that Fed's going to make it?" asked D'Arcy.

"Ivor asked us to call," said Daisy. "He'll be O.K."

At five-thirty the phone rang, and it was Keller. "Your tip was right on the button. He was there, sitting on the front porch chatting with the family. He was too surprised to see us to make any fuss. We've got him tucked away safe. I can ferry him down tomorrow if you want, or you can send somebody up."

"We'd appreciate a ferrying job very much," Rodriguez told him. "It's going a little hot and heavy here right now, Captain, and we're shorthanded."

"I bet," said Keller. "I've heard some about your neck of the woods. Kind of fast and furious. God knows this town isn't as little and peaceful as it used to be when I was a kid, but we're still a ways from being a big city. Well, I'll be with you sometime tomorrow."

D'Arcy and Rodriguez went home early. It had been quite a day.

◆

Sue was pleased to have an unexpected day off; she'd been thinking along the same lines as Ivor. She'd been looking at houses for more than six weeks, on all her days off, and it was difficult, causing all sorts of problems. There was the laundry, and all the mundane housework she usually did on Wednesdays taking up evenings instead. And by now she'd seen so many houses it was hard to keep them straight in her mind.

She had stuck with Mr. Parrott, as his company was a big one and carried property nearly all over the county. She phoned him early on Sunday morning and proposed that he show her houses all day. He seemed rather stunned, but gallantly agreed to give her his time up to three o'clock, when he had an appointment. He picked her up at ten.

By this time she had seen houses she liked, houses she didn't like, a lot of houses she could live with but wasn't especially enthusiastic about, and at least she had some clearer ideas of what she didn't want in a house.

He showed her another house in Toluca Lake which was possible, the four bedrooms quite small. He showed her a house in Burbank which had a wall of mirrors in the living room, ruling that one out completely. He showed her a house in Glendale which was very possible until she looked out a back window and discovered that there was a large public school playground just behind it; she could imagine the noise. She was beginning to feel terribly uncomfortable about going into peoples' houses with the people there, and having to be noncommittal without being impolite.

She was also feeling rather exhausted at one-thirty in the afternoon when they got back into his car, and he was looking a little cross. He said, "I have another property in this general area I can show you, Mrs. Maddox, but quite frankly I doubt if you'll care for it. It's been vacant for some time—"

"Let's go see it," said Sue.

He started the engine. "The former owner—an old lady—died several months ago. She'd neglected the place for some time, I'm afraid. It's sound enough—the roof's only three years old—but it needs painting and yard work. Her heirs live out of state, and they're anxious to sell, but— Well, there's a lot of potential value, but it does need a lot of work." They were driving up a main boulevard; he turned left onto side streets, climbed a curving rising blacktop road. "You aren't familiar with Glendale, are you? This is Verdugo Woodlands, a very desirable area."

When he pulled to the curb, at a corner where a narrow side street crossed, Sue looked at a very untidy front yard, patches of long-uncut lawn and overgrown bushes. But what she could see of the house looked interesting. It was an older house, a two-story white stucco house with a gabled roof and two little windows up under the eaves like eyes peering out. She went up the curving front path behind him eagerly. It was a dark, dank day, raining on and off.

Inside, at first glance the house was awful: chill and drear, and completely empty of furniture. But the lovely space, thought Sue; the size of the rooms, and all quite well proportioned— There was a big living room with a stone fireplace—a dining room—an old-fashioned big kitchen with plenty of room for a table—a study big enough to take all Ivor's bookcases. The wall-to-wall carpet was far from new, but there was plenty of wear in it yet, and it was a neutral dark tan. Up the rather narrow staircase with a wrought-iron railing there was a landing, a hall and four really huge bedrooms and two bathrooms. All the rooms needed painting or papering; the real ceramic tile in one bath was an unfortunate shade of green, but the other one had tan tile with a gold vein. There were big walk-in closets in all the bedrooms, and a window seat in one at the back. Sue knelt there and looked out to quite a large back yard with a chain-link fence all around it. The yard was a wilderness of overgrown shrubbery and flower beds.

But it was a *house*. The kind of house nobody built anymore, with the kitchen at the back, where it should be, cupboards galore, lots of storage space, big rooms.

"—Double garage," Mr. Parrott was saying. "An appraiser has just been over it, and structurally it's in excellent condition. But in view of all the work it needs—"

"How much do they want?" asked Sue.

"Too much, in my opinion. A hundred and five thousand. Of course the lot's a hundred and eighty feet deep. But the age of the place, and all the work it—"

"What are the taxes?"

"Fifteen hundred. Are you really considering—"

"I don't think we could afford it. But I like it very much." It would be a lovely house, warm and light and spacious, with the new paint and paper and furniture in place. *Too dear for my possessing,* thought Sue. Unless Mother sells the house on Janiel Terrace and comes in with us— All our furniture together wouldn't begin to fill the place, but— And all the work in the yard— But the beautiful big oak trees there, this quiet shaded street, the house on a corner with the nearest neighbor not close at all—

Parrott was eyeing her keenly. "I think they'd accept a lower offer. Start with ninety and dicker up."

Sue sighed. "I'll have to ask my husband. I want him to see it. Maybe, but I'm afraid not."

But she kept thinking about it after he'd taken her home. It could be such a beautiful house. A family house. Goodness knew both she and Mother didn't mind painting—any idiot could wield a paint roller. Get somebody to put the yard in shape to start with—things easy to take care of. Curtains—there must be twenty windows, some big ones. No carpets upstairs, but there were always sales— They needn't furnish all the bedrooms right away. There was that tile you could just stick on piece by piece. Hardwood floors all over. It was built ten times better than anybody built houses now.

Only it was too much money. Even if Mother sold the house— No, they couldn't possibly afford it.

Sue felt restless. She went out and got the car and drove up to Janiel Terrace to tell her mother about the house. She felt irrationally annoyed with her mother when she found the garage empty and the house locked. Where on earth was she on a dreary Sunday afternoon?

But suddenly she had to tell somebody, and it would be ages before Ivor came home. On impulse she drove over to Alexandria Avenue to see how old Mrs. Eady was.

As she'd suspected, Mrs. Eady didn't have the gas heater on; too expensive. She'd been sitting in the platform rocker, which she'd pulled into the front bedroom, and she was bundled up in two cardigans over her cotton dress; it was probably in the low forties, damp and chill. "It's so nice of you to come and see me," she said, surprised and very pleased. "I can't get over the way you've been so good and kind, you and your mother."

"We haven't done much," said Sue. "I wish—" But she knew there really wasn't any use saying to Mrs. Eady, Ask for some of that money being poured out to the ungrateful bums and lushes and professional welfare families, it's the people like you who deserve it. It wouldn't be any use at all. Old Mrs. Eady could never face her husband in the next world if she took charity.

She'd been reading a book; Sue moved it, sitting down on the bed, and it was Norah Lofts' *Bless This House*. "You know, it was providential," said Mrs. Eady, "that I found they didn't take my string bag. I always use it to carry books from the library. I don't know if I could manage more than one or two, on the bus, without it. And reading's about all I do these days—I always liked to read. And I always loved that book, I like to read it over again every so often. I was so pleased when I found my string bag in the closet."

"I've been out looking at houses—we're going to buy one. We're hoping to start a family sometime."

"Oh, my dear, I hope you do. Your husband's in the police too, isn't he? Bert and I were so sorry we never had any children— I always wanted a big family. What kind of house do you want?"

"Well, I saw one today I'd love—but I'm afraid we can't afford it." Sue started to tell her about the house. She thought suddenly, unfinished furniture. Places you could get good solid pieces, and save by finishing them yourself. And you could find good second-hand furniture if you looked—

◆

They'd been out all morning on the legwork, chasing up the names on that list of violence-oriented homosexuals. Nothing suggestive had showed except that two of them had solid alibis for the Noonan job.

By coincidence, they all showed up at The Grotto on Santa Monica about the same time: Maddox, D'Arcy, Rodriguez, Feinman, Dabney and Rowan—and pulled a couple of tables together. There was a waitress there who felt very motherly toward cops. They ordered absently, and Dabney said, "This is a hell of a way to have to go to work. All up in the air."

"Any suggestions for shortcuts?" asked Maddox wearily.

"It's the way we have to go, I guess. The only thing is, of course, queers are apt to spook easy and spill all they know."

"What we've got to bank on."

"Somebody," said Rodriguez, "ought to go back and mind the store. That captain from Stockton should be landing here with Wyatt any time."

He and Maddox stayed in, waiting. It was getting on for two

o'clock when Keller arrived. He was a big, broad, tanned fellow in natty sports clothes. "I haven't been down here for ten years," he said. "Hardly recognized the place, all the new freeways." He had Wyatt in cuffs.

There wasn't any reason to say anything to Wyatt, but Maddox did. Even an experienced cop, who dealt with the wild ones every day of his life, couldn't help wondering what made them tick: and of course it was parallel lines never meeting. The cop, oriented to a tidy routine of life, orderly motives: the outlaw moving as the wind listed.

"You had a job, Wyatt," he said. "You ran straight for a while." Of course they usually did, on parole. "Why the hell did you have to backslide?"

Wyatt raised sullen eyes. "I wanted to go see Mom. That lousy job—boss order me around all the time. I dropped all I had saved up in a lousy crap game."

It was an answer, if there was any answer. Rodriguez took him over to book him in, and Maddox talked shop with Keller until he got back. Keller had just said, "Well, I reckon to lay over and drive home tomorrow—any suggestion where I should go, get a decent bed and a good steak dinner?" when the phone buzzed on Maddox's desk.

"Sergeant Maddox."

"Juvenile reported missing," said Whitwell. "Just now. Off a locked estate up in Mount Olympus. Eight-year-old boy. What Carmichael says, it looks offbeat."

"We're on it. Send up all the squads you can round up!" Maddox was on his feet. "*Vamos,* César—this might be number three!"

———◆———

The Mount Olympus residential area, northwest and above Hollywood, was a millionaires' row. There were curving hillside avenues of big expensive homes, some big estates. The address was Jennifer Drive. When Maddox pulled the Maserati up in front, they looked at the place and Rodriguez said, "Number three hell, it's a snatch." The place might be an acre in size; there was an expanse of green lawn, a big clean-looking white Spanish house with a red tile roof.

It was raining again. It had been stopping and starting all day.

There were two squad cars in front of the tall iron gates. A six-foot chain-link fence circled the estate. Patrolman Gonzales was coming down to the gate, inside; he looked grim and agitated, letting them in with a key.

"Listen, these gates are kept locked. It looks like a snatch—but how could it be? The kid's only been gone under an hour."

"What have you got so far?"

"Enough to make it look damn queer. The father's Howard Lockwood, one of the directors of a big hotel chain. You see the setup—about all the money there is. They've got two kids, the boy Justin, ten-year-old girl Anne. Everybody's been home all day, in the rain. When it stopped raining a while ago the boy went out, take the dog for a run, just around the house." Gonzales turned. "There's the dog. What damn kind of dog, it didn't even bark—"

The dog, advancing slowly and imperturbably down the gravel path, was a very large St. Bernard. He came up and sniffed Maddox's shoes, turned his back and sat down to scratch an ear. Maddox eyed him with disfavor. As any burglar knew—trained guard dogs aside, and they were dangerous for laymen to handle—little dogs were more to be feared than big ones; they were readier to bark and bite.

"—When it started raining again, and he didn't come in, Lockwood went out and called. *Nada más.* He's nowhere. Lockwood searched the place end to end—there aren't any live-in servants—and then called us. It seems to narrow down to a period of about half an hour when he must have disappeared."

"All right," said Maddox. "There are cars on the way. Deploy them for ten blocks around. There could be an easy answer, he might have climbed the fence to pat a stray dog."

Gonzales made a derisive sound. "O.K. You'd better see the Lockwoods—they're trying to send us away now, to them it's a snatch."

The Lockwoods were nice people. The kind of people who didn't think money gave them any privilege, who would have been nice people whether they had money or not. But if money didn't make privilege, it made dangers; and they faced Maddox and Rodriguez in fright and panic.

"We shouldn't have called you." Lockwood was gray and taut:

a good-looking man about forty. "There'll be a ransom note. We'll have to wait. We shouldn't—"

His wife was a pretty brunette, pale and fighting for control. She let him do the talking.

"He's a very obedient boy—no reason to run away, that's ridiculous, imagining he should climb the fence and run off— I lost my head, I shouldn't have called you. And the kidnappers may be watching— I want you all to go away—there'll be a ransom note—"

"The jigsaw puzzle," said Mrs. Lockwood in a faint voice. "He was so interested in it. He and Anne were doing it together, he was bound to finish it today. He only—when it stopped raining—he only said, take Barnaby out for a few minutes' run—"

Maddox hesitated. He said, "You may be right, Mr. Lockwood, but there could be other answers here too. We don't know yet. But you did the right thing to call us in, whatever this turns out to be."

Lockwood turned away. "I can't stop it. I see. I can't give you orders what to do."

"But," said Rodriguez on the broad brick front porch, "how the hell, Ivor? Either a snatcher or our sex fiend, how? A six-foot fence, and the gate locked?"

"Let's look," said Maddox. It had not rained heavily today, just drizzled on and off. They collected Gonzales and four other patrolmen and made a foot-by-foot examination of the fence, the ground beneath.

About four feet down from the locked gate the fence bore marks; the ground beneath was soggy with mud and the fallen leaves of a big bush there, and there were gobs of mud, a few of the leaves, caught in the links of the fence, in five places up to the top bar.

"He climbed over," said Rodriguez. "That's what it could say, all right. But why the hell?"

Maddox stood in the light drizzle, looking at the evidence. It was evidence, of a somewhat nebulous sort. "I don't know why the hell, César," he said soberly. "But there it is. The kid climbed the fence himself—after something—for some reason, whatever. Nobody snatched him. He went of his own volition."

"The family—"

"Forget the Freudian double-talk. It wasn't a runaway. It's a decent family, he sounds like an ordinary decent kid, well brought up. Even an eight-year-old would plan a runaway, take his allowance money, clothes. He was just on a walk with the dog, in the yard. He had to make some effort to climb that fence— What the hell was on the other side to entice him? You don't bribe an eight-year-old with candy, the puppy. What the hell attracted him?"

"It could still turn out to be a snatch," said Rodriguez.

"Wait for it—but I don't believe it," said Maddox.

FIVE

By the time it was full dark, they knew that Justin Lockwood hadn't wandered off on some impulse, seeing a friend go by, or for any reason. They had a dozen squad cars prowling the streets around for blocks. They contacted the boys he knew who lived in the area—there were only three, and none of them had been out of the house that afternoon.

Lockwood had done a complete about-face and was demanding the FBI. Patiently Maddox explained to him that the Feds couldn't come into a case for twenty-four hours, when it could be presumed that the victim could have been transported across a state line. They put out an alert county-wide with a description, and then all they could do was wait. It was fifty-fifty, in Maddox's estimation: a snatch or the sex nut.

He got home at eight o'clock, and told Sue about it over warmed-over creamed chipped beef. She told him about the house; she wanted him to see it. "That's too much money," he told her.

"He thought they might come down. It's such a nice house, if it was just given some tender loving care."

And the station would call him if anything broke, but he called in at midnight to ask. Brougham told him there'd been another heist, a liquor store on Sunset, and that was all.

Once he got to sleep he had a vague nightmare which fled out of his mind when Sue woke him at seven. It was raining gently. He left before she did, and was just sitting down at his desk when Rodriguez and Feinman came in, D'Arcy and Rowan drifting after them.

There were two manila envelopes on his desk. The one on top was the lab report on the examination of Clifford Jaynes' apartment. It didn't amount to much. Nothing whatever that could link

Jaynes to the homicides had showed up. They had picked up a few latent prints. Some of them belonged to one Alan Seibel, who had a little rap sheet: enticement of minors into lewd acts, public brawling, public drunkenness; he was, of course, a known homosexual. And that said nothing here or there.

The other manila envelope was from the coroner's office: the autopsy report on Louise Sexton. It had come up yesterday afternoon; he hadn't had a chance to look at it.

Another burglary had been reported, also yesterday afternoon, and they hadn't done a damned thing about it—all of them roaming around the streets up in Mount Olympus.

"We ought to know one way or the other by noon," said Rodriguez, "or am I woolgathering?"

"Joe, you'd better go get a statement on this burglary," said Maddox. "It isn't the Herschel truck team, and I don't suppose we can do a damn thing about it, but we ought to preserve the image by the citizenry." He passed over the address.

The Sexton inquest was scheduled for ten o'clock. It was Dabney's day off, but Maddox had had Whitwell call him in to cover the inquest, in case the coroner wanted full police evidence. They had this new heist, and all the sex nuts still to find and question, and the Martin-Butler thing was still up in the air. "Damn it," said Maddox, "somebody ought to go out to that Firestone plant, see if Coker's been to work—maybe pick him up."

Then the phone rang on his desk. "Well, now we know," said Patrolman Ben Loth. "A couple of P. and R. men just found the Lockwood boy."

"And I had the gut feeling," said Maddox. "Where and how?"

"Up by the road in Wattles Garden Park. Looks just about like the other two."

"That's the pattern. Same time, same M.O. All right, we're on the way." Maddox stood up, his eyes savage. "Number three, César. Rout out the lab and call the morgue wagon."

Wattles Garden Park was above the hillside residential area to the north of Hollywood Boulevard, in a suddenly hilly terrain that rose abruptly to the winding streets off Mulholland. It was not a heavily wooded area, contained mostly low brush, a few young trees, and was not much used by picnickers; a few bridle trails ran through it. The black-and-white was waiting at the top of Hillside Avenue; there weren't any roads in but a rough trail. Maddox parked the Maserati beside the P. and R. pickup and Loth led them up the little path a hundred yards to where the Parks and Recreation men stood. The two men were upset and angry.

"I read about the other ones in the paper," said the older man. "By God, guys like that they oughta hang! Kids!"

It was the Lockwood boy all right: the brown pants, yellow knit shirt, brown shoes and socks, brown and yellow cardigan: brown hair, four-feet-eight, eighty pounds. He was lying on his side by the path, and Maddox and Rodriguez didn't need a doctor to tell them he had been strangled manually. The doctor would say what else. This time it looked as if no clothes were missing.

"Goddamn it to hell," said Maddox very quietly. "And we'll have to go and tell them, and poke around, and there are just no Goddamn leads on this at all." He lit a cigarette with a savage snap of his lighter. "*Except*," he said, "except—"

"Oh, yes," said Rodriguez. "*¿Y cómo es posible?* It makes no sense at all, Ivor."

———◆———

"I'd just like to know what they expect people to do," said Alfred Brannon querulously. "We bought this house twenty-three years ago; in fact, just finished paying for it. It was a nice quiet neighborhood then. Now the taxes so high we'd like to sell and find a cheaper place, out a ways, but what we'd have to pay, no way could we do it. Seven burglaries in this block the last six months. I retired last year, I'm on pension, and what can I do?"

"Yes, sir, I know," said Feinman.

Brannon was a plump, red-faced old fellow, sitting in the middle of a sagging couch in the living room of this old frame house on Virginia Avenue. His wife, even plumper and rosier, sat beside him. "You said this was about five o'clock yesterday afternoon?"

"You look," said Mrs. Brannon suddenly, "just like that fellow used to play the sergeant on Adam-12. Mac, they called him."

"I'd just like to know how they expect people to *manage*," said Brannon. "I went to a thing at the high school, police sergeant there, how to burglar-proof your home. Sure. Easy to tell somebody about the dead-bolt locks. Do you know how much those damn things cost? I've never been handy with tools. I'm still paying installments on that—a hundred and ten bucks it cost. Screens. Do you know what aluminum screens cost? Forget it. Bars on the windows? A fortune. What it comes down to, we just don't go out much anymore. Never after dark. Where's to go, anyway, with all these filthy movies they're making?"

"Yes, sir, I know," said Feinman patiently. "Can you tell me what the fellow got away with?"

"Not much, thank God—there wasn't much here to get," said Brannon. "Broad daylight! Like I say, we don't go out after dark. Just been to the market, pick up a few things— We came home about a quarter to five, I ran the car into the garage and got the groceries out of the trunk, we go in the back screen door, and by God, here's the kitchen door broken in, half open, and we knew right off— Marge let out a scream and I go running for the front, never crossed my mind he'd still be there—and this guy comes out of the bedroom and charges right into me, like he's tackling somebody in football—a big guy, he knocked the wind out of me, I fell against the TV. Might've brained me." There was a three-inch cut on Brannon's temple. "Why, he might've hit Marge too, except she'd run into the bedroom from the back hall—and by the time I could get up, he was long gone out the back door."

There was a lab man coming to dust the door for prints, and elsewhere, but it looked as if it had just been kicked in. Unfortunately, some of the cop shows on TV gave the laymen pointers on that kind of thing.

"What did he get?"

"The bedroom was a mess, drawers all pulled out," said Mrs. Brannon. "All my good jewelry, not that I had much—my mother's set of garnets, her diamond ring, my pearl necklace— thank goodness I was wearing my engagement ring! I had forty dollars hidden behind a picture in the bedroom"—one of the first places anybody would look, of course—"and he took the portable radio. I think that's all."

"If you can give me a description of the jewelry, we'll get it on the hot list right away. It may show up in a pawnshop. Mr. Brannon, could you tell me what he looked like?"

"I can. He was a young punk, maybe nineteen, twenty, and I think he was high on some kind of dope, his eyes were all wild and starey. He had kind of a fat face and long dirty blond hair right down to his shoulders. These damn good-for-nothing *kids!*" said Brannon. "I don't know what's happening to kids these days, I swear to God!"

Feinman sighed. It was a very run-of-the-mill burglary, the kind that happened nearly every day somewhere in the city. The burglars, operating more and more by daylight, were getting more violent these days, and most of them were amateurs without cunning. This one sounded like just such another one, maybe with a habit to support, picking up the little loot as he could. He hadn't got much here.

But Brannon had a point, of course. In the unlikely case that they caught up to the lout, a judge would put him on probation and turn him loose. The judges accepting the plea bargaining, reducing charges, reversing evidence on technicalities and turning the outlaws out to roam were in effect sentencing the Brannons and all the decent people like them to indefinite sentences locked up in their own homes, afraid of the dark.

———◆———

"I'm sorry to have to ask you to answer questions right now," said Maddox. "It's useless to offer you our sympathy, but for what it's worth— Do you feel able to talk to us, sir?"

"All right," said Lockwood stiffly. "I'm all right." They were sitting in his beautifully appointed study in the big Spanish house on the hill, surrounded by deep leather armchairs, a mahogany desk, fitted mahogany cocktail cabinet, walls of books. Gray light streamed in the window, but it had stopped raining. "I understand —you want to start your investigation."

"We think your son is the third in a series of similar murders. You may have read about the other two boys—"

"Yes," said Lockwood. "Boys—in the streets down there. Liable to—run into that kind? I'm afraid I didn't—take much notice. The kind of thing couldn't happen to—couldn't happen— Oh, my God."

It was eleven-thirty. The mobile lab truck had come out, the men had taken photographs at the scene; the morgue wagon had come for the body. They had taken the P. and R. men back to the station to make statements, leaving that to Daisy and Sue. Maddox had asked priority on the autopsy, and then they had come up here to break the news to the Lockwoods. Mrs. Lockwood had collapsed, and their doctor was with her now upstairs.

"Are you all right, sir?" asked Maddox after a moment.

"Yes. Yes. I want to help you—however I can. But I don't understand how Justin—a man like that up here—"

"Mr. Lockwood, you said a moment ago, boys on the streets down there. Not exactly, you know. They were both well-brought-up boys, with good school records. They'd been warned about not talking to strangers. One of them was very shy. We've been wondering just how this man managed to get hold of them, to entice them into his car—we think that's how it was done. On each occasion he encountered them on their way home from school, and it's practically certain they must have been taken away in a car. It was the same pattern—both boys held overnight and the body left somewhere the next morning, where it would be found at once. But in this case we've come across something rather queer. It's a virtual certainty that your son climbed the fence out there to join the man voluntarily. He went of his own volition."

"That's not possible," said Lockwood.

"It's certainly a twist. We'd like you to think, if you will, what could possibly have been an attraction to him. A much younger child, it might not take much—candy, a puppy, a kitten—but an eight-year-old, no. What were—"

"Of course he'd been warned," said Lockwood in a stronger voice. "Money carries its own responsibilities—and burdens, Sergeant. Why do you think I kept that gate locked out there? Is it any wonder the crime rate is so high when the death penalty isn't used, when a lifer's eligible for parole in seven years? Justin knew he was perhaps more vulnerable than boys whose fathers hadn't as much money. God knows I didn't try to frighten him. He wasn't a boy easily frightened. But he knew that. He wouldn't have—just unthinkingly—climbed that fence to a stranger for *any* reason, Sergeant. That's unthinkable."

But he did, thought Maddox. "What were his interests, Mr. Lockwood? What did he like to do, play with?"

Lockwood stirred in his chair. "What's any normal eight-year-old interested in? He went to St. John's Episcopal Academy—he was a good student, brightest at arithmetic—he liked the beginning science courses, pretty simple but he— But he reads well too, he likes—liked—books about mechanical things, he was good with his hands. Oh, sports, of course, like any boy"—he smiled a ghastly little smile—"baseball, he was an avid Dodger fan. Animals. He'd just started taking riding lessons, and he was looking forward to taking fencing next semester."

Maddox ran a hand through his hair. "Had he ever climbed that fence before?" he asked suddenly.

Lockwood raised his head and looked at him, but his eyes were unfocused. "Why, yes," he said. "Yes. The gardener told me about it—he was amused. He said, 'That's a good boy you've got there.' It was typical that Justin hadn't told me until I asked. He was a brave little boy, Sergeant."

"Why did he climb the fence?"

"He saw a girl from down the street—the Tennant girl, she's older and bigger than Justin—whipping her puppy, and he got over the fence and took the whip away."

"I see." Maddox exchanged a glance with Rodriguez.

"I'm sorry," said Lockwood, standing up. "I don't think—I can stand any more—right now. If you'll excuse me—I ought to go to my wife."

"Certainly," said Maddox. Lockwood went ahead of them down the hall to the square tiled entry; the doctor, a spare dark man, was at the foot of the stairs.

"I've given her a sedative, Howard. I think you'd better have one too. Come on up, let me settle you down—you're not doing any good this way." He took Lockwood's arm, just glancing at the two detectives.

They got into the Maserati, past the newly hired uniformed security guard at the gate. Maddox rolled down a window for air and they both lit cigarettes.

"This one was out of the original area," said Maddox. "Old middle-class Hollywood. Millionaires' row."

"Yes, but what does it say? He's maybe just riding around when he gets the urge, anywhere? We don't know how many kids he may have tried to pick up, anywhere else, who wouldn't come close enough and never told anybody about it, before he did get hold of Frost and Noonan." After a minute Rodriguez added, "Riding around on his lawful occasions? I've just had an idea."

"We could use one."

"They were nice kids, as you just said. Raised to be polite. They wouldn't have responded trustingly to the anonymous stranger, but somebody familiar—somebody they could place— might be different. The driver of an electric company truck, phone company van, post office truck, gas company—"

"Yes," said Maddox. "Oh, yes. And some of those in a kind of official uniform, César. Looking all the more upright and respectable. But anyone on a regular job like that—how'd he conceal the boy? Don't answer me. Leeway on times, on a job driving around. He could knock him out, tie him up, take him back to his own private place until after hours. There was evidence that both boys had been bound and gagged."

"But, *condenación,*" said Rodriguez, "this one, yesterday? How the hell, Ivor? I see what Lockwood means—that kid, young as he was, had had it drilled into him that he could be a target for kidnappers—he'd probably have been even warier than the other ones about strangers. I don't see him eagerly climbing that fence because a post office van stopped and the driver asked where the Smiths live, come closer, little boy, I'm hard of hearing."

"No," said Maddox, "but I'll tell you something I can just see. Maybe. As a wild surmise. I can see, say, a gas company truck, or the post office van, stopped out here, the driver tinkering with the engine. And talking to the boy through the fence. And asking if he'd come and hand tools or something. Lockwood says the boy was mechanical. He might have climbed the fence without thinking to help the nice man."

"I might buy that. Or something like it. But what are we talking about? Men in those jobs are screened, aren't they?"

"You know as well as I do not every sex freak starts out as a teen-ager. This could be a first time round for our boy, or he's been a peaceful secret fag and just now suddenly getting the bigger kick out of killing. It could be he's never attracted the law's notice for anything before."

"That's a sweet thought. No record on him at all."

"It happens."

"Is this bright idea worth doing anything about? What could we do?"

"Damn all," said Maddox. "I wouldn't like to haul in every truck driver, repairman, from all the utility companies, the post office, and spend six months talking to them in the hope that eventually one of them would say, 'How'd you know I did that?' And I've just had another idea we can't do anything about."

"Yes?"

Maddox sighed. "Those boys—nice, well-raised boys. Knowing the good guys from the bad guys by their white hats. I just suddenly remembered one of the classic cases—before your time or mine. The Chessman case. You know, especially in this town, there are places you can rent any sort of fancy dress you want. Among other things, police uniforms. Do you think any of those boys would have hesitated a minute, a car pulling up, and a uniformed officer calling, 'Can you give me some help, answer some questions?' And especially that would explain Justin. He'd have been over that fence right now, to the good guy."

"*¡Por Dios!*" said Rodriguez. "That's a very nasty idea, *amigo*. But a very simple one. What do we do about all this?"

"Not a damned thing," said Maddox. "You know as well as I do, it's usually the tried-and-true routine that breaks cases. On one like this, the odds are that this joker has given the warning rattle before and he's in our files somewhere. For something. We go on hauling in these men and leaning on them and hope sooner or later we'll come across him and break him down—or at least find enough evidence for a charge. And if this is his first time round, there's no way on God's green earth we can spot him cold, unless fate trips him up. And another sweet thought, which I had before—he may be new in town. He may be in somebody else's records, New York or Miami or Seattle. And if so, there's no way to find out, because while we can see a pattern, it's not a distinctive enough M.O. to pass on to NCIC."

"I see it, I see it," said Rodriguez. "Are we going anywhere?"

Maddox started the engine.

They went back to the station to see if the lab men had spotted anything useful at the scene. But as so often happened on this job, they were immediately deflected to something else.

When they came into the office Sue said, "Thank heaven you're back. We didn't quite know what to do about it. We left a lab team there, but—"

An old white-haired man was slumped in Maddox's desk chair,

his head on the desk; he was sleeping peacefully, a slight smile on his face.

———————◆———————

Sue and Daisy had been the sole occupants of the office when Whitwell called in a new homicide—Crescent Heights Boulevard. Sue had never been alone on a homicide, but Daisy was a veteran; they took her car. It was one of the new high-rise apartment buildings; they went up in a silent elevator to the ninth floor. Patrolman Rinehart was waiting at the end of the corridor.

"I was kind of stymied," he said. "Times it's handy to have a partner. But the old guy seems pretty tame—it was him called in, you know. So I took the chance and called you from the squad."

The apartment was furnished in violently modern style, with a distinctly pornographic poster plastered on one end wall. Sprawled in the middle of the living room floor was a young dark-haired man in skin-tight black slacks and a white silk shirt. Parts of the shirt were stained red now; he lay on his back, eyes wide on the ceiling. Sitting in an armchair across the room was a tall old man with white hair. He looked at them in surprise.

"Dear me," he said, "I didn't imagine that they would send policewomen. How very unpleasant for you, ladies. I'm so sorry. I shall try to make everything as clear as possible. My name is Cameron, James Cameron. The young man on the floor is Robert Windrow, and I shot him about half an hour ago. I had a very good reason. But now perhaps we had better go back to your station and you can summon my attorney. I'm feeling rather tired and I shall be glad to be in jail and able to rest."

They looked at each other, and at the corpse. There was a .38 Colt revolver on the coffee table. Daisy slid it into an evidence bag. She told Rinehart to go back to the squad and call up the mobile lab. Then they took Cameron downstairs and drove him back to the station. He said courteously to Sue, "My attorney is Caleb Gardner, in Beverly Hills. You will find the number in the book. I wish you would call him now."

The next time they looked at him he had gone sound asleep on Maddox's desk.

———————◆———————

He blinked at Maddox and Rodriguez and smoothed his white hair. "I beg your pardon—that was rude of me. I expect you'd like me to make a statement. It's all very simple. You see, there was really nothing left. Nothing to mean anything. My wife died last year— I believe it did shorten her life, the grief. He was our only child. We'd had such high hopes for him. The business may just as well go to my cousin John—I have made my will. So there was no reason I should not take the matter into my own hands. I employed a private detective to locate Windrow, and when I received his address yesterday I simply called him and made an appointment. He was a very easy person to approach, you see, he was a dealer in narcotics."

Maddox raised an eyebrow at Sue, who went out hastily. "Yes, sir?"

"My attorney can give you all the details. I really am feeling too tired to talk much more now." He sat back and shut his eyes. Sue came back with a Xeroxed page and gave it to Maddox. Windrow had had quite a pedigree, with LAPD and Beverly Hills. About seventeen counts of various narco charges and one of homicide.

"You'd better get down what he's said so far," said Maddox. "We'll be that far ahead." Sue typed up what Cameron had told them, and Maddox made him read it carefully.

"Yes, that will do very well," he said, and brought out a pen and signed the statement in careful copperplate. About then a bony red-haired man came in explosively, stopped short and surveyed the tableau, and said, "James, you are a Goddamn fool and I wish I had your guts."

Cameron looked at him calmly. "Kindly don't be stupid, Caleb. I'm seventy years old and it's time I had a rest. I don't feel any interest in the business now. And there was no one left who could be harmed by my act. You understand, it wasn't revenge? It was simple justice. Where the authorities refuse to act, ordinary men must somehow create simple justice. The other two were only weapons—he was the one who conceived the murder." He looked at Maddox. "I really am very tired, sir. I would appreciate being taken to jail."

He did look exhausted, and they obliged him. When Rodriguez had led him out, Caleb Gardner sat down suddenly in D'Arcy's desk chair and said, "I suppose you remember the case."

"What case?"

"You don't. I suppose in all the welter of crime going on—and it wasn't your jurisdiction. Well. Cameron married late. He's a wealthy man—a big plastics corporation. Good businessman. They had one son, Martin. A fine boy. Bright boy—he was twenty-one. They lived in Beverly Hills. Martin was going to U.C.L.A., going in for archaeology, of all things. Short and sweet—that's a big campus. He and a friend of his, Ron Decker, dropped in to see some casual acquaintances, boys they'd met on campus—boys shared an apartment. Martin and Ron didn't have any idea they were mixed up with narcotics. Apparently the boys had double-crossed Windrow, shortchanged him on a deal for heroin, and he sent a couple of thugs to rough them up. Happened to be that night. The thugs got a little confused and roughed up Martin and Ron worse than the other three. Martin died of a fractured skull and Ron will be paralyzed for life."

"I don't think I want to hear any more," said Maddox, his eyes cold, "because I can guess the rest of it."

"Maybe not quite. The police were a little slow, but they caught up in the end. Windrow and the thugs were charged with homicide and conspiracy to commit. The trial got delayed. And delayed. Finally it got under way and dragged on for a couple of weeks. They were all found guilty. There was an appeal, and they got a new trial. It was set three months ahead. It went on for a week, and then the judge found something wrong in the transcript and broke it up and ordered a new one. That finally got under way last month—over a year since Martin died—and they were found guilty again. And then the judge ruled that one of the prosecution witnesses hadn't been fully informed of his rights, and reversed the verdict, and they walked out free as air."

"Now you know why cops get ulcers, Mr. Gardner."

"They'll have to prosecute him, of course. But I hope to God it gets a big play in the media. Maybe one of these days the grass roots in this country will grow enough moral indignation to oust some of these petty tyrants playing God—and getting taxpayers' money for it." Gardner stood up. "Anyway, now you know."

◆

Maddox sat there for a moment after Gardner had left; he felt tired, vexed and perplexed. One thing he knew: whether Cameron made the headlines or not, the Lockwood murder would. Reporters were already calling in; by tomorrow they'd be flocking around, pestering them for latest news.

They would all be out doing overtime tonight, finding more of the fags to lean on. On this kind of thing, their street informants were a broken reed; this kind of killer was very much a loner, and nobody but himself knew about his secret urges. His vulnerability was his very perversion; men like this were not stable, and under questioning he might easily give himself away, with the merest expression, a gesture, an answer—and then they would know, and persist, and with luck break him down to confess. Or they might not. This kind of thing was a bastard to work.

He straightened up. On his desk was the other manila envelope that he hadn't had a chance to open: the autopsy report on Louise Sexton. For a moment his hand stayed inert on it; for a moment it did not seem important how Louise Sexton had died, or that she had—as compared to three little boys abducted, frightened, hurt and abused and killed before their lives had got under way. Then the instincts instilled in him by twelve years of being a reasonably good cop moved in him, and he opened the envelope.

It wasn't an elaborate report; evidently there hadn't been much to say. She had died of a massive skull fracture, in lay terms smashing in the temple and frontal bone. There were bruises on the body, detailed, but they had all been made post mortem. She'd been a healthy woman; no indication of chronic ailments. The time of death was estimated as between 6 and 9 P.M. last Tuesday night. Present in the stomach was a small amount of alcohol, about equivalent to two cocktails, and a partly digested meal consisting of beef, tomatoes, bread, potatoes and cake.

"Now do tell," said Maddox to himself softly. "Indeed. And damn all this rain—" It was three-thirty. He got up and ambled over to Sue's desk. "We'll all be out overtime tonight. I'll take you out to dinner and then you can go home."

"Fine," said Sue. "Do you think we could possibly make a formal offer of eighty-five thousand? And keep fingers crossed they'd take it?"

He scowled, rubbing his stubbly jaw. "If I ever get a chance to talk to your mother— Let me think it over."

It was still overcast, but not raining. He went up to the boulevard, turned on Outpost and further up hit Mulholland. It was an old road but well maintained, and not narrow. He had a good idea of about where the Chrysler had gone over, and presently parked and crossed the road, pacing along with his eyes on the ground. He identified the place by all the used flashbulbs littering the edge of the road and on down the bank.

He eyed the terrain. He could see the flattened underbrush, the great patch of oil where the car had hit and come to rest. But from the edge of the road here all the way down, there wasn't a sizable boulder, a thick bed of rock, any protuberance the car might have hit, to spring the doors and throw her out. He edged down the steep slope, looking on all sides. There was nothing but underbrush and a few loose small rocks.

"Very, very funny," he said to himself. He started for the road again and discovered that while it had been easy sliding down, it would take a major effort to pull himself up. He was panting when he regained the road, and sat in the car getting his breath back. He thought he could bear to know a little something more about the background of Herbert Sexton. Had somebody said Eugene, Oregon?

Well, take Sue out to dinner and then get back to the legwork. So often it was the legwork that broke cases.

◆

Sue's mother called her at eight-thirty. "Well, I went and looked at your house," she said. "Your Mr. Parrott was very nice. You could do a lot with it, Sue—it's certainly got potential, as he kept telling me. All those marvelous big rooms. I was itching to get at that poor living room with gallons of white paint. And I love the window seat. But it's an awful price."

"They might take less. I want Ivor to offer eighty-five. But you know, Mother, if you sold your house—"

"Now let's not get into that again, for goodness' sake. There's no point, you know how I feel."

"Yes, I do know how you feel," said Sue, helpless to prevent her instinctive reaction even though she knew it was the wrong way to go about it. They were too much alike, tending to the emotional arguments while pretending to be logical. So, knowing it was simply fuel to the flame, she said, "Yes, I do know. You'd love to be in the middle of a family again, and have something to do, and you know we'd all love being together, we get on beautifully. But you've got it in your head we're being charitable, which is absolutely ridiculous. Nobly offering to take on an obviously senile senior citizen as a burden—"

Mrs. Carstairs of course fired up instantly. "Now I don't think anything of the kind, and doesn't it occur to you that I enjoy being independent? Young people deserve their own private homes. Nobly offering, indeed! I'd never think such a thing of you and Ivor, but I'm blessed if I'll intrude—"

"Your middle-aged ideas on us," said Sue crossly. "Honestly, Mother! That's just *it*—you'd be such a help! If you sold the house—"

"There's really no point in arguing about it. I'm not going to change my mind."

"Oh, you—you're as bad as old Mrs. Eady," said Sue.

Her mother laughed. "Calm down, Sue. You sound so much like your father when you get mad. I saw her today, poor old dear. Your protégé. I made one of those bundt cakes, and of course I couldn't possibly finish it myself, so I took her half. She's taken a cold and feeling pretty miserable. You know she can't go on like that, she probably hasn't enough blankets or clothes—"

"I did think about filling in the application for welfare and getting her to sign it as police business about the burglary."

"That's quite bright, Sue. But how could you explain the checks?"

"Yes, I know. All printed so clearly, Aid to the Indigent. She'd be furious."

"Well, I've got a new detective novel, I'm going to bed to read. Don't fuss, Sue. It'll all come out all right in the end. Things usually do. If a thing is meant for you, it'll come."

"Good night, Pollyanna," said Sue.

———◆———

They roped the night watch in, doing the overtime. This kind of legwork was tedious; often you had to go back and back, hunting down one man to question, before finding him. It took time and patience.

One man they were looking for interested Maddox slightly

more than the rest: one William Naldauer. He had only one count of enticing a male juvenile, but he had used force; and he was presently working for a TV repair service. His parole record said he was an excellent electronics technician. Any little boy these days would be more than familiar with the brightly painted truck carrying all the gadgets, the friendly jump-suited figure who turned up to fix the set in time for a favorite program. It could be a useful gimmick.

But they hadn't found Naldauer yet when he and Rodriguez finished questioning a just possible suspect who turned out to have a solid alibi for Sunday afternoon. It was eight-forty. They let him go, and came out of the interrogation room to see if somebody else had turned up anything. Nobody was there but Brougham waiting for something new to go down. He glanced up at Maddox from his paperback.

"The desk just called. The A.P.B. just turned up Scott Coker. Squad spotted his car in the lot of a bar down on Florence, and they picked him up. They just delivered him to Wilcox Street."

"Oh, dandy," said Maddox. "Is he drunk?"

"Uh-uh. They nabbed him just going into the bar."

"The end of a perfect day," said Maddox. "I suppose we'd better go see him. It'd be nice to get one wrapped up."

He and Rodriguez drove over to the jail. They could only hold Coker for twenty-four hours without a charge; they'd better talk to him. He was brought up to an interrogation room and they had their first look at him.

He fitted Ruth Butler's description like a glove. He was at least six-three, and must weigh two hundred. He had a round head with a thick neck, and huge hands; he sat and rubbed his hands along the sides of his thighs. He was dressed neatly enough in tan slacks and shirt.

"I dunno what the cops want of me," he said.

"Oh, you know," said Maddox easily. "About last Tuesday night, Scotty. Now just why did you want to rape that woman? She was a nice woman. She'd offered you a job, hadn't she?"

"I never did anything like that."

"Don't be stupid," said Rodriguez. "The other one's still alive, you know. She can identify you, she had a good look at you."

"We can guess how it went," said Maddox. "She called you—

you had an ad in the paper offering to do painting—and she asked
you to come and look at the job and give her an estimate. And
you said you'd come on Tuesday night. You've never been in trouble before, Scotty—always held a regular job, lived straight. What
set you off?"

"I didn't. I didn't do that."

"You left some fingerprints on the knob of the back door."

"I never had my prints took."

"No, we know. But if we get a warrant to arrest you, we'll take
them now and they'll match up, won't they?"

"You can't arrest me for nothing."

"Look," said Maddox. "It's the way my partner says. The other
woman's alive, and we'll ask her to look at you, and she's going to
say, 'He's the one.' Isn't she? Isn't she?"

Coker stopped rubbing his pants legs and put his hands together
in his lap. "Oh, I guess she will," he said miserably. "I guess she
will. And I wasn't even drunk. I don't know why I did such a
thing. It was all mixed up with Madge. That's my wife."

"Suppose you tell us about it, Scotty."

"Madge was too good for me. I knew that. High-yaller girl, and
she graduated high school and all. But I was crazy about her—I
was makin' good money at Firestone—I got her to marry me. But
she's a managing woman. She got to be boss, and I don't care, it's
not in me put up with a bossy woman. No way do I. I never in my
life thought I'd take a hand to my woman, but some ways it's all a
woman understands. I didn't want to do that—I had to get down a
few drinks to do it—and then that night—that night—it was a week
ago last night—I belted her some, she naggin' at me about spendin'
for liquor— I never used to drink much before we was married—
and she walked out on me. Yelled she was gonna divorce me, and
packed a suitcase and walked out." He took a breath. "She never
come right out and said it, 'I'm too high-class for the likes of you,'
but she might's well have. So I guess I got drunk that night.

"That lady, she called next night. About painting her house. I
said I'd come by and tell her how much. That day, I went in a
place for lunch and ran into a guy I usedta know, old neighborhood down in Vernon I usedta live. You know, I never in my
life took any dope before. Never wanted to. But he had some stuff

on him, just grass, nothing big, and I bought a couple joints off him.

"It's funny, what it does to you. I didn't feel especially different, I felt O.K. I thought, Nothin' much to this stuff, and I drove up to Hollywood just thinkin' about this job and Madge and the divorce and how mad I was at her. I remember goin' in there, and how she said it'd be painting both the apartments in that place, big job. And then all I remember is she was sayin', 'Don't you come any nearer, don't you touch me'—*just the way Madge always said it*. I wanted love her up—an' all of a sudden she changed right *into* Madge, an' I was gonna show her what kind of man she walked out on, I was gonna show her—"

"You did," said Maddox. "Do you remember the other woman?"

"Kind of. She bothered me, interfering like. I knocked her down. I don't know how I ever come to do a thing like that. I'm sorry. I'm sorry it happened."

"That's not much good now, is it?" asked Maddox.

"No, sir. I just thought I'd say it."

They'd driven over in Rodriguez' car; they went back to the new station and Maddox said, "Little something I forgot to do. See you in the morning, César." There was no hurry about the warrant; get the machinery started in the morning. He went into Communications and sent a telex to the chief of police in Eugene, Oregon, asking for any information they had on one Herbert Sexton, description appended.

◆

On Tuesday morning, with D'Arcy off but probably coming in, another heist and another burglary overnight, and nothing having come in about the county-wide hunt for the Herschel van, Maddox found just one communication on his desk.

It was a telex from the chief of police in Eugene, Oregon. It said that Herbert Sexton had been indicted for fraud over a land deal twenty years ago; he had beaten the rap, but had had a somewhat unsavory reputation. The chief had no more on him there, but believed Sexton may have been in other trouble elsewhere in the state and suggested querying NCIC.

"Well, just fancy that," said Maddox. He went down to Communications and consulted NCIC, with all its handy computers.

Five minutes later NCIC handed him the record. Sexton had been charged with fraud over a land deal seventeen years back, paid a large fine, escaped jail; charged with misrepresenting land offered for sale, the case thrown out; charged with bigamy, eleven years ago, the bigamous wife suing for money she claimed he had extorted from her; he'd served a year in jail on that. The charges were in different Oregon towns. There was a Canadian count: fraud in a land sale. He'd beaten that rap too.

"Well, I will be Goddamned," said Maddox. "So the money-hungry daughters were right after all."

SIX

Rodriguez and Feinman had just come in; Maddox beckoned them and passed on the interesting news. "Well, I'll be damned," said Feinman. "So he is a con man after all."

"Not necessarily," said Maddox. "Just a shrewd operator—eye to the main chance. As far as the bigamy goes, we don't know the background, could have been an honest mistake."

"The operative point," said Rodriguez, "is that significant little bit in the autopsy report. He said she was on her way to have dinner out. On the contrary, it seems she'd had dinner. With him?"

"Um, yes," said Maddox. "Even that he could disclaim knowledge of. He says he didn't come home until five o'clock."

"Do you think he killed her?" asked Rodriguez.

Maddox ran a hand through his hair. "How the hell do I know? The accident looks very funny—but freak accidents happen. An army of experts could all have different opinions. Why should he have killed her? All we've heard, everything was lovey-dovey with them. If he is something of a con man, they very rarely go in for violence. He seemed to be getting anything he wanted from her."

"She could have found out something so it wasn't lovey-dovey," said Feinman.

"True. I'd also like to know about her will. Find out who her attorney was from the daughters."

"They probably held the funeral yesterday."

"Um," said Maddox. "Without knowing any more about it— and we can do a lot of wild guessing—I'd have a bet it's the kind of thing the D.A. wouldn't touch with a barge pole. All ifs and maybes and could-bes. But right now Mr. Sexton goes on a back burner. If he did somehow arrange that accident, he's not about to arrange another in the next week. Our sex fiend is something else. I want to find this Naldauer."

Rodriguez nodded seriously. "He could be hot for it. So do I."

"Wyatt's being arraigned this morning, D'Arcy's on that—he'll come in later. The rest of you can get on to the next names on the list."

Naldauer, of course, had just turned up as they worked their way alphabetically down the list of names; and Maddox liked his TV connection very much. It could so easily be the gimmick to attract the little boys. They'd tried Naldauer's apartment last night with no luck, but he worked for a big electronics repair service company, and he was still on parole; almost certainly they'd find him at work.

The company office and shop were on San Fernando Road in Glendale. As Maddox parked in front, they both noticed the trim gaily painted truck standing in the lot: ANDERSON'S TV AND ELECTRONIC REPAIR SERVICE. Together with the friendly uniformed driver, a thing to attract a small boy. Had it?

"Listen," said Anderson worriedly. He was a scrawny little man in the forties. "I didn't want to take him back. A thief or something, that's a little different. But I got no use for the fags, and the ones like him, go after the kids, aughh! His parole officer argued at me, but I wasn't going to. Only I got to say, a real good electronics man, they don't walk in every day, and he's good. I'm not going to say I like having him around, but there it is. Do you think he's done something again?"

"We don't know, we'd just like to talk to him," said Maddox. "Do you keep a log for your trucks—record of service calls?"

"Yeah, sure. How many calls, where to, and so on. One thing, we do all the work for the biggest company handles TV insurance around here. You want I should call Naldauer in?"

"That's right." It wouldn't be much use to check that log for the Friday when Harold Frost was picked up, or a week ago Friday when Freddy Noonan vanished. Naldauer lived in an apartment on Mariposa, not all that far from the general area; if he picked up the boys on impulse, he'd already been in that area on the job, and fifteen minutes added to this service call, fifteen minutes to that, would have given him time to immobilize the boys, take them to his apartment. Probably most people there were away at work all day. A lab examination of the truck—well, the lab sometimes pulled off seeming miracles, but they couldn't make bricks without straw.

Twenty minutes later a truck twin to the one in front pulled in and a man got out of it. "What's with the call?" he asked Anderson. "I got eight more calls to cover."

"Some cops want to see you," said Anderson shortly, and went back into the office.

Maddox and Rodriguez looked at Naldauer with interest. Again, you couldn't have placed him on looks. He wasn't bad-looking: twenty-eight, five-ten, a hundred and sixty, brown hair and blue eyes. He had a thin nondescript face, but hardly one wearing a mask of evil; his mouth was wide and mobile. He returned the stare warily, and a little muscle at the corner of one eye jumped in a nervous tic.

"I don't know why you want to see me. I'm still on P.A., I'm clean."

"Then you won't mind answering some questions," said Rodriguez, "will you?"

"That depends." Naldauer turned and went into the building. "No sense standing out here in the cold." It hadn't made up its mind whether it would rain or not today. There was a coffee machine against the wall; Naldauer fished in his pocket, came up with a dime and drew a paper cup of coffee.

"So where were you on Sunday afternoon?"

The muscle jumped again. "Why? Why should I tell you?"

"Because you're still on P.A. and don't want to go back to the joint. The other boys there may not be Sunday school teachers but they don't like your kind worth a damn, they give you a rough time, don't they? Where were you?"

"At home, that's all. My apartment. It was raining, I didn't go anywhere."

"Can anybody back that up?"

"How? I live there alone. But I was there. I tell you, I'm keeping clean."

"That your car in the lot—the blue Chevy?" They knew it was; the D.M.V. had told them. "Mind if we have a look at it?"

"Yes, I mind. You've got no right to persecute me—so I've done the time, they let me out on P.A., I'm in a regular job and you've got nothing on me. I answered your damn questions. You haven't got anything on me." And all the while the muscle twitched convulsively.

Without looking at each other, Maddox and Rodriguez gave him friendly smiles. "That's right," said Maddox. "We were just asking, is all."

"Nothing to worry about," said Rodriguez. "You cooperated fine."

They went out to the Maserati. "He's hot," said Maddox. "I like him. He's nervous as a witch, trying to put up a front."

"Come down on him just the right way, he'll likely fall apart and tell us all about it," agreed Rodriguez. "How do you want to do it? Give him rope? He thinks he's off the hook. The rest of the day, and pick him up as he comes off the job, lean on him good and hard?"

"It's one way. Meanwhile, he's busy. If maybe not concentrating on the electronics as close as usual. I think we'd like a look at his pad. Let's see if we can get a warrant."

They were both feeling rather excitedly hopeful on the way back to the station. Naldauer was very nervous of cops; he had the right record: it could be they were going to be lucky, the routine turning up their boy without any more slogging than this.

At the station, however, they found D'Arcy just in, with a problem.

◆

D'Arcy had obligingly turned out to represent the police at Randolph Wyatt's arraignment, to save somebody else's time. It was a purely formal ritual; it was very unlikely there'd be any questions asked by the magistrate. He got down to the courthouse in good time; the deputies had brought Wyatt and several other men from various jails around, and had them waiting on the front row of seats. For a wonder the judge arrived promptly, but five other men were brought up before Wyatt.

As a matter of fact, D'Arcy wasn't thinking much about the scene before him, the dingy old courtroom, the prisoners lined up for the somewhat archaic ritual. He was thinking gloomily about his latest girl friend, Joan Berry, and concluding that it really wasn't good enough, wasn't going anywhere. She worked for the phone company, a split shift, and was off on Thursdays; she was also attending a secretarial course at night school; and in the three months they'd known each other they had managed to get together for just three dates. It really wasn't good enough. She was a marvelous girl, a very sweet girl, but—

He heard Wyatt's name spoken and focused his attention. The judge was droning out the charge, and suddenly Randolph Wyatt blurted out, "That's a damn lie! Homicide? I never killed anybody!"

The judge admonished him, finished the ritual; bailiffs and deputies came forward. Wyatt looked around desperately, and recognized D'Arcy as one of the men in the detective office on Sunday. "Hey!" he said. "This is all wrong! You tell that sergeant I got to see him. I never killed anybody! I did that food-chain store on Tuesday night, that's all— I thought that's what you dropped on me for! Where's the murder come in? I never even fired that gun! You tell that sergeant—"

◆

"But listen," said D'Arcy, "somebody identified him, didn't they? From a mug shot?"

"On the Jiffy market job," said Maddox. "On account of the snake. And damn it, everything coming at us hot and heavy—after we picked him up, there was time to collect the formal evidence. The search warrant for his apartment came through on Sunday and we haven't executed it yet. There wasn't a gun on him when he was picked up. It looked so damn cut and dried—Mapps. We haven't had an autopsy report yet—but I should have talked to Ballistics. Only the Lockwood thing— Damn it, I'd better see Wyatt."

He'd be back in jail now; fortunately, only a couple of blocks away. Maddox drove down to what had been their dreary old precinct house for so long and asked for Wyatt to be brought up. He hardly recognized him as the sullen young man he'd talked to briefly on Sunday.

"My God, am I glad to see you, Sergeant! So the other guy told you— Listen, I didn't believe it, that judge says homicide! What homicide—when? I never killed anybody in my life! Sure, I did that food-store job, you got me on that, but I never—"

"What gun did you have on that?"

"Colt .22," said Wyatt promptly. "I got it at a pawnshop. I lent it to my brother-in-law up in Stockton. I suppose he'll still have it. Just since Saturday. Listen, what's this homicide I'm supposed to have done?"

"Heist at a liquor store on Sunset, last Friday night. The owner was shot."

Wyatt sagged with relief. "Oh, hell, then I'm O.K. Thank God, then I'm O.K. I couldn't have done that, I went up to Stockton Friday morning on the bus, I got there about noon. My brother-in-law met me at the bus station. Listen, nobody in my family ever been in any trouble with the law, they're all do-right people— they'll tell you. They'll tell you I was there."

"Well, I'm damned," said Maddox.

He went back to the office and looked up the reports in the current files. Feinman was there and he blew off a little steam. "I know we've been busy, but for God's sake, somebody ought to have caught this! Like to think we're such a damned efficient force —kind of damned boo-boo a Keystone cop might make! Everard, I'd forgotten his name. One of our rookies." Everard was on swing. He'd be out of bed by now. Maddox got on the phone, told the desk to get hold of Everard. When he came on, he sounded apprehensive: had he done something stupid to annoy the brass? "Just a couple of questions," said Maddox. "That heist last Friday night. Could you identify the man?"

"My God, no, sir. It was raining like hell, and dark. He was just a shape running out of that store. I couldn't even make the car he took off in—Ford or Chevy, tan or white."

"Yes," said Maddox. Somebody should have remembered the car, when it turned out that Wyatt didn't have one, and at least asked about it. "But you are sure of what Mapps told you—about the tattoo?"

"Oh, yes, sir, absolutely. I'd swear to that any time."

"O.K., thanks." Maddox put the phone down, immediately picked it up again. "Talk about slipshod detective work— Get me R. and I. downtown. . . . Ballistics, please. Whatever the autopsy report on Mapps has to say, the coroner's office would send any slugs out of him to R. and I. I just hope there were some in him and we don't have to go crawling all over that liquor store. . . . Maddox in Hollywood. Did you get sent any slugs for testing out of a Willis Mapps, heist victim last Friday? . . . You did. Good. What were they? . . . Oh. Thanks very much." He put the phone down. "Smith and Wesson .32. Two slugs in good condition, they can match the gun if it turns up. Hell!" He took up the phone again and told the desk to get him the Stockton Police Department. Keller was in, and he broke the news.

Keller was astonished, and said he'd go and ask. "I thought you had some good solid evidence," he said, sounding aggrieved.

"Occasionally we like to prove we're human," said Maddox. "Let me know, thanks. So let's go do what we should have done two days ago, Joe. Isn't it the truth, a stitch in time saves nine."

They went to Wyatt's apartment and found it was his former apartment; the manageress had bundled up all the personal possessions in it for storage in the basement. She was much annoyed at having to give the police access. And there wasn't much there, and no gun of any description.

"One of the other snakes," said Feinman. "Jerome Simms is the likeliest. He's got a couple of counts of armed robbery."

"Indeedy," said Maddox. "But just to be on the safe side, we'll put out an A.P.B. for all of them. This on top of everything else— wasting time." It was two-thirty and he hadn't had any lunch. Rodriguez had got deflected onto helping Rowan question another suspect. Maddox drove down to The Grotto and had a sandwich while Feinman had coffee. Just as he was finishing the sandwich, he remembered that he hadn't put in the application for that search warrant on Naldauer's apartment, and cursed aloud. It would be unlikely to come in before tomorrow morning now.

They got back to the station in time for Keller's call. "Well, they all say Wyatt was there, Friday noon, and never out of sight more'n a couple of minutes till I picked him up on Sunday. How come you goofed over it, hah? I took it for granted—if I'd just asked them then, but you didn't say—"

"Yes, yes," said Maddox. "At least we caught it in time. Will you get statements and send them down, please? We'll have to correct some legal paperwork." All the red tape was something else. Wasting half the day on this!

Rodriguez came back just before four, and they drove over to the TV shop in Glendale. Naldauer got off work at five; they sat in the car and waited for him. When he drove into the lot, in the truck, they got out of the car and were waiting for him when he came up to the Chevy. He slowed, and stopped five feet away.

"What the hell do you want now?"

"Some straight answers, Naldauer." Between them, asking curt alternate questions, they let him know what they had in mind. Where had he been the afternoon of December thirteenth when Harold Frost had been abducted? A week ago last Friday when Freddy Noonan vanished? Last Sunday afternoon when Justin Lockwood— The media were really giving that a play, and sudden fear leaped into Naldauer's eyes. What kind of proof could he offer that he didn't know anything about those boys?

"You're crazy," he said. "That's nuts. I'd never kill a kid. Why the hell would I have to go picking up—" He stopped and licked his lips. "You've got nothing on me, because I don't know a damn thing about those kids. I was at work when those first two—"

"What about Sunday afternoon?"

He shook his head. "None of your damn business. You got nothing on me."

"We've got an eye on you, Naldauer," said Maddox in a cold voice. "Don't forget it." They let him get in the car and drive off; he killed the engine once, crashing gears, and probably could have kicked himself.

"Oh, I like him," said Rodriguez happily.

"That search warrant should be in tomorrow morning."

It was twenty of six, but Maddox had to ferry Rodriguez back to his car. They pulled into the lot at five past, and Maddox wouldn't have stopped the engine except that somebody waved at him from the back door of the station and came hurrying up to the car.

"That other detective said you might be back. I was watching for you." It was the studio security guard, Earl Harkness. "Look, I played it just the way you said to—"

Maddox was resigned to more overtime. He lifted a hand at Rodriguez and said, "Come on in where it's warm."

"I tried to play it cool," said Harkness in the office. Everybody else was gone and the night watch hadn't come on. "I met up with Erhardt again yesterday afternoon. I told him I'd been thinking over what he said and I thought I could help him. I said I knew somebody who might put me in touch with a guy like he's after."

"Good. Did he bite?"

"He sure did. It's crazy—he doesn't really know me from Adam, just come out with a thing like this— Anyway, I asked where we should meet, I bring this guy to him, and he said his photographic studio, say eight o'clock, when I had it lined up I should give him a call."

"Fine," said Maddox. "You call him and set it up for tomorrow night. You meet us here, and we'll see if we're good enough actors to put him in the trap."

"I just hope I don't give it away. My God, I never thought I'd get mixed up in anything like this!"

"Give you a story to tell," said Maddox. "You make the date and let me know how it goes, whether he agrees to it."

"O.K., I'll give it a try. I'll let you know as soon as I set it up."

Maddox watched him out. He was tired and he'd be glad to get home, though there was a little warm satisfaction in him that they were probably going to nail their sex fiend soon. There was no rest for the wicked. He proceeded out to the front hall, the part of the building open to the public, where the watch commander's office was located. On duty this shift was a veteran officer with the unlikely name of Thackeray. Maddox sat down, lit a cigarette and explained about the hit man, and Thackeray was amused.

"You picked anybody out to do it?"

Maddox had spent ten minutes here on Saturday, studying the photographs. "Fellow I don't recall seeing around—Edward Vargas. He looks like a gangster."

Thackeray guffawed again. "Rookie, on this shift. He's got a college degree in liberal arts, with a minor in English literature. He told me after five years on a campus he thought it'd be an easier life dealing with criminals than college kids in a classroom. You want to brief him?"

"I'd better." Thackeray went out to summon the squad in, and there was a little delay before Vargas appeared; he'd been manhandling an obstreperous drunk uptown. He looked, face to face, slightly less gangsterish than his photograph, and he had a deep voice with a slight midwestern accent. He listened to Maddox in surprise and gave him a grave smile. "Well, I never went in for theatricals much, Sergeant. How should I play it—dese and dose and youse guys?"

"A little old-fashioned, I think. Practice looking sinister and dangerous. This Erhardt seems fairly naïve. We'll wire you for sound, and for God's sake, remember you can't lead him on. Get him to do the talking—spell it out."

"Oh, sure. I know all the ins and outs of entrapment."

"Er, belatedly I ought to apologize," said Maddox. "Picking you by your face, as it were. That is—"

Vargas chuckled cheerfully. "That only a mother could love. Don't worry, I've lived with it long enough to be used to it."

◆

Feinman, having spent the afternoon on the legwork and having an hour at the end of shift, wondered about shortcuts. That Simms was the likeliest one for the liquor store heister who had shot Mapps. If they could clean that up— They had Simms' most recent address from his parole record. It was Tyburn Street over in Atwater. He drove over there to see if Simms was home.

He found that it was a big old-fashioned two-story house with an ancient landlady who rented out rooms. "Mr. Simms?" she said, peering nearsightedly at Feinman. "Oh, he moved out. He just got married, you know. A month or so back. Seemed like a nice young man, always so cheerful. He introduced me to his bride, seemed like a nice girl, her name's Edna or Julie or something. . . . Oh, I don't know where they moved, I'm sorry."

◆

On Wednesday morning, after Ivor had left, Sue began to catch up on a number of jobs she'd been neglecting for too many past Wednesdays. But as she washed windows, changed the bed, got the laundry ready to take out, her mind kept presenting her with little snatches of ideas about that house. Which was absurd.

She emptied out the dirty water from the living room windows and ran fresh for the bedroom windows, adding vinegar, and quite without volition she thought, The bedroom with the window seat has got to be Mother's: the second bath right across the hall. A bold yellow striped paper, and you could get coordinating fabric to upholster the window seat. Plain white paint downstairs. Mother's bedroom carpets would do upstairs for now—later, watch for sales. One of those big round oak tables would be nice in the dining room, but they cost a fortune. The kitchen badly needed new vinyl flooring—possibly those stick-on tiles would do—and it was big enough to take a gay patterned paper on the walls, the cupboards plain white enamel—

It was completely absurd, she told herself crossly, because it was *too much money*. She wanted Ivor to see the house— Maybe they'd make the offer, but the people probably wouldn't accept it. What she should be doing was letting Mr. Parrott show her the possible houses again. That one in Burbank would do, and it was sixty-three thousand dollars and didn't need a thing done to it, though she didn't like the color of the master bedroom. But it had such poky little rooms—

◆

The search warrant for Naldauer's apartment was on Maddox's desk, and he and Rodriguez got there by nine o'clock. The night-watch report was a little less monotonous; for a wonder there was no new heist, but a body picked up in an alley, looking like a teen-ager dead of an O.D., another burglary, a hit-run with one victim dead.

The place on Mariposa was an old tan brick building housing perhaps thirty apartments. They looked for an owner or manager on the premises, to show the warrant, and the middle-aged woman behind a door labeled *Manageress* peered at it in astonishment, asked a lot of questions, finally spent fifteen minutes hunting keys and panted up the stairs with them to unlock the door. "I don't know what we're coming to when the police can come right into a person's own home like this—you better believe I'll tell Mr. Naldauer you was here!" She panted away again; the apartment was on the fourth floor.

It was a very small apartment, with a bedroom about ten by ten, a tiny slice of kitchen with an eating area that barely accommodated a card table and two chairs. Even the small living room was bare, with only a couch and armchair, one small table with an ashtray and lamp.

"Doesn't waste money on luxuries, does he?" said Rodriguez. There was a small closet just beside the front door; they looked there first. If he had stashed the boys here until he was off the job, there might be some evidence; they might be getting some-body up here to dust for prints.

The evidence that came to light, however, didn't need a lab man to interpret. *"¡Caray!"* said Rodriguez, looking into the closet. "So that's what he spends money on." Sitting in its box on the floor of the closet was an expensive movie projector, sixteen-millimeter and looking fairly new. They hauled it out, and behind a couple of coats, flat against the wall, was the rolled-up screen, also looking new. That was all the front closet held; they went looking in the bedroom.

In the bedroom closet, which was tiny, were only clothes, shoes on the floor. The cheap painted double dresser held underwear, handkerchiefs, shirts in the three top drawers. In the bottom drawer were four round cans of movie film, not labeled.

"Take a bet?" said Maddox.

"No way. But if that's his kick, there must be somebody else involved. In homicide? I don't—"

"Could be the photographer doesn't know about the homicide." Maddox pried the top off a can and unrolled a couple of feet of film, holding it to the light. It was sixteen-millimeter; the frames were small but clear enough. "Oh, damn it to hell and back!" he said softly.

"What is it?"

"Sodom and Gomorrah," said Maddox. "And a dead end for us, but some more work. Take a look if your stomach's strong enough."

The film, of really excellent quality, consisted of a series of sequences of naked men, women and children, with a few animals thrown in for good measure, performing a variety of sexual perversions. The background looked like a private house or apartment, with leopard-patterned drapes at one window. Naldauer was definitely one of the performers.

This kind of thing was made, and sold for sometimes hefty sums; often to groups, private clubs. There had always been a trade in undercover pornography, but these days it was a good deal more hardcore, because much of the tamer variety was openly available at the corner drugstore, the nearest theater.

"My good God in heaven!" said Rodriguez, disgusted, putting down the film. "Talk about getting sidetracked!" But of course they couldn't just walk away and leave it; it was on their beat, and there were boys and girls in that film as young as the three dead boys. There had been cases of parents hiring out their children for this kind of thing; it paid good money.

They went through the place very thoroughly then. There didn't seem to be a scrap of paper in the place, an address book, a phone book. They pulled contents out of drawers. They looked at the back of kitchen cupboards; eventually they started feeling inside pockets and shoes in the closet.

It was Rodriguez who came up with the envelope, carelessly left in the pocket of a sports jacket in the closet. They weren't thinking about fingerprints right now, and looked at it interestedly.

It was a business-size envelope, with a printed return address which had been crossed out, no new one substituted. Inside there was just a page torn off a memo pad, with a large hasty scrawl across it. *You can pick up another 50 if you turn up Sun. for new sequence. One p.m. Don.* The crossed-out address was *Photo Enterprises,* an address far out on Santa Monica.

As they headed out there, Rodriguez said, "Funny about Sexton."

"I haven't forgotten him. If she did leave him any money— See her attorney. But with practically no evidence, I don't think the D.A.'d like it at all."

Photo Enterprises was housed in a rather small modernistic building, gray with white trim, with its own parking lot. They went into a long, narrow reception room, with a counter across one wall, which was neatly decorated on three sides with, evidently, examples of what the business dealt in. There were colorful postcards of every tourist attraction imaginable; and there were color slides made for Viewmasters, for home projection, of the same subjects and others. There was the Hollywood Bowl, Farmers' Market, the beaches, the mountains, the parks, the Arabian Horse Farm, the planetarium, hotels and theaters, and not so much as one artistic nude.

A blonde female who wasn't as young as she was trying to look appeared behind the long counter, from some back premises. "Oh, can I help you?"

Maddox produced the badge and she looked frightened. "Who owns this business?"

"Why, Mr. Bush. Mr. Adam Bush. Why? He's not here right now. What do you want him for?"

"Do you hire photographers to do all that?" He gestured at the walls. She looked confused.

"They free-lance. I mean, they know the kind of thing we want, and submit things. Photographs. Sometimes there's a special commission."

"Is one of your photographers named Don?"

"Don—" Her mouth hung open briefly. "The only one I can think of is Don Rudd."

"Fine," said Maddox. "Have you an address for him? Let's have it, like a good girl."

"I don't know what Mr. Bush would—but I guess it's all right, for the police. It's in the book anyway."

It was Sunset Boulevard, nearly out into West Hollywood, not a new apartment building but one of the old ones with a remodeled front; the rents would be fairly steep. "We're in the wrong racket," said Rodriguez.

By the mailboxes in the lobby Don Rudd lived on the top floor. There was an elevator. As they walked down a plushly carpeted hall toward the apartment door at the very end, Maddox said, "Place is soundproofed. Ideal for this caper." He pushed the bell.

After a moment the door opened. The thirtyish man who faced them could only be described as winsomely handsome, with soft girlish features, a small red mouth, thick blond curly hair. He was very dapperly dressed in a poem of brown shades, deep brown slacks, creamy beige shirt, dark beige jacket. He said, "Yes? What can I do for you gentlemen?"

But Maddox was looking over his shoulder, to where leopard-patterned draperies were pulled across a big picture window. "Oh, how very nice," he said. Just now and then the guardian angels came through and they got a break. He smiled tenderly at Rudd. "In, my friend. We've got a few questions for you."

"Who *are* you? You can't come pushing in here—" Rudd stared at the twin badges. "Oh," he said. "Oh." He backed up and sat down on the couch. "I'm not saying anything," he said. "You can't make me say anything."

Not having a warrant, they couldn't open drawers or closets, but they had a look around, and in the dining area Maddox let out a relieved *whoosh* and said, "Somewhere up above, César, is a corps of good deceased cops looking after us and sending us the breaks when they can. Thank God, this messy thing with all the red tape is now out of our hands."

Rudd had been readying a parcel for mailing, and by its shape and size it was obviously a can of sixteen-millimeter film. It was addressed to The Candle Club, at an address in Richmond, Virginia. "Oh, happy day," said Rodriguez. "So it all belongs to the Feds and the post office. Let's call and tell them about it—I know they'll be charmed to have something to do."

In a little while, they got the FBI and a postal inspector. They were all resigned at the red tape winding out into the distance. They found an address book with a list of club names and single names, evidently steady customers. They found an account book with a lot of names in it, with various amounts noted against them. Let the Feds try to locate them, the various performers. Doubtless there would be juveniles removed from parents and guardians, the charges and trials at the Federal level. Mercifully it wasn't any responsibility of the Hollywood precinct.

"All we want from Rudd," said Maddox to the FBI man, Canotti, "is an alibi for Naldauer. To clear him out of our way. We thought he was hot for our sex maniac, but it appears he was nervous about this operation instead."

"Sure," said Canotti. A couple of the Feds had gone back to Mariposa Street to commandeer that film. Possibly Naldauer had taken part of his pay in copies of the films, to enjoy at private showings. They picked up Naldauer off his job too, and confronted him with Rudd.

"It's pretty meaningless to sit there pouting," said Maddox to Rudd. "You're finished, and you might as well tell the truth. Was Naldauer here last Sunday afternoon, making movies?"

"Well, all right, he was," said Rudd sulkily. "But I'm not going to say one word more. I want a lawyer."

"And that is that," said Maddox. "Let's just hope we come up with another hot suspect for our own little problem. Do have fun, boys."

"Thank you so much," said Canotti bitterly.

They went back to the station at four-thirty, having skipped lunch entirely, and found they had a new one on hand.

"Oh, Harkness called in," said Daisy as Maddox came past her desk to the drinking fountain. "He said to tell you it's all set up. He'll be here at seven."

"And when I'm going to get any dinner— A new one? For God's sake, what now?"

———◆———

The call had come in at ten-thirty, from the squad car first on the scene. Feinman was the only one in.

It was Catalina Street, another of the run-down residential areas of old Hollywood, run-down not because the residents were careless but because many of them couldn't afford to keep the property up. This was an old bungalow, needing paint, on a narrow lot.

Patrolman Keeler, who had seen most of the things there were to see on this job, looked oddly pale. "It's a mess," he said to Feinman.

Feinman went up on the porch. The door was open behind a screen door. Patrolman Gomez was somewhere inside, and he was saying, "Would you like me to call a doctor, sir? Mr. Foley—"

Feinman edged in the door, and then stood aghast at the scene. Over the years he had seen about all there was to see too, but he didn't remember anything quite like this.

It was—or had been—a pleasant, shabby, comfortable living room. A worn rug, miscellaneous old furniture, down at the end of the long room a built-in sideboard, a round table and chairs.

Sprawling half off a big upholstered armchair was the body of an elderly woman. She was fat, gray-haired; she had on a housedress and thick cotton stockings; her felt slippers had fallen off, and her dentures had dropped out of her mouth onto her chest. Her throat was cut right across, and the fountain of blood had sprayed her clothes and the carpet and the chair and the other body.

The other body was a child—couldn't be more than two or three, thought Feinman numbly. A little blonde girl. She was wearing denim pants and a flowered top, not that you could see much of it. Her throat was cut too, and she was lying up against the armchair.

The man sitting at the dining table was moaning over and over, "But why did anybody have to *kill* them? Just to rob us? But she wouldn't have opened the door to a stranger—she always kept the chain on! Why did anybody have to *kill* them? She wouldn't have opened—she always kept the chain—"

Feinman drew a long breath. He said to Gomez, "Call up a lab unit. Just quick, what've you got?"

"He's Jack Foley. That's his daughter and mother-in-law. His wife works. The old lady looked after the little girl all day, lives here. He forgot his wallet and came home to get it. He says he wasn't gone an hour, they were fine when he left."

"My God," said Feinman. "Go call in."

———◆———

"I hope this is going to be all right," said Harkness uneasily.

"You got him convinced enough to set up the meeting," said Maddox. "Take it easy. You'll be O.K."

Harkness kept casting uneasy glances at Edward Vargas, who seemed to be taking the whole thing as a joke. Somewhere he had found an old suit jacket with heavily padded shoulders, a broad chalk stripe, and he had slicked his black hair down with brilliantine. "You got carried away," Maddox told him.

Vargas gave him a sinister hard stare. "George Raft," he said. "My brother's got a thing about old movies, books of stills."

"Well, I doubt that Erhardt knows much about modern hit men, let's hope you impress him," said Maddox. "Come on—zero hour."

"I just hope to hell I don't give it away," said Harkness.

They had Vargas wired for sound with a mike hidden inside his tie and a tiny recorder in his breast pocket. With the folded handkerchief outside it didn't bulge. They were in Harkness's Chevy, sitting outside the narrow store front on Santa Monica Boulevard. They couldn't see the sign, but it said *Erhardt's Photo Salon*. It was ten to eight.

Reluctantly Harkness got out, and Vargas hopped after him. "Good luck," said Maddox, and settled himself to wait.

He slid down in the seat and somewhat sleepily thought about what they had to work. The endless routine. Sexton—that was queer. Very nebulous. That Herschel van was probably in a garage or under cover somewhere except when it was being used. And just what in hell had been so attractive to Justin Lockwood that he climbed that fence, eagerly going to meet his destroyer?

Wyatt—that was really very funny. Sue wanted him to go and look at this house. It sounded rather impossible, and one hell of a lot of money, a pity she'd set her heart on it. Of course, if that stubborn lady Margaret Carstairs would come in— He grinned to himself. He knew very well that she had a great big soft spot for Ivor Maddox—funny thing, so many females did, he'd never understand why, and just a good thing Sue wasn't jealous—and somehow he'd argue Margaret around. It was nice enough to have Sue, but it would be all the nicer to have a real family again—

He woke with a start as they bundled into the car, shutting doors with exaggerated care, talking in low voices. "I think we did it," said Vargas. "I'm a lousy actor, but that guy'd believe anything."

"Let's get back to the station and hear the tape." Maddox sat up.

"Oh, he'll be here awhile—he said he was going to develop some negatives. Might as well play it here. I think it's all right," said Vargas. "He came out with everything without any prodding —her name and address, and the going price. My God, how naïve can you get?"

"Sensational novels," said Maddox. "The burbling media. Unrealistic movies. People swallow all sorts of things. So let's hear what you got."

It came over quite well. There was no suggestion of entrapment; Erhardt had a strong, clear voice, talking about that bitch, the big life insurance, and making the offer, two thousand to take her off. She had a beauty parlor on Vermont, an apartment on Edgemont. He just wanted to know when the hit was due, to set up an alibi for himself, just in case the cops got to wondering.

Vargas came over in a sinister growl, unexpectedly impressive. "You missed your vocation," said Maddox.

They waited until ten o'clock, when a light came on in the front of the studio and a figure came out, reaching in to switch out the light before pulling the door shut with a bang. Maddox slid out of the sedan. Vargas came behind him.

The figure turned toward the compact car parked ahead of Harkness's. "Sorry, Mr. Erhardt, you're not going home tonight," said Maddox, and turned a pocket flash onto the badge. "You're under arrest, for conspiracy to commit a homicide, and we've got all your recent remarks down on tape."

Erhardt, anonymous until now, not really visible in the darkness, was a very tall, broad fellow. He said blankly, "What?" And then he let loose a string of colorful observations.

"Come on, Erhardt." Maddox opened the door of the sedan, the roof light flashed on, and Erhardt recognized Harkness.

"You—" he yelled. "It was you—" Quite unexpectedly he swung on Maddox, knocked him against the car; Vargas grabbed him and was caught off balance when Erhardt backhanded him; he went sprawling.

"Oh, hell," said Maddox. Erhardt was in the act of turning, starting to run. Maddox took one long stride, caught him by the shoulder, hauled him around and brought one up from the ground. Erhardt collapsed face down, out cold.

SEVEN

Maddox was supposed to have Thursday off, but with everything they had to work, the routine on the sex killer, he came in. Well, he would take part of the day off; Sue wanted him to look at that house, and the real estate agent had agreed to show it to him at three o'clock.

Feinman and D'Arcy had spent most of yesterday on the new homicide, and briefed him on that succinctly.

"It's a wild one," said Feinman. "This Foley works at a men's store on Hollywood Boulevard, his wife works at The Broadway, the department store. They moved in with her mother, Mrs. Teresa Duval, when they got married three years ago. Mrs. Duval looked after the little girl all day. Ordinary people, there wouldn't have been much of value in the house—but we know how much that means. Foley left for work about half past eight, around the same time as his wife. And it wasn't until he got there he found he'd left his wallet in his other suit. It wasn't that far to go, he came home on a coffee break to get it. Say nine forty-five. And there they were with their throats cut and the house ransacked."

"He keeps saying, 'She'd never let a stranger in,'" said D'Arcy. "Always kept the chain on, answering the door. Implication being, which he says isn't possible, somebody she knew, and they were killed so they couldn't identify the burglars. But a two-year-old, for God's sake?"

"The jungle," said Maddox. "The wild ones getting wilder. I suppose it's early to ask if the lab picked up anything."

"They got some latents, they're still sorting them out," said Feinman. "It was all too possible, of course, that all the prints belonged to the family. The neighbors on one side were home, didn't see or hear anything. It narrows down to a little over an hour when it must have happened. I still haven't talked to this Mrs. Kettleman, on the other side—she's not home, but her next-door neighbor says she thinks she was yesterday morning. It's unlikely she can tell us anything. She'd have come over when she saw all the squad cars, the mobile lab. They couldn't have got a hundred bucks in loot—what was in Mrs. Duval's handbag, a Masonic ring of Foley's, a couple of pieces of modest jewelry of his wife's, a portable radio."

"And I'll take no bets the lab comes up with anything useful," said D'Arcy. "I would take a small bet that whoever did it was high on something. It had the earmarks—he didn't give a damn what he did. Berserk. Out of control."

"Yes," said Maddox. "In the middle of the morning. And is that anything new? See what the lab turns. And damn it, I asked for priority on the Lockwood autopsy. Hasn't it come in yet?"

"The desk just sent it up," said Sue crisply behind him, and handed it over. "They've usually got a bunch of bodies stacked up down there."

"So they do." That teen-age body looking like an O.D. hadn't got identified yet. Maddox slid the report out of the envelope and scanned it hastily, handed it to Rodriguez. "Well, there you are. More of the same. He was bound and gagged, beaten, sodomized and strangled. And the underclothes are missing. All right, on a third count that ties it up—a fetish symbol. It's ninety-percent sure he's kept those clothes. So, I know it's going to slow it down, but from now on, every man that looks at all possible for it, we get the search warrant. Because, you know, it was twenty days between Frost and Noonan—but then only ten to Lockwood."

Rodriguez looked up from the report. "He may be going right over the edge, fast?"

"A psychiatrist I'm not," said Maddox. "He's been over the edge some time, wouldn't you say? But he seems to have a gimmick—no trouble getting hold of them. I still can't get over the Lockwood boy climbing that fence—but it's no good speculating, let's just clean up the damned list and hope he's on it. And that we'll turn some evidence." He stabbed out a cigarette, lit another.

"I've got to get a follow-up report written on Duval," said Feinman, and moved back to his desk. Rodriguez, D'Arcy, Rowan and Dabney collected hats and coats and started out. Maddox looked up the number in the book, dialed and got Thelma Troy at an address in West Hollywood.

"Mother's attorney? Alan Hancock, Fairfax Avenue," she said promptly. "You're *not* just letting it go as an accident? You're doing something about it? We told you, there's something terribly wrong about it! What are you—"

"Now, Mrs. Troy, don't leap to conclusions. There's a certain amount of red tape to these things." He cut her off politely and phoned the attorney's office, surprisingly got a secretary who said, sounding surprised, that if it was police business—he did say police?—she supposed he could see Mr. Hancock at ten o'clock, if it wouldn't take too long. What was it about? . . . Oh, Mrs. Sexton. In that case, she was sure Mr. Hancock would be very pleased to see him. Would he mind spelling the name?

Maddox raised his brows at the phone: Hancock harboring doubts too? The phone buzzed at him and he picked it up. It was the D.A.'s office; a pert voice put him on Hold, returned three minutes later to say that Mr. Bigelow would be right with him, and four minutes later to say brightly, "Here's Mr. Bigelow."

Maddox placed Bigelow as one of the bright young men down there, ambitious, quite reasonably honest, inevitably tinged with politics. "It's about this James Cameron," he said. "After looking over your reports and—er—reviewing the events leading up to the homicide, the District Attorney feels it would be in the best interests of everybody concerned to reduce the charge to voluntary manslaughter. He'd like to discuss it with you, if you—"

Maddox grinned mirthlessly at the phone. "Oh, yes, indeedy. Let's not make a big thing out of it, play it up that the sole motive was the court's apparent inability to shove a trio of killers inside even on a minimum sentence. The natives are getting a bit restless over that kind of thing lately."

"If you could come and discuss it," said Bigelow remotely, "he can give you half an hour, say at one o'clock."

"Very big of him," said Maddox gently. "As you know, there's not one damn thing I can do about it if that's the way he decides to play. Trying to argue me around that it's the thing to do will get you nowhere."

"Then we'll expect you at one o'clock," said Bigelow.

———◆———

D'Arcy went out to the front hall to get a pack of cigarettes out of the machine, before starting out on the sex list again. As he passed the desk, Whitwell looked up from the phone.

"Say, that A.P.B. just turned up your moving van," he said. "Squad just called in."

D'Arcy spun around. "Where?"

"In a junkyard down in Inglewood. You didn't say what to do about it, they just reported noticing it." He handed over the address. D'Arcy went back to tell Feinman.

"I'd better go down and have a look. But this is a funny twist."

The city fathers wouldn't have liked it called a junkyard. There had to be repositories for the junked cars, other large items, on their way to being recycled into scrap metal, but the planning commission tried to hide them away nowadays. This one was hidden away behind a board fence; its chain-link gate bore the sign BEN'S METAL SALVAGE. D'Arcy could see how the patrol car had spotted the van: it was close up to one side, inside the fence, and a good bit higher: the HERSCHEL'S FINE FURNITURE sign was clearly visible. These few blocks were a wilderness of warehouses, small manufacturing plants, one lumberyard. D'Arcy parked, walked back to the gate and went in. There didn't seem to be anybody around. He had a look at the van, and wandered around among junked cars and outbuildings until he came across a little gnome of a man in a white jump suit just going into a trailer parked at the far end of the lot. He showed him the badge.

"Well, what in hell do cops want of me? Come in, sit down." Evidently he lived in the trailer, which was shabbily homelike inside. "Yeah, I run this place. My name's Ben Summers. It's a living."

"The moving van out there—furniture truck. How long have you had it and where'd you get it?"

"Oh, that. Well, I don't usually come by such a thing. It'll take a month of Sundays, break it up. But they'd got stuck with it, and I was willing to oblige."

"Who? When?"

"Hold your horses, I'm fixing to tell you. It was last Saturday. Couple of young fellows come in. That thing had died on'em a couple blocks away, up on Florence. They had a look, figured it was on its last legs, after they got it around on a side street, the cops yelling for obstructing traffic and all. I was handy, they come to me and says would I take it, only I got to hold it till they get it unloaded. It was full of furniture."

"Oh," said D'Arcy. He thought, That latest job—that poor damned old lady they'd cleaned out—that had been last Friday, hadn't it? The van still filled with stuff from that job?

"I took a look and said sure. They had to get a tow service to bring it in, hell of a job. That van has had it. Don't see how the engine kept going as long as it did. They came back on Tuesday with another van, not so big, and unloaded what was in the big one, and I paid'em fifty bucks and that was that."

"You didn't give a receipt? No names mentioned?"

Summers shrugged. "It's strictly cash and carry, son. Why'd I bother? They called each other Tony and Jay. Jay was black, I guess the other one might've been Mex or Italiano."

D'Arcy was exasperated. "Didn't you get any more information on it? What company it belonged to? Any registration?"

"Listen, they were junking it, son. Which cancels the registration. They said they worked for a secondhand furniture outlet. That's what was in it, a load of old furniture."

"Oh, hell," said D'Arcy. "We'll have to take a close look at it. It was being used to transport stolen goods. Have you got a phone?"

"Is that so? Help yourself." The phone was on the table in the kitchen. D'Arcy used it to call the lab. It was just possible that there'd be some latents left in the van; it was just possible that one or more of the wholesale burglars was in Records.

Waiting, he went and had a look at it himself. It had seen a lot of hard usage. The gauge showed just over two hundred thousand miles. There wasn't any registration in it, and the plates had been stripped off. "Hell," he said again. This put them (barring the possible latents) right back where they had been. At least the Herschel sign had been a lead. Now the burglars were using another van they knew nothing about at all. He went back to the trailer and asked Summers if he could remember anything about it, but Summers hadn't taken much notice. He guessed it wasn't as big, it was white or some light color anyway, he didn't remember any sign on it.

D'Arcy left the lab man busy with fingerprint powder and went back to the station.

━━━◆━━━

Feinman was methodical by nature, and tenacious. Before getting back to the sex list he wanted if possible to see Mrs. Duval's next-door neighbor, Mrs. Kettleman. He liked to clear up as he went, cover all bets. But just as he got up to leave the office, the desk buzzed him. The A.P.B. had turned up Andrew Sigworth down in Boyle Heights: a car from the headquarters beat was bringing him in.

Feinman was mildly annoyed. It was nearly a certainty that the snake they wanted, for the heist and Mapps' murder, was Jerome Simms; but they had to be thorough and go by routine.

Fifteen minutes later the downtown patrolman dropped off Sigworth, who was even more annoyed than Feinman.

"What the hell do you crazy cops think you're doing? Grab me off the street and bring me to hellengone up here? I'm absolutely clean, I was on my way to work, damn it, and what the hell do I tell the boss?"

"We just want to ask some questions." Sigworth had a very small record, one count of B. and E., petty theft. "Where were you last Friday night, do you remember?"

"For God's sake! Yes, I remember. I was at my sister's birthday party and the whole family was there too and could tell you. Of all the damn stupid things. Listen, damn it, this construction crew I'm on just got back to work today after all the rain, I haven't earned a dime in nearly a week, and now the cops have to grab me for nothing!"

They hadn't, of course, had a valid address for any of these three besides Simms; and of course now they hadn't a valid address for Simms. That had been the reason for the A.P.B.'s. Feinman asked Sigworth for an address and he gave one down in Boyle Heights. "All right," said Feinman. "Thanks, that'll be all for now, you can go."

Sigworth, who was a small wiry man, practically bounced in the chair beside the desk. "If that isn't just the hell like cops! So I can go, can I? Ten miles up here they bring me without even a please, and now I can go! Where? On the Goddamn buses around here, take me three hours to get back to my car! Did I ask to come up here? Could you have asked the stupid question on the phone? Cops!"

Feinman realized he'd had rather cavalier treatment, and called up a squad to ferry him back to Boyle Heights.

About then D'Arcy came back and told him about the van. Then a messenger came in with the autopsy report on Willis Mapps. There wasn't anything in that except the description of the slugs, which they already had. The same messenger had something for Daisy Hoffman, who looked at it and said a few unladylike things.

"Called to testify at that damned Telfer trial starting next week. You know it'll drag on and on. Especially as he's got that shyster Van Allen for his attorney."

It was ten-forty. Rodriguez and Rowan had come in, each with a potential suspect for questioning. Feinman and D'Arcy followed them out to the interrogation rooms to help lean on them.

The one Rodriguez and Feinman talked to, Charles Mosely, struck them both as a strong possibility for their sex killer. He had only once committed a homosexual attack, but that had been on a twelve-year-old mentally retarded boy last year, and he had used threats and violence. He was twenty-two, a senior student at L.A.C.C. majoring in higher mathematics and science, and quite obviously felt himself to be enormously superior to the plodding stupid cops. He answered questions contemptuously, bored; but like most of this kind, he was highly unstable. He was also nervous, but whether he was habitually fidgety and twitchy or whether they were getting to him about the murders, it was hard to say.

They liked him quite a lot for it. He lived with his parents on Curson Avenue. They let him go about noon, and put in an application for a search warrant on the Mosely house. It might come through by four o'clock or so.

The one Rowan and D'Arcy talked to turned out to have an alibi for last Sunday. They all went down to The Grotto in D'Arcy's car for a hasty lunch—days seemed to slip by fast when there was a big job like this on hand—and came back to their respective cars, to start out again. Feinman went down to the mens' room in the front hall, and when he came back Rodriguez was waiting for him, hat in hand.

"New call."

"Oh, for the love of God!" said Feinman. "Can't we finish one thing at a time ever?"

"No rest for the wicked," said Rodriguez.

It was only about six blocks down Fountain, one of the garishly painted new jerry-built apartments built around an inner courtyard. There were outside stairs going up to covered balconies where the rows of front doors to the upper apartments made little rectangles of different brilliant colors. The uniformed man was up on the right-hand balcony talking to a woman. Nobody else was around. Feinman and Rodriguez climbed the stairs and went down to them. They were outside an orange-painted door about halfway down the balcony.

The woman was in the mid-twenties, a good figure in a navy pantsuit, dyed red hair, a little too much makeup, shallow blue eyes. She was looking horrified, and interested, and scared and a little smug all at once. "—Can't get over it!" she was saying. "Nonie and Gordon! I just can't believe it. Like I told you, I heard them going at it—arguing, you know—when I left to get my hair done and go shopping, that was about ten o'clock—and then—"

"These are the detectives, Mrs. Herter. They'll want to hear about it and ask some questions, if you'll just—"

"Oh, sure," she said. "Certainly." You couldn't have driven her away with a pitchfork.

The apartment door was half open. From here they could see the upper half of a female body lying about five feet from the door. There wasn't any screen door. Rodriguez shoved the door farther open with one foot and they went in. The body was that of a young woman lying on her back with her head nearly touching a big stereo console. She had been a good-looker, with short black hair, a slim curving body, very white skin. She was fully dressed in red slacks and a white long-sleeved shirt. There wasn't any blood, but her skull seemed to have assumed a peculiar shape, one side of her forehead sunk in. There was a large and heavy hammer lying right beside her.

They went out to the balcony again. "Can you tell us her name?" asked Rodriguez.

"Sure. Nonie Hart. She'd lived here about two years. She was a waitress at The Crystal Room, and what she got in tips—! I heard them when I went out. Her and Gordon. Fighting. It was just lately they used to fight, I don't know what about. See, we live in the next apartment, and you can hear sounds through the wall, if people are yelling or something, but not any actual words. My husband said the honeymoon was over." She tittered.

"This Gordon—Nonie's husband?"

"Oh, they weren't married. He's just a live-in boy friend. You know. I don't say I exactly approve of that, but a lot of people don't think anything of it, it's just the way to go now. Gordon—"

"Gordon who?"

"Oh, Roberts. Of course he wasn't making as much money as she was, he goes to L.A.C.C. part time and has a job as a parking lot attendant somewhere. Maybe that's what they argued about."

"You knew them pretty well?"

"Oh, well, just like anybody living next door. I'd run into her in the laundry room sometimes. But I'd never've thought Gordon would do such a thing! I just couldn't believe it. See, when I left about ten I heard them. Yelling at each other. Like I say, just the last couple of weeks they'd been doing that. I thought probably Gordon'd be moving out, she'd got tired of him. But I never would've thought— Then I came home just now, well, it's been a while, I called the cops and waited— Maybe it was twenty minutes, half an hour ago—and when I came past the door there, just like you see, I saw her lying there, and I said Nonie and she didn't move, so I went in and looked at her— Oh, Lord, I knew she was dead, and he'd killed her! A murder, here! Gordon! I never would have—"

Feinman said to Rodriguez, "At least, not very abstruse."

"Unless it turns out to have a twist."

"Don't say it." Feinman looked at the patrolman, a new face to him. "You're new on the beat."

"Wallace, sir. I just got transferred from Rampart."

"Oh. Well, chase down to the squad and ask the station for a make on Gordon Roberts' car, and put out an A.P.B. on it. And have them send a lab truck." Open and shut as it looked, they had to collect all the evidence for the possible trial later on. The reports had to be written, the statements taken, the copies made, all the red tape wound up.

"Mrs. Herter," Rodriguez was saying, "I'm afraid we'll have to ask you to come in to the station to make a statement."

"Oh, sure." She was intrigued with his dapper moustache, suave appearance. "Certainly. I'll be glad to. Oh, wait till Bob hears about this! A murder! I can't get over it! But Gordon, he always seemed like such a quiet fellow, the few times I talked to him—nothing much to say for himself. I can't get *over* it!"

◆

About four o'clock D'Arcy and Rowan emerged from another session with one of the men from the list, which had been completely unproductive and a waste of time. Dabney had just been talking to the lab, and said, "Well, they picked up a few good latents in that van. Remains to be seen if they'll be any use. They also picked up the remainder of a couple of joints from the front seat. If that says anything."

"Interesting, if useless," said D'Arcy. He sat down at his desk and lit a cigarette. The phone buzzed on Maddox's desk and he made a long arm and reached it. "D'Arcy. Oh, for God's sake. All right, send him in when he gets here. Talk about getting sidetracked. A squad just picked up Bruce Young in a market parking lot."

"Well, we do have to go by the book," said Rowan. "I know it's a hundred to one it's Simms we want, but all these damned snake tattoos—if we don't clear the rest of them out of the way definitely, it could raise some doubts at the trial. And it is homicide."

"Yes, yes," said D'Arcy. It had to be done, but with all the rest of the routine piling up on them, it was a nuisance.

Young didn't have much of a record—grand theft auto, B. and E. He'd been surprised to be stopped by a squad car and brought in; he said aggrievedly he was just on his way to pick up a six-pack of beer, it was his day off, and he hadn't been in any trouble and hoped he wasn't. "Just a couple of questions," said D'Arcy. "Where were you last Friday night?"

Young thought. "Oh, lessee," he said. "One day kind of like another. Friday. Oh, I remember, I was at the beach."

"At the *beach?*" said D'Arcy. "In all that rain?"

"Well, I was with my brother-in-law and a couple of his friends. They like to surf-fish, and they claim rain makes good fishin', kind of drives'em in toward the beach, see. But we didn't

catch much, at that. Oh, sure, they'll all say I was there. Did you
think I'd done something?"

"Just clearing you out of the way," said D'Arcy. "Let's have
some names and addresses."

———————◆———————

It was four o'clock by the time the preliminary work on Nonie
Hart was done and Feinman had written an initial report. The
search warrant on the Mosely house hadn't showed up, and it had
started to rain again. Feinman was a methodical man and liked to
take things in order, and now he took advantage of a slight lull
to go out and drive back to Catalina Street in the hope of finding
Mrs. Kettleman.

The house next door looked dark and shut up, and he wondered suddenly if the Foleys were there at all. He thought about
that living room, and wondered exactly what you would do after a
thing like that happened. After the police had finished with all
their work and the bodies were taken away, there was still the
physical mess; police, lawyers, didn't do anything about that. All
that blood. Not exactly, or just, a disgusting mess to be cleaned up
so you could go on living in that house. They hadn't mentioned
any relatives; maybe they were staying with friends.

There weren't any lights on in the front of Mrs. Kettleman's
house either, and the rain had darkened the day; but he went up
on the porch and rang the bell, and in a minute the door opened.
"Yes?"

"Mrs. Kettleman?" He brought out the badge. "I'd like to ask
you some questions if it's not inconvenient."

"But what on earth about? I've just this minute got home.
What's happened?"

Feinman made a quick decision. He knew from Foley, a chance
remark, that Mrs. Duval and Mrs. Kettleman had been old
friends, neighbors for years. You never knew with a woman, they
might be cool and collected as could be, or they might go into
galloping hysterics. "There's been a robbery next door," he said.
"Yesterday morning. At Mrs. Duval's."

"A burglary? For heaven's sake! All this awful crime around—
oh, poor Tess, and all the doctor bills she's had lately too— My
goodness, I must go and see her. But for goodness' sake, don't

stand there on the porch, come in." She let him in, switched on lights; it was much the kind of homely, comfortable room as the one next door had been before it was invaded. Mrs. Kettleman was a large-bosomed ruddy woman with untidy white hair and a gentle voice. She sat on the couch, Feinman in a chair opposite. "As I said, I just got home—I drove down to Anaheim yesterday to see my daughter, it's a little drive of course, and the time slipped by and I don't like to drive at night, so I stayed over. And they're having a white sale at Buffums', so we went there this morning and I never started back until after two. But what's all this about a burglary? As if they needed any more hard luck—when did it happen?"

"Yesterday morning. What time did you leave?" asked Feinman.

"Oh, it was just nine o'clock. The chime clock went as I was going out, and it's a good timekeeper. I'd just made sure the front door was locked *and* the windows, planning to be gone all day, and I— Oh, my goodness!" she said suddenly. "My goodness gracious! I wonder—I might have been quite wrong, I did think—but I was rather in a hurry to get started—"

"You noticed something next door?"

"Well, I—yes, I did. I didn't think much about it except to think they must have moved back closer, because I hadn't seen her since they moved away. But of course she wouldn't have anything to do with the burglars."

"Who, Mrs. Kettleman?"

"Why, Sally Ann Thompson. Such a pretty child she was. Of course, as I say, I hadn't seen her in a couple of years. But I might have been wrong."

"Where did you see her? And just who is she?" Feinman was a little confused.

"Oh, well, that's a little complicated. You see, Tess Duval's older brother married a second time after his first wife died. And she had a family by her first husband, and Sally Ann was her granddaughter. They used to come and see Tess sometimes, but after her brother died they moved to Covina or somewhere, and never got up here. It was yesterday morning, I was just saying, as I was seeing the windows were locked, I saw a girl I thought was

Sally Ann just going up to Tess's front porch. There were a couple of boys with her—teen-agers, you know."

"About nine o'clock?" said Feinman.

"That's right. But about the burglars— Oh, I must see Tess— what a dreadful thing—"

Feinman knew he was being a coward. But he got up rather hastily and said, "Well, thanks very much, Mrs. Kettleman, I won't bother you any longer now."

"No bother—" she burbled gently the few steps to the door, and he managed to escape before she could get out any direct questions.

---◆---

Maddox had started out the day with Louise Sexton's attorney. He was a slim dark man with shrewd dark eyes and a flat voice. He listened to what Maddox had to say and nodded. "Very interesting. I may say I was a little concerned about the marriage. Not greatly, because Louise had a good deal of common sense where money was concerned. But she'd certainly fallen for the man—quite starry-eyed," he said dryly. "Good-looking man. I'd known Louise—and her first husband—for years, and I wondered about the, er, financial status. She came in to make a new will after they were married, and I asked her outright about the financial arrangement between them. He'd simply moved into her house. She was pretty evasive. I suppose her daughters had already given her a hard enough time, she didn't want another lecture from me." He smiled faintly. "She just said Howard's assets were tied up in land mostly, but he expected to negotiate a big timber deal very shortly. Meanwhile, I'd have a guess that she was paying all the household expenses."

"Yes. The will?" asked Maddox. "What's in it?"

"I said she had common sense. She was infatuated with the fellow, but after all, the money was her first husband's and should go to the girls. In round terms, there's about four million. All of it in gilt-edged stock except for a thirty-unit apartment in West Hollywood."

"How very pretty," said Maddox. "Where's it go?"

"She left Sexton half a million and the rest divided between the girls. I am—um—interested to talk with you, Sergeant. I've had both the girls at me this week. Isn't there some way to prevent him getting the money, something queer about the accident. Er—do I take it that the police think so too?"

Maddox contemplated his cigarette. "There's something queer about that accident all right, Mr. Hancock, but as a lawyer you'll understand that—as far as I can see—there'd be absolutely no use trying to prove it. It's all very iffy. Expert accident investigator on the stand: 'Are you absolutely certain that there was nothing present in the terrain of the accident which could have caused the driver's door to spring open before the car reached its final resting place?' Expert: 'Oh, well, I couldn't say absolutely.' No. We could poke around and get more chapter and verse on Sexton's background, which might show him up as a crook and quite possibly an exploiter of women. But even that's opinion and hearsay, and not every crook by a long shot ever commits homicide. There's really nothing to disprove the story he tells except the presence of that undigested meal in the stomach, which makes it look as if they'd had dinner at home."

"But you think he set the accident up?" asked the lawyer softly.

"I'm morally convinced of it. It'd be a very freakish accident to have happened that way. But there are just too many little ifs and buts to say positively it couldn't have happened that way."

"For the money? Very likely she'd told him about the will."

Maddox shook his head. "I don't know, and I don't suppose we'll ever know, Mr. Hancock. But there are a few suggestive facts—and I've got a few ideas. If he is an out-and-out con man, well, it's very rare for them to use violence. They're often rabbits when it comes to physical courage—they rely on charm and cunning, not physical strength. And then there's that meal—and the story he told. It's just barely possible he might have planned to get rid of her, enjoy the money alone. But I don't really think so. She was infatuated with him, she was providing him with an excellent living, everything was rosy, what more could he want?"

"If she'd just found out something about him?" suggested Hancock. "Oh—if he had a letter from the bigamous wife, or an old pal, and she came across it and realized what he was—" He sighed. "I suppose we'll never know. There was a cleaning woman came in twice a week, but the last time she'd have been there would have been the previous Saturday, and anyway Louise wouldn't have been having an argument with him in front of her."

"Did she read other peoples' letters?" Maddox smiled and shrugged. "I keep coming back to that meal. If he'd had a plan, it would have been the hell of a lot smoother than the story he told. If he's a con man, he's relied on his wits and cunning all his life. No, I think the whole thing was forced on him somehow."

"Forced—"

"I couldn't guess how. A sudden quarrel—even the letter-reading idea— It could be she suddenly realized his big timber deal wasn't materializing, and wondered about it—if she had money sense, woke up to realize he wasn't contributing. Almost anything. And—what? He struck at her in a temper, knocked her against the hearth? Hell, I haven't even seen the house. She could even have slipped and fallen against—um—what? That massive a fracture—something broad and big—"

"The bar," said Hancock quietly. "I wonder. They had it specially made, for the den. It's a solid slab of petrified wood, absolutely smooth, top and sides. About five feet long and four and a half high."

"Oh, that would do," said Maddox. "If he didn't kill her accidentally, it happened some way that would be awkward to explain. What with the girls screaming that he's a crook stealing from dear Mama. Whatever, he set up the accident. The quick, clever mind building that story—and overlooking the little detail of the meal, which would show at the autopsy. He put her in the car, drove down there—in gloves—you seldom get anything but smudges off a steering wheel, you know. And that's a damn dark road, no lights. He couldn't tell that he'd picked the one spot where there weren't any convenient boulders or trees. He sent the car over, and then he rolled her down after it. And walked home. If Thelma hadn't called him, he'd have called her about midnight, asking if Louise wasn't coming home soon. And there's no way to prove all that in court."

"Very likely not," said Hancock. "That's the police opinion?"

"It's my opinion as a police officer. I'm seeing an assistant D.A. this afternoon about something else, and I'll put it to him, but I think he'll agree. Really no point in trying to hang it on him. Waste of taxpayers' money to bring in what would be in effect the Scottish verdict, Not Proven."

"It's a damn shame," said Hancock seriously. "She was a nice woman. Nicer than her daughters. I'm damn sorry to see him get that money. If he was charged—"

"And convicted, he couldn't profit from the crime. But if he beat the rap—which would almost certainly happen—" Maddox grinned. "The lawyers would end up with all the money, the girls trying to prevent him from getting anything."

Hancock laughed. "You're probably right. Let me know what the D.A. thinks, will you?" He stood and offered his hand.

"If it's any consolation to you, I'm morally sure the man never planned to kill her. He just—tidied up, after the fact."

"Well, morally—" said Hancock, and left it at that.

◆

Maddox dropped into a coffee shop for lunch and went on to the interview with the assistant D.A. Neither of them enjoyed it much. Maddox was feeling considerably annoyed about the reduction of the charge on Cameron, and he had a shrewd suspicion that Cameron would deplore it too. He had made a gesture to publicize the state of the courts, and of course the court, in the person of the D.A., was hastily scrambling to nullify the gesture.

"We also considered that a plea of not guilty by reason of insanity—"

"Oh, you can shove that one," said Maddox pleasantly. "Cameron has too much guts to buy that. As I said, I can't do a damn thing to stop you trying to cover up, but don't ask me to like it."

After that he got onto Sexton, and Bigelow kept looking gloomier and gloomier, shaking his head dismally. "There's simply not enough evidence," he said.

"I know. I just thought I'd put it to you."

"Forget it. You may not altogether approve of some of what we do, Sergeant, but now and then we do try to think about taxpayers' money," said Bigelow sardonically.

When he left the courthouse it was raining again, and he'd have to hurry to keep the appointment with the real estate agent. To see Sue's house.

Looking at the house in the cold and dank light of a gloomy day, he was dismayed. He thought it was a disaster of a house; after all her looking, why she had to pick a place like this— Dimly he saw what she meant: big rooms, the deep backyard, the space. But it needed just about everything done to it, paint, yard work, cleaning. Apparently an appraiser had passed it as structurally sound; at least the roof wouldn't leak. Well, women were funny, the best of them. When she'd set her heart on the place it was a pity they were asking such a price. At least there was room for all his bookshelves.

"You can see the potential value," the real estate agent was saying.

"Oh, yes. Offer them eighty-five thousand," said Maddox absently. The chain-link fence had reminded him of Justin Lockwood; he hadn't noticed the window seat at all.

"I rather doubt— Well, we can start with that, of course. Very well, I'll submit the formal offer today."

Back in the Maserati, Maddox thought, But the other house— It was about time he really tackled Margaret Carstairs and soft-soaped her into agreeing to do what they both knew she really wanted to do, damn it. She'd always listened to him before she listened to Sue. The house in Hollywood ought to bring at least fifty thousand, which would be a long step on the way. And for some incomprehensible reason, Margaret liked that dank mansion too.

Through increasing rain he drove back to Hollywood. It was a quarter to five when he pulled up in front of the old house on Janiel Terrace. He got out of the car, and then he noticed that the garage door was up. Funny—she always closed it as soon as she put the car away. The car was there, her old tan Dodge.

He went up to the porch, rang the bell. He rang it four times. The door was locked, behind the screen. She didn't fraternize with neighbors, had old friends living farther away.

He went round to the back door, and beyond the screen saw the kitchen door not only ajar—

It had been savagely kicked in, and hung drunkenly. "Margaret!" he called, and silence answered. There had been no little dog to bark at burglars—

He pounded through the kitchen, down the hall, glancing into the bedrooms—nothing— She was in the living room. She lay awkwardly, crumpled against the TV console.

For one moment it was fifteen years ago and the high school principal was nervously, miserably telling him how Mother and

Dad had been killed in the air crash— Experience and training steadied him. There was a pulse. He went to the phone in the hall, called for an ambulance. He called the station, and got Rodriguez.

"For God's sweet sake," said Rodriguez. "O.K., I'll get the lab. You know we'll get nothing. My God, I'm sorry, Ivor—hope she'll be all right. Do you want—"

"That's right," said Maddox. "Get Sue. And—stand by, César."

"Will do. Hang on."

And he knew his girl, she wouldn't pass out or go into hysterics. This was one they'd have to get through together, and be glad they had each other.

EIGHT

He was waiting for her when she got to the hospital, at the end of a long corridor in the Emergency wing. He held her hands tightly. "Now, love, we don't know anything yet. It may just be concussion. Looks as if she interrupted the burglar and he just hit out in panic."

"Burglar!" said Sue. She let him sit her down on the vinyl-padded bench there, light her a cigarette. She said, "That old house! She had new locks put on—but that was ten years ago after Dad died. If Gor had been there— But, oh, Ivor, if you hadn't found her she might have been there for hours—all night—"

"Somebody will tell us something sometime, I suppose." They sat there for an unspecified time, until a tall white-coated man came up and said, "Mrs. Maddox? I'm Dr. Bernstein."

"How—what—"

"Your mother has a depressed skull fracture. We're taking her into surgery to relieve the pressure as soon as possible. You understand, I can't give you any definite assurance—it'll take time. We should know soon if she'll come out of it without impairment."

"Yes," said Sue numbly.

"But you can't do anything to help her, sitting here worrying," he told them practically. "We'll be doing all we can for her, and as soon as we know anything definite you'll be informed."

They drove back to the house on Janiel Terrace separately. Rodriguez was there with a man named Lopez from the lab, who was busily dusting for latents. That was a hope, but you went through the motions. They told Rodriguez what the doctor had said and he just shook his head. "I hope she'll be all right, Sue. It was the fairly crude thing, the kitchen door kicked in—he must be middling-big and strong."

That rang a very faint bell in Maddox's mind, but he couldn't think why right now. He said to Sue, "I don't need to tell you the first thing we want. Give you something to do." She nodded silently.

"Look, she'd just come in from the market." She indicated the bag of groceries on the kitchen counter. "L-like old Mrs. Eady. I'll look, Ivor." She came back in twenty minutes and said, "I've made up a list, the best I could. But it's funny not more *is* gone. It looks to me as if he was just in the process of hunting for loot, when she came in, and he just took what he had and ran. Grandfather's diamond stickpin is still right there in the box with all Grandmother's diamonds, and Mother's good diamond watch. What is gone is odds and ends. My father's watch—that was in the little jewelry box on the dresser, he just snatched that up and took the whole thing. It's a solid gold pocket watch with his name engraved on the back, Austin B. Carstairs. And another thing that would have been there was Mother's high school graduation ring—Hollywood High, 1944, and it's got her initials inside, M.E.F.—her maiden name was Forsythe, you know. Besides that, only the tape recorder's gone. It looks as if he was just rummaging around when—"

Maddox was grimly pleased. "Yes, and that gives us something more than we had." All of the collected loot, from the many casual burglaries they had had in the last month or six weeks, was hardly individually distinctive enough for a pawnbroker to identify it, inform the police; the casual burglars seldom had a connection with pro fences, relied on pawnbrokers. But those two pieces at least would be very readily identifiable; they'd go on the hot list right away.

"We can't—" Sue was looking at the door hanging loose on one hinge in dismay. "Ivor, we'll have to stay here tonight, we can't just leave that. The n-next thing, we'd have the wholesale burglars cleaning out all the furniture. Tomorrow—somehow—get the door fixed, the lock—"

Rodriguez and Lopez went away, and she looked in the freezer and got them a dinner neither of them remembered afterward. She put clean sheets on the bed. Presently they called the hospital and an impersonal nurse told them that Mrs. Carstairs was out of surgery and in Intensive Care, still unconscious.

And Maddox couldn't just take time off the job to sit holding her hands and worrying; the never-ending routine was there to be done, all they had on hand to work. She understood that, his good girl. Maybe by morning they'd know.

He remembered to tell her about the offer for the house. She just nodded listlessly.

◆

On Friday morning Feinman, driving through another spate of foglike rain, was thinking about that, hoping Sue's mother was going to be all right; they thought a lot of her, he knew. Hell of a thing—the kind of thing happening oftener and oftener to the honest citizens.

He was on his way to Covina. Foley had called the night watch last night to report that he and his wife were staying with her sister in Burbank, in case the police wanted them, and left an address, a phone number. Feinman had talked to him this morning, and Foley had had to think awhile before he remembered Sally Ann Thompson. "Oh," he said. "The Thompsons. We sort of lost track of them after my wife's uncle died. He's Carl Thompson, I think he's a C.P.A." He hadn't asked why Feinman was interested; his voice was dull.

Thompson was in the phone book, an address on Glendora Avenue; Feinman got there about ten o'clock. It was a small office but well furnished, looking fairly prosperous, with a middle-aged woman and a girl in the front part. They looked at the badge with fascinated eyes, and the woman led him back to Thompson's private office without question.

Thompson was a scholarly-looking man in the forties, with horn-rimmed glasses, worry lines searing his forehead. He sat back and regarded Feinman in surprise at the question, and pain came into his eyes. "Sally Ann," he said. "Why? Why are the— You've come to tell me she's dead. Haven't you?"

"Why, no, sir," said Feinman, surprised in his turn. "Her name just came up in connection with a case we're working. She is your daughter?"

Thompson sighed, took off his glasses and stared down at the pile of tax forms on his desk. "I suppose it isn't a new story to you," he said. "Yes, she's my daughter. Our oldest child. I—we don't know where she is. She left home last year. I don't need to tell you how frantic we were, her mother and I—sixteen— We told the police, but I don't suppose there's much they can do, and it wouldn't be so important to them. Do you want to hear all this?"

"Go on, sir."

"She was—such a sweet child, when she was younger. But after she got into junior high, she changed. Overnight, it seemed. All the—the nonvalues they seem to teach—what she got from the other kids—nothing right or wrong, do your own thing—you know the line. She turned so rebellious, disobedient—we couldn't seem to do a thing, she wouldn't listen to us whatever we tried. Oh, we suspected she was using marijuana—and the boys—" Thompson shut his eyes. "We don't know where she is," he said flatly.

"I see," said Feinman.

"There's a girl," said Thompson, his eyes still shut. "Angela Wood. She and Sally Ann were friends in school. As far as I could make out, the Woods don't care what Angela does, or where or when, so I imagine she's content to stay at home. I think Sally Ann contacts her sometimes. Once, about six months ago, she called us and said Sally Ann wanted us to know she was O.K., but she claimed she didn't know where she was."

"Yes," said Feinman. "Where'd I find her?"

"She's still going to high school, I think." Thompson opened his eyes and sat up. He said precisely, "For what it's worth, I'll tell you this. We took the two younger children out of public school and they're going to a private religious school. We had to give up the second car to do it, but I would say it's been worth it." He didn't ask about the case Feinman was working, or why he was interested in Sally Ann at all.

◆

Sue sat on the hard bench along the wall of the hospital corridor and lit another cigarette. She was smoking far too much, but it was something to do with her hands. It wasn't any use, mindlessly worrying, a waste of time; you knew that logically, but you couldn't control your mind.

The house. Ivor had made an offer for it. The house wouldn't mean much at all if Mother wasn't there to share all the fun of fixing it up the way it could look. If— She'd always be thinking,

Mother would have loved this, or Mother would have approved of that. They probably wouldn't get the house anyway if those people held out for more. Buying their own house—

She felt suddenly, violently, that if they were going anywhere she wanted to get right away from this sordid, dirty, violence-ridden city, the endless job of dealing with all the dirty little people— so many they saw, not even consciously vicious or evil, just the random impulsive giving in to temptation that ended in viciousness and evil. Just living in the middle of it, it rubbed off on you.

The nurses passed up and down the hall, fetching and carrying, paying her no attention. She lit another cigarette and realized she hadn't finished the last one. When she saw him coming up the corridor she could have wept just for the look of him, the lithe spare figure, black hair untidy again and his mouth a little grim.

"They don't know yet—I saw the doctor about an hour ago, but—"

"Well," Maddox said, "I thought I'd better see that you get some lunch. Get yourself all run-down and anemic and you never will start a baby. I managed to get hold of a carpenter who's supposed to put a new door on this afternoon. You can always get an emergency locksmith."

He urged her up and down the hall to the elevator, and they met the doctor just coming out of another room, halfway down the corridor. "Can you tell us anything?" asked Maddox.

Bernstein said, "There's a good chance. She came through surgery just fine. We just have to wait."

◆

Feinman looked at Angela Wood and she looked back at him a little scornfully, hand on one hip. They were in the office of the girls' vice-principal at West Covina High School. She said, "Oh, Sally's folks are real squares, I don't blame her for getting out. What a drag, she couldn't do anything hardly, way they ordered her around. I wouldn't know where she is, sorry." She was a big girl, with a lot of black hair and a fine olive skin; she was dressed —if you could call it that, he thought—in ragged blue jeans and a sloppy peasant-type seersucker blouse and dirty sneakers over bare feet. He wondered how the hell the schools had fallen so low to allow that kind of thing.

"Mr. Thompson thinks you know where Sally Ann is," he said evenly.

"Oh, he does. Well, I can't help that." Her gaze was insolent. "What the hell does a cop want with Sally Ann?"

"That's our business," said Feinman, and added in a softer voice, "and get that tone out of your voice when you're talking to a police officer. If you were one of mine, God forbid, you'd be getting your ass flattened regular until you remembered to be polite to your elders and betters. I suppose it's years too late to change you, but I don't have to take your insolence, so keep quiet."

She stepped a pace back and stopped chewing gum for a moment. She even looked a little uncertain. "Where's Sally Ann?" asked Feinman.

Angela looked at the floor. Unexpectedly she said, "They cared what happened to her. You know? Like, they worried about her. All the rules. It was a real drag." She drew a shallow breath. She said, "Sometimes it seems like nobody gives a damn what I do or don't do."

"Do you know where she is?"

Another minute, and then she said, "Sometimes she calls me. Now and then. So far as I know, she's shacked up with Sam Mendez, but I don't know where. The phone number's four two seven nine four three two." She turned and went out, and the door shut hissingly behind her.

◆

At about the same time, Daisy Hoffman and D'Arcy were having a look at another result of the confused morals of modern youth.

Patrolman Gonzales, cruising up Highland on his regular tour that morning, had idly noticed an ancient green Ford sitting alongside the entrance to the Hollywood Bowl, which of course would not be open for business for some months. He had cruised back into town, wandered down Hollywood Boulevard, made the usual circle up to Vermont, down to Santa Monica, up Cahuenga. He got sent to a bag-snatching incident on Sunset, and later to a fight in front of one of the twenty-four-hour porno theaters. He took a drunk up to jail, and went back on tour again. About one-fifteen he came up past the Bowl again, one end of his route, and the Ford was still there, so he pulled up and went to have a look at it. There was a dead body in the front seat, so he called the station.

At first they weren't sure it wasn't another homicide, so they were careful. D'Arcy gingerly got a front door open, got the glove compartment open, found a registration. Gordon Roberts, an address on Fountain. That rang a bell in his mind; he'd heard something about Nonie from Feinman. It looked like an O.D. of some kind. He was a young fellow, blond, dressed in slacks and turtleneck sweater. He was lying across the front seat, and when D'Arcy had got the door open the body slipped a little and the corner of some paper showed under one shoulder.

Daisy edged it out from under the body, and it was a dirty envelope with the words *To the Police* scrawled across it.

D'Arcy arched his lank length over her shoulder and they read the letter together—a much-folded sheet torn out of a loose-leaf notebook. It had no salutation, and the writing was painful and childish.

"You get told by everyboddy its olfashioned to beleve theres right and wrong, its just to get happyness however so long as you dont hurt annyboddy else and that sounds fine like it should be so. You beleve it. Its real square about all the stuf about virginity and living in sin. Everythings OK so long as you like it and its not hurting other peeple. My own ma she thinks that way too and so I got very much confused before it hapened. I dont know anny way to explane it. Except to say that Nonie thoght that way and all of a suden I found I didnt because it was funny wed ben living together a year and it was fine only I found she was making it with other guys and I didnt like it. She said about free spirrits and no harm to annyboddy but it was to me because I felt she belonged to me and noboddy else. I wanted her to mary me and then she couldnt go with other guys and she laughed real hard and said why not. And she wouldnt get tied up. But I couldnt stand for her going with other guys and we had a figt and Im pretty sure I killed her. Im sory about it all which I dont guess is anny good now and she had some sleeping tabblets so I am taking all of them and I guess that will finish all the troubel." It was signed a little more carefully, Gordon E. Roberts.

D'Arcy straightened up and grimaced. "Besides the obvious comment on the schools—he was a part-time *college* student?—I heard about Nonie yesterday from Joe."

"Yes," said Daisy, and her eyes were sad, and for a moment, despite her curly blonde head, you could believe she was a grandmother. "These poor damned kids, thinking all the hedonistic quote-unquote freedom is something new—never even dimly realizing that the rules and regulations are there because of what human nature is."

They called up the morgue wagon, and the garage to tow the car in. They'd have to ask the school for his mother's name and address, notify her.

———◆———

The search warrant for the Mosely house had come in this morning, and Rodriguez and Dabney went to execute it. Mrs. Mosely wouldn't let them in until she'd called her husband to come home. Charles Mosely had his own room; if there was anything to find, it would be there, and they looked. "He don't like anybody touching his things," she said. "You better be careful."

There wasn't anything suggestive immediately visible, but they found a locked suitcase under the bed. They forced it open as she protested loudly. Inside was a stack of homosexual literature and pornography, nothing else. "I take that garbage away from him when I find it," said Mosely, looking tired. "But what can you do, he's twenty-two. I never thought a boy of ours—" He left it at that.

There was nothing linking Charles Mosely to the murders.

There had been a little activity overnight. Another report of some nut firing a gun at a couple sitting in a parked car. There had been another heist; the victim couldn't even say whether he was short or tall. Unless they had something definite to go on—like the snake—that was just the same sort of job as the sex list, haul in men with the right records and lean on them.

The latent prints from the van hadn't shown in their records, so they'd been sent to the FBI; this morning they got the kickback, and the Feds didn't have them either.

Rodriguez, Rowan and Dabney got on with the sex list, and

broke for lunch. Rodriguez had just got back to the station with another suspect, at two-thirty, when Feinman called in.

"I've been on a little chase," he said, and explained. "Now I've just got the address of this trailer park from the phone company, and I'm here, and I don't think I'm a nervous sort of fellow, César, but I think I'd like some backup. It's a pity George is still in the hospital, he's bigger than the rest of you, but I guess you'll do. Who else is there?"

"What are you about to tackle?" asked Rodriguez. "A conclave of armed hoods?"

"Something a little wilder, I think. You might bring D'Arcy along."

"He seems to be out—" But just then D'Arcy and Daisy came in. "O.K., he's here, I will. Where?"

Feinman told him. It was an address in Eagle Rock.

When they got there, in Rodriguez' car, they saw what Feinman meant. It was an old, very shabby, run-down trailer park way up above the freeway, in the oldest and slummiest part of town. It looked as if it were overdue for an examination by the Board of Health. There were about thirty old trailers, never the kind to be dignified with the name of mobile home, in two rows, with about ten feet between them. There was a good deal of litter all over, and from one of the trailers at the far end loud rock emanated.

Feinman had to lead them a quarter block away before they could hear him. "This Sam Mendez—his father owns this place. He hardly gave me the time of day—he lives in one of the front trailers, and he doesn't like cops coming around. The only thing I got out of him, he lets Sam and his girl friend use one of the rear trailers—that, I take it, is where the rock is—and he thinks there's two-three other people there now."

"And just why are we interested in Sam Mendez?" asked D'Arcy. Feinman told him. "Oh. Oh, I see. Rather a tortuous sort of route, but I do see. The chain wasn't on the door."

"I just hope," said Rodriguez, "that everybody else living here doesn't gang up on us. From the look of the place, they're probably all welfare bums who don't like cops much either."

They marched down the narrow aisle between the rows of trailers, the rock getting louder. It was coming from the end trailer on the left. There was no remote hope of penetrating it with a knock; Feinman tried the door, it opened and a blast of noise rushed out. They braced themselves and filed in the narrow door.

Five people were in there, in a cramped space perhaps ten by forty. One of them appeared to be comatose on a built-in bunk: a man, lying face down. There was a couple sitting on the floor against the stereo, arms around each other, giggling and drinking beer out of cans: a blonde girl and a fat young man. Another girl sat at a card table at the other end of the trailer, drinking a glass of wine; and a third man was getting ice cubes out of a tiny refrigerator. Nobody noticed they had company until Feinman reached to turn off the stereo. The sudden silence hit like a bomb.

"Hey, man! Why'd you—" The fat young man stared up at them. His eyes were bleary, and he stumbled to his feet. "Who the hell're you?" Of necessity they pulled out the badges, and Feinman asked for Sally Ann.

Just for a minute the badges seemed to quiet them down, and the blonde girl admitted to being Sally Ann Thompson. Feinman asked her, "Were you up in Hollywood on Wednesday morning? Maybe stopped in to visit an old acquaintance?"

Her eyes held sudden shock. Not a man given to using ESP, Feinman suddenly understood the expression: it was the naïve surprise of a child who thought she had been so clever, at the instant comprehension of adult authority.

She turned, grabbed up something from the bunk and tried a blind rush past them for the door. Feinman caught her by one arm, D'Arcy by the other. She dropped what she was holding. The fat young man began to roar and came at them, flailing his arms wildly. The other two just stared. The cramped space made things awkward, but Feinman got the fat one under the jaw and knocked him down, and he fell against the bunk and didn't get up, scowling and rubbing his face. Sally Ann began to scream, and Rodriguez slapped her smartly.

Feinman bent and picked up what she had dropped. It was a portable radio, and there was a strip of adhesive tape with the inked name *Foley* on its bottom.

They were all a little high, if just on the liquor, and the law took a dim view of questioning subjects in that state. Feinman found a public phone and called up a wagon, and sent them over to the jail. They followed the wagon back to Hollywood and booked them in.

---◆---

Maddox went back to the hospital before the end of shift. Sue was still just sitting there, but he couldn't do anything about that. He found a coffee machine in the lobby and brought her some. A nurse stopped and said, "Really, Mrs. Maddox, you're doing no good by staying. We'll let you know the moment your mother's conscious. She's past the worst of the shock now."

A little color came back to her face at that. After a while Maddox took her out for dinner, made her have a drink first; she got some of the food down. They went home to Gregory Avenue. It was raining again, and she kept shivering, even with all the heat on. "That house," she said, "when it happened once, it could happen again. People living alone—"

"Now, love, don't borrow trouble."

She was taking a shower when the phone rang, and he ran for it. It was Parrott. "Well," he said, "I'm afraid they won't go for eighty-five. I talked with them on the phone this afternoon. They're saying now a hundred."

"I see," said Maddox. "Well, just at the moment there are—um —family circumstances which make this a little uncertain anyway. We'd better just leave it for the time being."

"Oh." Parrott sounded taken aback; apparently he'd been looking forward to an enjoyable session of dickering. "Oh, well, all right. I'll tell you one thing. Nobody's going to buy that house right from under you. Confidentially, it's the first offer they've had and quite possibly the only one they'll get."

"I see," said Maddox. "Well, I'll get back to you sometime."

Neither of them slept very well. He was in the middle of a confused dream in which Sue was telling him that he had to burn the house down because the locksmith was in jail, a proposition he found reasonable except that he couldn't find any wallpaper, which for some reason was necessary to the operation, when he suddenly came full awake and realized that the phone was ringing. Sue sat up in bed. He fumbled at the bedside lamp, flung the blanket off and ran for the living room. "Yes?"

"Mr. Maddox? I'm glad to tell you that Mrs. Carstairs is conscious and the doctor's quite pleased with her. We were given to understand that the police want to interview her. I'm afraid that won't be until later, but the family may see her for a very few minutes when you care to come in."

Putting down the phone, he looked at the clock. It was twenty past six.

◆

She still looked white and ill, and they had shaved some of her hair; there was a bandage around one temple. There was an intravenous needle in one arm. She gave them a weak smile, and her eyes were clear. Sue bent to kiss her. "You gave us a real scare, darling."

"Me too," said Mrs. Carstairs faintly. "Just got home from market—bag was too heavy, couldn't close the garage door—so went in, and saw the back door—"

"You take it easy," said Sue. "We can hear later."

"Never crossed my mind—still there— If Gor had been there, he'd have warned—but—"

"Don't try to talk too much, darling. You're going to be fine."

"Like you to catch him. He was—big young lout, blond hair to his shoulders—came at me, knocked me right down—"

The bell rang in Maddox's mind. He said, "Margaret, you're not fit to look after yourself. That's the damnedest, craziest thing I ever heard, you just walking in like that when you saw you had a burglar. A five-year-old would know better."

A small twinkle showed briefly in her eyes. "Yes, Ivor. Know better—the next time, won't I?"

In the corridor, Sue gave him a blinding-bright smile and let out a long, long sigh. "Just for once, darling, I could eat a perfectly enormous breakfast."

◆

Saturday was supposed to be Feinman's day off, but he had followed his nose on this case and wanted to see the outcome of it. He came in, and Rodriguez told him about Mrs. Carstairs. "Good news. Ivor called—they'll be in a little late."

"Good news," said Feinman seriously. He sat down and pulled the phone closer. "Let's see if the younger generation's sobered up enough to be talked to." He got the jail and asked questions. "All ready and waiting for us. The matron thinks the girl was strung out on PCP—the rest of'em were just half drunk. God knows what they'd had on Wednesday."

"And if that woman hadn't just happened to glance out the window, we'd still be groping in the dark on that one." But as they started out, Maddox and Sue came in.

"Say, Joe—I just realized what rang a bell in my mind. You were on a burglary the other day, where the couple came in and found him on the premises. Described as a big young fellow with long blond hair."

"The Brannons, yes. Why?"

"It sounds like the same one caught Sue's mother, by her description. He may be an amateur, but he could graduate to something more—the violence in him, no hesitation to strike out. Any leads? I didn't think so. Well, let's hope the identifiable jewelry will give us one."

Feinman and Rodriguez went over to the jail. Sam Mendez, the fat young man, wouldn't say a word: he just scowled at them. Sally Ann said too much. "Mr. Foley gave me that radio a couple of years ago. Honest he did. It wasn't new, but they were going to get a new one and he gave that to me. I don't know why you had to come busting in there yesterday, we weren't doing anything. We never did anything anyway. You can't pin anything on us." Then she said it all over.

"Then you don't mind if we ask Mr. Foley about the radio, do you?" said Feinman. "Good, we'll do that." But he looked at her in some wonder. In spite of all that cops see, there is usually something worse coming up. All that blood, in that comfortable homelike living room. She didn't look as old as seventeen; her blonde hair was stringy and dirty, and she sat sullenly chewing her nails like a five-year-old.

The one who had been passed out was Ken Murdock. He hadn't anything to say either. The other couple was something else again: Linda Mercer and Tim Kruger. Tim said they'd hitched to California from back east, and met Sam and Sally Ann a couple of weeks ago at a rock concert. They needed a place to stay, they were broke, and Sam said they could stay in an empty trailer there till they could pick up some bread some way. "I'd even applied for a job at a gas station up the street. Hell, we didn't have a buck between us." That must have been the ultimate sacrifice. Linda and Tim were much the same kind as Sam and Sally Ann, but there seemed to remain in Linda a few shreds of a basically sound middle-class background. She was the one who spilled it in detail.

"I mean, I never heard of such a thing," she said mournfully, twisting a lock of her dark hair round one finger. "I thought it was the awfullest thing I ever heard of. I mean, Sally Ann and Sam seemed to be the greatest, giving us a place to stay and all, real free spirits, they were hanging real loose, really living it up and forget about tomorrow. But I really got shook, Sally tell me about that." She peered at them through the tangled hair. "I mean, you got to have the bread to get things. They get food stamps, that's O.K., but it doesn't buy everything. Ken, he's kind of a funny one, he wanted some coke that day. He knew a dude in Hollywood owed him some bread and they went over there to find him—"

"They, who?" asked Feinman.

"Oh, Sam and Sally Ann and Ken. But they couldn't find him, and all of a sudden they were riding around and Sally Ann recognized the street, some kind of relatives of hers lived there and she figured the old lady'd let her in and they could see what was there they could hock. And she did, only I forgot to say by then Ken was kind of high. He doesn't go for grass usually, just coke when he can get it, but Sam had some grass and he had a couple joints. They went in, and Sally Ann said the old lady couldn't make out what they were doing, looking for stuff, she was real funny and stupid, and then she was scared. And it was Ken said she'd tell who was there, better shut her up. But I guess, I mean the old lady didn't know who Sam and Ken were, and I guess Sally Ann was kind of shook, way he did it. I mean, an old lady and a baby— And she didn't know where Sally Ann was living, did she?" It was a vague plea for common sense. She abandoned that lock and started on another. "And they didn't get anything anyway. There was twenty bucks in the old lady's bag, was all, and a couple pieces of junk jewelry Sam hocked for another ten. But I thought that was just awful. I mean, killing people like that."

"If we get all that down on paper will you sign it?" asked Rodriguez.

"Sure. I, you know, liked Sally Ann real good till that happened. But I mean, after that it was kind of different."

When the matron had taken her away, Rodriguez expelled breath in a sigh. "*¡Santa Maria!* The jungle getting wilder all the time. But that should tie it up."

"If she doesn't decide to go back on it and side with the free spirits against the establishment," said Feinman.

"So let's get it typed up and get her name on it quick," said Rodriguez.

———◆———

Sometimes Saturdays came on hot and heavy. They would get a series of quiet ones, and then suddenly all the wild ones in the jungle would pick Saturday to do their thing. Possibly it was because even the ones who were holding jobs were mostly loose on Saturday to follow their impulses.

It was raining in a halfhearted way, and very dark. They were still out on the sex list, and Maddox and D'Arcy knocked off for lunch late. They'd just got back to the station at two o'clock when a call came in: a heist and a shooting, an address on Ardmore. "A heist?" said Maddox. "That's all old residential." They headed for it, and D'Arcy said querulously he was getting tired of rain.

The squad was waiting, with Patrolman Gomez in it. "The ambulance came before you did. She was bleeding pretty bad, I thought she'd better have attention first. The other one's up in her apartment, pretty shook. They both live here—Mrs. Lyle and Mrs. Thornburg—they'd been out shopping together in Mrs. Lyle's car. Came home a little while ago, put the car in the garage, started in the back, and a guy holds them up. Mrs. Lyle screamed and hung onto her bag when he tried to grab it, and he shot her. I don't think it's serious, but she was bleeding."

The apartment building was an old one, garages at the back, a narrow drive. When they talked to Mrs. Thornburg she was more indignant than frightened. "What we're all coming to I can't think —criminals roaming the street like animals! At our own back door! We had a lot of packages to bring in, likely take two trips, and we never saw him at all till we got nearly up to the door. He pointed a gun and said, 'I want all your money,' and Clara screamed when he grabbed her bag, and he *shot* her—he *shot* her! And the next minute he just ran down the drive and disappeared—and I was so frightened," said Mrs. Thornburg, looking mad instead, "that I dropped the package of brand-new sheets I'd got on sale *right in the mud* by the driveway, and I—"

"Could you describe him, Mrs. Thornburg?"

"Indeed I can. He was a black man, sort of thin and tall—not as tall as you," she said to D'Arcy. "He had on a bright yellow raincoat. Recognize him? By a picture? Well, I don't know about that. But I must say, what we're coming to when two respectable women—"

It was obviously going to be one of those things they couldn't do much about. They went back to base and Maddox called the hospital. Mrs. Lyle was resting comfortably; they'd taken a bullet out of her shoulder and she would be sent home tomorrow. Maddox asked them to send the slug to the lab, but he hadn't much hope of dropping on the gun that had fired it.

He grinned across at Sue. For the moment, it didn't matter. Everything was—what did the old song say?—copacetic.

The door from the front hall opened and Frank Cooper came in. He was carrying a raincoat over his arm, wore the same white jump suit with *Frank's Union Service* stitched on the pocket. He recognized Sue and went up toward her desk. "Say," he said, "I said I knew you couldn't do anything about this, but it's a damn nuisance. I wrote to the company about it, the damn machine color-blind, but naturally I haven't heard from them yet. And it's only been about forty bucks so far, but that's so far. If this joker keeps handing me Xeroxed dollars in the self-service machine, I could be in trouble."

Maddox came up, Sue introduced them, and Cooper produced nineteen more black-and-white dollar bills. Maddox laughed and Cooper looked annoyed. "Well, technically," said Sue, "it is counterfeit money; you should contact the Secret Service."

"Which reminds me," said Maddox, "I ought to go and visit George in the hospital tonight. I think he goes home tomorrow, and I hope we'll have him back on the job Monday. Oh, I can hear what the Secret Service would say."

"Technically speaking," said Cooper, looking more aggrieved, "it's the damn company's machine, and if it's set up so it takes counterfeit money the damn company's responsible. I just thought you ought to know."

"If I were you," said Maddox, "I'd start worrying about something else."

"What?"

"That your amateur counterfeiter doesn't get the bright idea of Xeroxing fives, tens and twenties. He could supply a regiment from your self-service tank."

"Oh, my God," said Cooper.

"I also wonder," said Maddox, "if he—and maybe some of his friends—are patronizing other stations. Though I suppose we'd have heard about it. Take the funny money to the Secret Service, Mr. Cooper."

"But," said Sue when Cooper had gone, "don't they look *queer?* Black-and-white dollars."

"No queerer than the green ones with nothing to back them up," said Maddox. "Reason your house is priced so high. I meant to tell you, they refused eighty-five."

"Oh. I thought they would."

"But you never know," said Maddox vaguely. "Hold the good thoughts." The phone buzzed on his desk.

"Your team of burglars has been busy again," said Whitwell. "Place on Micheltorena Street. People just came home and found it. This is one hell of a caper, isn't it?"

"Oh, for God's sake. You may say so. And not one damned lead—" After the Herschel sign had fallen through. They had never followed up on all the James Wheelers, but it was unlikely that was the real name of the fellow who'd bought the first van.

Maddox went out to Micheltorena Street with Rodriguez. It was a pleasant small house on a neatly landscaped lot, and Mr. and Mrs. William Leaman were still too stunned to be angry.

"Just over to Lydia's for the day," said Leaman. "We left about noon, got back half an hour ago." It was a quarter to five. "But— *everything*— My God, when we moved here the movers took a day just unloading it all—"

The house was completely bare. This time the wholesale burglars had taken furniture, stove, refrigerator, washer, dryer, and even a little electric broiler oven. "But I can't even fix anything for dinner," said Mrs. Leaman blankly. "Just canned goods—but no way I could cook—"

That was when she looked in the pantry cupboard and discovered that they had taken all the canned goods too.

Only the neighbor on the right side was home, an indifferent old fellow smoking a pipe and reading a German Bible. "Oh, yeah, I saw the truck," he said. "Coming and going. Didn't know the Leamans were fixing to move. The fellas in that truck, they had to make three trips altogether, get everything moved."

NINE

Sunday morning broke bright and clear and very cold, which was normal for southern California after a rainstorm. They were all in except Daisy; it was her day off. The night watch had had a slow night, a heist in a public parking lot, another felony hit-run with no witnesses.

Feinman was getting out the final reports on the Duval case; together with Linda's statement, the reports would all get down to the D.A.'s office tomorrow, and it would be out of their hands. "And it'll be interesting," he said to Maddox, "to see if Sam and Sally Ann get charged as accessories, or what. And I can't understand why that A.P.B. hasn't turned up Jerome Simms." Sometime today he would be calling Thompson to tell him about Sally Ann; that kind of thing was another unpleasant job cops came in for.

"Didn't you say you'd found out he'd just got married? Maybe they're still away on a honeymoon. The A.P.B. hasn't turned up the other irrelevant snake either—what's his name?—John Winter."

"That's so." Feinman bent over the typewriter again.

Rodriguez came in about nine with another one off the list, and Maddox backed up the questioning. Neither he nor Rodriguez thought this one, Fred Chesney, was a very likely suspect. He had a barely normal I.Q., he was phenomenally ugly, and he wouldn't find it easy to attract well-raised little boys. Especially, thought Maddox, somehow to charm Justin Lockwood into climbing that fence. They let him go.

The jail called. Sam Mendez was now eager and willing to make a statement. Feinman, looking resigned, got his coat and went out. Three minutes later the desk relayed a new call—an eight-year-old boy abducted—and Maddox and Rodriguez were out of the station like scalded cats.

This time they were only minutes behind. It was Woodland Avenue off Laurel Canyon Boulevard, and Patrolman Carmichael gasped out the story as they ran up the walk to the front porch. "I wasn't three minutes away, the call was logged at nine forty-three and I was here by nine forty-seven. Kids playing in front, the younger one came in and told his mother the other one was taken off in a car. If we get out an alert right now—"

The couple's name was Tansy, and they were trying to keep their heads. "—Just playing outside before we left for church," she said, a slim dark woman, her voice taut. "After all this rain—yes, Sherman's eight, our other boy Jason's five, it was Jason came and told me some man had grabbed Sherm into his car. I called my husband—"

"No, Mama! He didn't!"

"—The police, and—"

"Mrs. Tansy, we'd like to get an alert out right away, there's a chance they can be spotted— Give us a description of the boy, what he was wearing, please."

"Yes, he's— Sherm's about average size for his age, blond, hazel eyes, he's got on a navy suit and white shirt and black shoes."

Maddox jerked his head at Carmichael, who ran to get that on the radio. Within minutes every patrol car in the Hollywood-L.A. area would be on the lookout.

"But, Mama, it wasn't—nobody hurt Sherm—"

"We'd warned him about strangers," said Tansy distractedly. "He's not—not an outgoing child, I don't know how anybody could just grab him, he's not a baby, and we didn't hear a thing— Jason just came in and said a man took Sherm away—"

"Sherm wanted to go with him!"

For the first time Maddox and Rodriguez took notice of the five-year-old between his parents. Maddox squatted down to see eye to eye with him. "O.K., Jason, how did it happen?"

"Me and Sherm was out in front, we wasn't doing nothin' because Mama said keep clean for church, I was just on the front porch—and—and Clancy come into our yard, the doggie lives next door, and Sherm just went to pet him. And the car come and stopped and the man opened the door—and it musta been somebody Sherm liked real good because he run right over and got in the car—"

"Oh, Jason, that's not so, Sherm wouldn't just go off with a stranger—you made that up!"

"Didn't either! Sherm was real glad to see him!"

"Did you see the man, so you could tell us what he looked like?"

"I was on the porch. I dunno."

"What was the car like?"

Jason wriggled. "Uh, it was white."

Maddox stood up and looked at Rodriguez. He said, "The pattern. What the hell, César?" But there was no time to speculate now; they could just hope, being on this within minutes, they might spot him and get him before he gained his private place and was under cover with the boy. They added the white car to the alert, and waited.

Fifteen minutes later they thought they had him; when the call came, Maddox and Rodriguez broke the speed laws back to the station. Patrolman Keeler had spotted a white sedan with a man and a boy in it, the boy crying, at Beverly and Vermont, and brought them in; the boy had tried to run when he got them out of the car.

The man was well dressed, looked like a solid citizen, and he was upset. "What the hell is this, anyway? Who do you damn cops think I am, anyway?" His name was William Koenig and the boy was his son, a boy older than Sherman Tansy. "I'd just gone to get him—deserves a good hiding—we had a family spat last night and he got out and went over to a pal's house—never found he was gone till this morning, and we were wild, and then he called and said he was sorry—we were just on the way home, and what in hell—"

"Why'd you try to run when the squad car stopped you?" Rodriguez asked the boy.

"Gee, I was afraid Dad was gonna have me arrested!"

That was a dead end. It was just past a quarter to eleven then, an hour and fifteen minutes by a conservative estimate since the boy had gone, and they knew that the odds were he and his abductor were somewhere under cover now. It might look as if there was a great gap between Harold Frost and Freddy Noonan from mid-Hollywood, and Justin Lockwood from Mount Olympus, and now Sherman Tansy from Laurel Canyon, but on a map there wasn't such a great distance between—it was all upper mid-north Hollywood. His private place might be anywhere in a radius of a hundred blocks around, the crowded blocks of Hollywood with apartments rubbing shoulders with single houses. There was no way to know, or look.

Maddox and Rodriguez went back to talk to the Tansys. They were asking for the FBI now; Maddox told them the plain kidnapping wasn't likely. Tansy was the manager of a big chain market, no millionaire. "You probably read about the other boys. That's what this looks like—the same pattern."

"*That*," said Tansy. "Oh, my God! A thing like that!" Mrs. Tansy rocked back and forth in agony.

"There's been a pattern to it," said Maddox. "Apparently the man has some, er, gimmick which attracts the boys—"

"Sherm would *never* go off with a stranger voluntarily—no, it's not possible—"

"And all I can tell you, Mr. Tansy, we'll be looking, we'll be doing what we can, but we've got no leads at all on this joker. I just want you to—be prepared for what might happen."

"Oh, God," said Tansy. "Oh, God. Why us? Why Sherm?" It was the question people would ask.

And Maddox said to Rodriguez, back at the station, "Will you tell me how the *hell*, César? This just reinforces what we got on the Lockwood kid, and the gimmick probably worked on Frost and Noonan too. For God's sake, how the hell does he do it? These were all city kids, forewarned by their parents—cared-for kids, carefully warned against the strangers! And this character drives up, opens the car door and says hello, and they run to him as if he was Santa Claus! How the hell?"

"I can't even begin to imagine."

◆

If the pattern held, the body of Sherman Tansy would turn up somewhere nearby early tomorrow morning. All the rest of that day the alert was still in effect, but everybody knew it was an empty gesture, that by an hour at least after the boy got into the car, he was off the street and held in the killer's private place.

Feinman had missed all the excitement, being over at the jail. He heard all about it, rolling forms and carbon into his typewriter, and after the appropriate comments said, "What Sam Mendez was after was trying to pave the way to getting out from under. Claiming he and Sally Ann were scared to death of Ken Murdock, afraid to cross him, afraid he'd kill them if they didn't go along." Feinman was disgusted with people. "I wouldn't take a bet that the D.A. won't play along if they turn state's evidence, and let them loose on probation on a plea bargain. And the good God knows what other mayhem they'll get into in the future, just through their damned irresponsibility. But he wants to make the damned statement, we have to oblige him."

About two o'clock a squad car called in: Rinehart had spotted John Winter's plate number, stopped him and was bringing him in. Feinman muttered, "Busy work—clearing up as we go along." Everybody but Maddox and Sue was out on the sex list, Maddox waiting to sit in on the questioning of men dropped on and brought in. It would be a great big miracle if one of those they had an address for turned out to have Sherman Tansy bound and gagged and visible when somebody knocked on his door, but that wouldn't happen: miracles were few and far between.

Rinehart brought a man in and said, "You'll have to sort this one out. It's the right car, he matches the description, and you can get fake I.D. pretty damn easy. And get tattoos taken off."

The man was looking both annoyed and amused. He did match Winter's description very generally, but looked older. "My name's Reeder," he said mildly, "Henry G. Reeder," and he pulled out a wallet and began to drop I.D.'s on Maddox's desk, Social Security card, driver's license, credit cards. "If the car was stolen—but I don't see how. He had all the transfer forms, the pink slip, he signed everything and I mailed them to Sacramento myself. I haven't got the new registration back yet—you know what the mail's like—and that was two weeks ago."

He was the assistant head librarian of the Burbank Public Library. "What about the car?" asked Maddox.

"It was advertised privately in the *Times*. We wanted a second one for me to drive to work. Yes, that's right, his name was Winter— I went to look at it at an address somewhere on Kenmore. He said he was going to Florida, he even showed me a plane ticket. That was two weeks ago last Friday."

"Well, we're very sorry you were inconvenienced," said Maddox. "These things do happen. We were looking for him to ask a few questions. We'll"—he smiled—"get the plate number off our list right away."

"Thanks," said Reeder dryly. "It's been a little experience, Sergeant. I hope somebody's going to drive me back to where I left the car."

When he had left Maddox said, "I suppose Winter did go off to Florida. Having the plane ticket—well, Simms has got to be the boy we want for that anyway." He yawned and shut his eyes. "Damn it, damn it, what the hell can his gimmick be, that this bastard can look at a kid and—Pied Piper of Hamlin, damn it. It was just possible he'd used the sudden violence on the Frost and Noonan boys, but now, knowing about the Lockwood boy, and Sherman, it's likely they fell under the spell too and just climbed into his car—damn it, it doesn't make sense!"

Sue sighed and looked at her empty desk. "There isn't much for me to do, Ivor. I want to go to the hospital—if you need me you can catch me there or at home."

"Go, go," said Maddox. "You might drop in and see George— lying down on the job, leaving us shorthanded." Some sort of complication had developed with Ellis's gunshot wound and he was still in the hospital, with no certainty as to when he might get out. "Him lying there being spoon-fed by nurses and waited on hand and foot while everything piles up here—" It was automatic, off the top of his mind; Sue knew he was worried to death about that boy, and nothing, nothing they could do to help him, find him.

———◆———

Rodriguez brought in another one, and they didn't waste much time on him; he'd taken to guzzling wine since his latest arrest and wasn't really likely for their boy. "Why the hell are we bothering to lean on them today, César? The one we want is busy with Sherman—we ought to rout out every squad car and have a look at all the addresses we've got. On the long chance—"

"It'd be something to do," said Rodriguez. Feinman came in with a man in tow.

"Go by the book," muttered Maddox.

"You don't think he's on the list?" said Rodriguez.

Maddox stood up restlessly and rattled the coins in his pocket, going over to the window. "No, *amigo,* I do not. I haven't thought so for some time. I think he's a stranger in town, and we haven't got damn all on him, don't know enough about him to ask NCIC is there anybody like this with a record anywhere—from New York to Miami to Chicago. There's just no way, damn it. No way." D'Arcy came in alone, sat down at his desk and lit a cigarette. "And you know what's going to happen next. Tomorrow morning that poor damn kid's going to turn up just like the other three, with some of his clothes missing, and it'll give us another great big blank—no leads any more than we had on the others. Damn it, we'd have a better chance of getting somewhere if we went out and bought a crystal ball!"

"Play the cards we've got," said Rodriguez.

"With him holding all the aces—*and* the jacks," said Maddox. The phone buzzed, and he looked at it wearily, didn't immediately reach to pick it up. It was Rodriguez who answered it.

"Yes, what? . . . O.K., the address? . . . We're on it."

"New one down," said Maddox without much interest.

"Assault of some kind. Hillside Avenue."

"Do tell," said Maddox.

Rodriguez raised his brows at D'Arcy, who got up. Feinman started his captive toward an interrogation room, and after a moment Maddox trailed after them.

◆

"There's an ambulance on the way," said Patrolman Wallace. "I think the girl will be O.K.—he doesn't look so good."

"Please—" said the girl.

They were in the living room of the house on Hillside: an old sprawling Spanish house with a lot of old dark furniture and Oriental rugs. Wallace had let them in; the girl had managed to call for help, and the door had been unlocked. They didn't know any names yet, or any circumstances. The girl was huddled on the couch, her dress half torn off her, blood on her face; she held the torn dress up with automatic modesty, didn't seem aware of the blood seeping along one side through the light blue nylon. "Please," she said. "Ray—"

The young man was a lot worse off. He was lying on his side in the dining room, blood all over him and around him; it looked as if he'd been stabbed. He was unconscious, but had a thread of pulse.

Rodriguez bent over the girl. "Miss? We're police. Can you tell me your name?"

"Gloria—Considine," she said. "Please, help Ray. He was hurting Ray—don't know who—rang the bell and just— Mother and Dad—over at Aunt Grace's. Got to—get them. Please help Ray. They had—awful fight, Ray trying—"

The tears were sliding down her cheeks now, and she began to sob. "He raped me. He raped me—but Ray—"

There had certainly been a fight here—chairs and tables knocked over, lamps, ornaments scattered all over where they'd been sent flying, a couple of area rugs in folded heaps. The ambulance came. Fortunately there were a couple of trained paramedics in it with a lot of equipment, for as they were getting the man onto a stretcher he went into cardiac arrest and they worked desperately on him for five minutes before they brought him back. The girl had passed out by then. When they had him fairly stable, the paramedics loaded them and started off, siren screaming, and then Rodriguez and D'Arcy looked around, trying to find out whom to notify.

It was D'Arcy who had the elementary idea of looking at the outside of the front door, and there was an engraved brass plate that said *Mr. and Mrs. G. M. Considine.* So then they found the phone, a phone index beside it. There was only one Grace listed, a Grace Boyle in Bel Air, so Rodriguez called there and asked for Considine. Cops were used to breaking bad news.

"My God!" said Considine. "But how could—who would— They were just there together when we— My God, we'll be right back—"

Rodriguez and D'Arcy were still there, with a couple of lab men starting to poke around, when the Considines drove up in a Caddy Seville and rushed into the house. They were handsome, well-dressed, successful people by their looks, and they were bewildered as well as frightened. Rodriguez told them their daughter would probably be all right, she had told the police she had been raped, but was only superficially hurt.

"Oh, my God," they said together, and he added, "But in broad daylight—quiet Sunday afternoon—who—how did he—"

"The little we got, evidently he rang the doorbell and when she answered it he pushed right in. It's possible it was someone your daughter knew, of course. Can you tell us who Ray is?"

"Ray Felton—he and Gloria are engaged. You said he was hurt?"

"Yes, sir, pretty badly. He'd lost a good deal of blood, he went into cardiac arrest before they got him in the ambulance. It was touch and go for a few minutes. He—"

"Oh, Christ, he's only twenty-two," said Considine. "A nice young fellow—good boy—they're going to be married in June— My God, Chrissie, I've got to call his parents—" He made for the phone.

"They'll be in Hollywood Receiving," said D'Arcy helpfully. She had sunk down on the couch and was holding her head. "Mrs. Considine, we don't want to bother you in an emergency like this, but sometime soon we'd like you to look around and tell us whether anything is missing. It's possible he came to burglarize the place and just took advantage of your daughter's presence to rape her."

She nodded silently. Considine came back and said heavily, "They'll meet us there. What—what do we do about you?" He looked at the police. "Nothing like this—ever came my way."

"We'll be here for a while yet, sir. Looking around for fingerprints, anything else. We'll see the doors are locked when we leave."

"All right, thanks," said Considine.

Half an hour later Rodriguez checked with the hospital, talked to a doctor. The girl had indeed been forcibly raped, and stabbed shallowly in the side and shoulder. Young Felton was still on the critical list; he had been stabbed some forty times, all over. They were pumping blood into him now. The rape had been a brutal one; the girl had been a virgin, and was considerably torn.

Rodriguez passed that on to D'Arcy, who grunted. He was watching the lab men dusting the dining table. He said, "Three long blocks down the hill, César. All the porno theaters along the boulevard. I saw a graph the other day down in Vice at headquarters. Very interesting. Relative proximity of forcible rapes to the porno houses. And the judges in the ivory tower say there's no connection between pornography and sex crimes. Just since it's been allowed out in the open, the sex crimes are up like a rocket."

"Let's start a crusade," said Rodriguez, "and hear all the sophisticated liberated citizens tell us what damned puritans we are."

◆

Just in thirty-six hours, Mrs. Carstairs was looking almost like herself, sitting up in bed with color in her cheeks, the intravenous apparatus gone. Only the somewhat rakish bandage proclaimed her an invalid. Sue had brought her an overnight bag from home, with a bed jacket and her robe, slippers, cosmetics, comb and brush, the book she'd been reading, her reading glasses. "Lifesaver," said Mrs. Carstairs gratefully. "I'll feel a hundred percent better with some lipstick on. But I'm going to look a sight until my hair grows out."

"Let it teach you a lesson," said Sue severely. "Talk about rushing in where angels fear to tread. At least Ivor thinks we may have a better chance of catching him, on account of Dad's watch and your high school ring."

"Good." By some miracle she was alone in the room, though a second bed was neatly made up by the window.

"And I was late, I'm sorry, they're going to kick me out of here in a few minutes, but Ivor and I'll be back tonight. I talked to the doctor and he said nobody could kill you with an ax."

"Not really, I suppose."

"Well, he said you have a very robust constitution. And you'll be in about another four days and then you can go home. But I don't know if you'll quite feel up to taking care of yourself right away—I can always come and get your dinner, or stay with you for a while."

"And what about Ivor?" asked Mrs. Carstairs.

Sue said half crossly, "Oh, Mother! You *see* how much easier it would be if we were all together—a regular family! Now, look, you are going to be sensible about it, aren't you? Sell the house, and come with us, and be a family again?"

Sudden tears came into her mother's eyes. "Oh, Sue, darling, I'd love to live with you and Ivor—if you're really sure you want—"

"Don't be an idiot! Of course we want you—madly," said Sue, and kissed her. "I don't know if we're going to get that nice house —wouldn't it be fun to give it a whole face lift?—but we'll find something. And thank God you've come to your senses. And I've got to run—it's four o'clock."

Her mother caught her arm as she turned. "Sue, if you've got time, would you stop by and see how Mrs. Eady is? The poor creature was on my mind the day the burglar came. I just don't know how she's going to manage."

"We'll think of some way to get her to take the help. Yes, I will," said Sue. "See you tonight."

She was feeling as lighthearted and happy as she'd ever felt in her life when she left the hospital—except for the dark shadow of the little boy lost, who was probably forever lost. She thought there was just time to go and see Mrs. Eady now. Ivor might be late. She also thought she'd take the rest of the fruit cake to her. Aunt Evelyn had sent an enormous one at Christmas, and the last quarter of it was in the freezer wrapped in foil. She stopped at home to get it, and drove over to Alexandria Avenue, parked in front of the poor little house.

There was a fat man in the yard next door, trimming some bushes. He straightened up and looked at her curiously as she started up the walk. "You know the old lady?" he asked.

Sue stopped. "Yes. Why?"

"Never saw anybody come to see her before, is all. I hope she's O.K. She got robbed again yesterday."

"What?" Sue moved toward him.

"Yeah. Hell of a thing. These Goddamn kids. I'd just stepped out on the porch, get the evening paper, it happened so fast I couldn't do nothing. The old lady was just comin' home, I guess, hobbling along with a little bag, and just about as she gets where you are now, a pair of great big kids—teen-age boys, you know— come runnin' up, and shoved her around, and grabbed her handbag. I come and helped her up, but they were long gone."

"Oh, no," said Sue. "Oh, no."

"She said they got all the rest of her money for the month. Damned shame," said the man. "These Goddamn kids."

Sue turned and ran up the walk, the two broken steps. "Mrs. Eady?" she called at the door. But of course there wasn't any lock on the door now that worked; she pushed at it, it stuck, but after a struggle she got it open and went into the bare living room.

The thick nauseous gas fumes caught her by the throat, and she saw that the kitchen door was closed, and she knew. But you always had to try. She flew to that door, shoved it in, stumbled over some clothes covering the crack, and holding her handkerchief to her face, fumbled at the handles on the stove, turning them off. She flung up the window, wrenched open the door to the back porch; cold fresh air began to blow in strongly.

Mrs. Eady had put a pillow on the floor in front of the open oven door and lain down herself prim and straight. She was quite dead.

Sue flew out the front door and down the walk. "I have to use your phone," she told the man peremptorily. He looked surprised, but let her in and showed it to her. She managed to dial the station, and she managed to control her voice over the big hard lump growing in her throat, until she heard Ivor's voice at the other end. She even managed to make him understand where she was and what had happened. But the lump got bigger and bigger, and she couldn't speak a word to the man. She stumbled back to Mrs. Eady's front porch and then into Mrs. Eady's living room with just the two religious pictures on the walls, and she stood there crying like a fool, the tears pouring down her cheeks. Through the open front door she saw the little blue Maserati slide up behind her car, and then a squad car ahead of it. He came in and took one look at her and put his arms around her tight.

"Now, love, now, love, stop that."

"I'm a fool, I know," she choked. "But she was so brave, Ivor—she tried so hard, so long. It was—the jungle. The jungle was too much for her—in the end."

He made her come out and get in his car, and gave her a cigarette. He went back into the house with the patrolman, who presently came out and used the mike in the squad car. The morgue wagon, she thought. After a while Maddox came back down the walk and got in the car beside her.

"Probably early this morning," he said. "I've got a couple of things I want you to look at, if you won't start crying again."

"I'm all right. I know she's better off."

He handed her a page. "She left both of these on the table in the bedroom, carefully weighted down with her library books."

It was a page torn from a linen-finish stationery tablet. She must have bought it specially; there hadn't been anything like that in the house. In the careful round script she had been taught at school so many years ago, she had written, "I hope the Lord will forgive me for this, but it is so hard and so long and I am tired. Now they have taken all the rest of my money and I would not have food the rest of the month, and I don't know what to do except this. I do not know if a minister would hold a service, but I would like one."

Sue blew her nose. "Here's the other one," said Maddox.

It was another sheet from the same tablet, the same careful script. It was headed, *Last Will and Testament*. "I have never made a will before and I hope this will be satisfactory. Someone told me once that in California a will all in your own handwriting is legal. There are no relatives to claim anything and all I own is my house. I would like to leave my house to the young lady from the police who was so very kind to me; her name is Mrs. Susan Maddox." Both the sheets were signed in a surprisingly steady hand, Constance Jean Eady.

Sue burst into tears again.

———◆———

A great wind got up in the night, and rattled windows and doors, tore down some trees and made sleep difficult. In yesterday's clear brilliance, the residents of sometimes smog-laden Los Angeles had been treated to a view of the back mountains, the great Sierra Madre range, glistening with new snow far down its flanks; the wind was very cold off those heights.

They generally set the alarm for seven, but it wasn't the alarm that woke Maddox. It was a persistent regularity of sound reaching down into the cocoon where he lay. Suddenly his conscious mind snapped on and he sat up, hearing the phone shrill again in the pitch-dark. He got out of bed and went to the living room. "Maddox."

"Bromfield, Sergeant." One of the lonely men who held down the desk in the lonely hours, taking the calls few or many, directing the squad cars prowling empty streets. "You're not going to believe this, but the Tansy boy's just turned up, and he's alive."

"Oh, Christ," said Maddox, and it was not a curse. "Where and how?"

"Corner of Hawthorne and La Brea. Don't cheer yet—from how I got it, it looks touch and go, but there was a pulse and they got him to the hospital fast. One of the squads spotted him in the headlights."

"What time is it?"

"Ten of six. It was about twenty minutes ago they called in. One thing they said, he was blue, and it looked as if he'd maybe been there most of the night. It got down to just above freezing. That might not help any. But I knew you'd want to hear."

"God, yes. Hold the good thoughts on it. Thanks." He could believe the temperature; he was freezing now. He heard Sue stirring, went in and told her about it, and turned on the heat all over the little house.

"It's an omen," said Sue, sitting up in bed and shivering. "We're due for some breaks. Did you ask if they'd called the parents?"

"Now, Susan," he said, "you've been an LAPD officer long enough to know that we always think of the citizens first."

◆

The Tansys, of course, were at the hospital when Maddox and Rodriguez landed there at eight-thirty. The doctor had already talked to them. He was a short, pudgy man named Holt. "I'm not handing out any guesses," he said. "The boy's had some rough treatment. He was bound and gagged, to start with, subjected to a beating or several beatings, burned with live cigarettes—at least that's what it looked like—and sexually abused. Then he was evidently lying in the street for some hours, and he's also suffering from exposure. I can't tell you when he might regain consciousness, or if there might be some brain damage." He shrugged. "There was one blow on the head, and head injuries are always unpredictable. At the best, he'll come out of it with no impairment at all."

"And be able to tell us something."

The doctor's eyes glittered coldly behind his glasses. "I would hope to God. Enough that you could nail this—psychopath and get him locked up. On the other hand, even if there's no physical damage, the psychological shock may have been so great that he simply won't remember."

"Hypnosis—" said Rodriguez. The doctor shook his head.

"I couldn't recommend it. Not for a child, if the psychological shock was that great. But that's speculating in advance. We'll just have to wait and see. And hope." He came out with them to the little alcove where the Tansys sat and waited.

"I don't need to tell you how we feel about this, Mrs. Tansy," said Maddox. "We're hoping he'll be all right just as much as you are."

"Oh, I prayed and prayed," she said in a muffled voice. "First to St. Anthony because he was lost—and now to the Blessed Mother because she knows how a mother—"

Her husband touched her arm. "Now, Helen, they don't want to—"

"Oh, no, Mr. Tansy," said the doctor. "Don't discount it. Prayer is a factor. It can be a big factor." He smiled. "I do a good bit of it myself, in the operating theater."

Gloria Considine and Ray Felton were in the same hospital, and so of course was George Ellis. Maddox and Rodriguez took blatant advantage of their special privileges and walked in on Ellis as he was eating breakfast. He hailed them enthusiastically. He was looking more like his usual ruddy robust self again. "When are they letting you out?" asked Rodriguez.

"Tomorrow, thank God. I'm going stir-crazy here, and damn what that doctor says, I'm all right. The damn shoulder's just stiff, is all."

"Adding insult to injury, if you ask me," said Maddox. "First you go roaring off helping out the Feds on what isn't our business at all, and then get shot up so you leave us shorthanded. Until some of those new recruits start tooling squads around and more men make plainclothes division, we need you, George. Wouldn't it be nice if headquarters sent us half a dozen new detectives?"

"Oh, you dreamer," said Rodriguez.

"I'll be back with you this week," said Ellis. "What's been going on?" They spent a while telling him, until a nurse chased them out.

Ray Felton was still on the critical list. Gloria Considine would be released today; she was sitting up in bed, very rational and anxious to answer questions. If she'd suffered any psychological shock —which she would have—she was coping with it.

"Any way I can help you," she said, brushing her hair back. "We were just sitting there on the couch talking when the doorbell rang. Well, three o'clock on Sunday afternoon—I opened the door. And he came right in, without saying a word—"

"Excuse me, Miss Considine, had you been outside within the previous couple of hours? Where he might have seen you?" Maddox, like D'Arcy, was thinking of those porno theaters down on the boulevard. Somebody stirred up, somebody looking at random.

"Why, yes—" She was surprised. "We'd been out in the front, looking at Ray's new car—but I didn't notice anybody around. He just came pushing in, and I said something, and Ray got up and asked what he wanted, and he just— I didn't believe it, you know these things happen but you never expect them to happen to *you*— he pulled out a knife, and Ray sort of grappled with him— I remember I tried to scream, but my throat seemed to just close up— They had an awful fight all over the living and dining room, Ray shouted just at first to call the police, but it was so fast, the next thing I knew he got hold of me, I couldn't see Ray at all and I was afraid—oh, I was so afraid he'd killed Ray, all the time he was—" She shuddered. "He never said a word the whole time."

"Can you describe him, Miss Considine?"

She nodded. "He was taller than Ray—Ray's five-ten. He was about six feet, and awfully strong—young, I guess maybe about twenty-five. He had dark brown hair and it was short, almost like an old-fashioned crew cut—you remember? He had kind of a broad face, without any expression on it at all—his eyes looked huge, all staring. I'm afraid I don't remember his clothes, a sort of beige shirt, I think."

"That's very good," said Maddox. "Do you think you'd recognize him if you saw a picture?" Automatically, of course, the same thought had hit both him and Rodriguez at once. A crew cut. Few young men these days flouted current fashion like that. But if that boy had just got out of prison somewhere, he might still be sporting the ultrashort haircut.

"Oh," she said. "Out of your records? I think so. I'd certainly like to try."

"Fine. We'll set it up. Whenever you feel like it."

They headed back for the office, and Rodriguez said, "Forget this damned list, and wait to see if the boy can give us something definite?"

"I think so. And hope those good deceased cops in heaven are smiling on us, César."

◆

About four o'clock that Monday afternoon Feinman went over to Micheltorena Street, by appointment, to talk to the Leamans again. The Leamans, their completely bare house being nonlivable, had removed temporarily to their daughter's home, but were back at the house today supervising the installation of a new door and new locks where the wholesale burglars had broken in. They had promised to deliver an itemized list of what had been stolen.

"I mean, I've heard of burglars," said Leaman, "taking all the valuables—but a whole house of furniture! A whole house!"

"Yes, I know," said Feinman. "And you're not the only ones."

"Well, I've made you up a list. Hope I remembered everything. At least we've got insurance, but when it might come through—" They were standing in the starkly bare living room; the carpenter was pounding lustily at the back door. The doorbell rang.

Leaman went to answer it automatically. "Hi, Mr. Leaman," said a cheerful young voice. "Say, I'm awful sorry to hear about your robbery. Mrs. Madden was telling me. I saw that moving truck here, and I thought you were gonna move, and I was sorry. You always pay right on time. It's four-eighty, like always."

"Sure, Ronny," said Leaman, and got out his wallet. The boy was about fourteen, sandy and freckled and round-faced. There was a bicycle at the curb; it had a burlap sack over the rear wheel stenciled *Herald-Examiner*.

"You saw the moving van?" asked Feinman.

"Yeah, like I said. The Leamans hadn't said anything about moving but—" Feinman showed him his badge and he said, "Oh, gee. Oh, gee, you're a cop?"

"What's your name, son?"

"Ronny Davidson."

"When did you see the van? Did you see anybody around it?"

"Oh, it was about three-thirty, I guess. I thought they'd got a wrong address, maybe. I'd been all up the block, I hit the Leamans last, delivering, and I saw that van drive up and park right in front when I was coming down that side of the block." Yes, thought Feinman, that was the van's third trip, to finish cleaning out the house completely.

"Was there a sign on the van?"

"Nope, didn't see any."

"Did you notice any men in the van?"

"Sure, that's why I figured they must have got the wrong address, the Leamans weren't moving. There was a guy got out just as I came up and threw the paper on the porch, and then he got right back in the van again."

"Oh," said Feinman. "Could you describe him?" This was, of course, grasping at straws.

"Sure," said Ronny. "He was a thin young black guy, and he had on a white jump suit, and it had on it *Zablowski's 76 Service.*"

TEN

"'Out of the mouths of babes and sucklings,'" said Maddox. "I will be damned."

"He hadn't realized that just a little detail like that might be a lead to them," said Feinman. "Thrilled to pieces when I said it could be."

It was after five, and getting on to the end of shift, but Maddox said, "So let's have a look." He consulted the phone book, and Zablowski's 76 Service Station was there big as life, out on Sunset nearly into West Hollywood. He got up. "Let's go talk to Mr. Zablowski."

It was dark when they got there, but the station lights were on. Maddox pulled up away from the pumps and they went looking, found a big, broad dark man bent over the engine of an old Ford sedan in the garage. "Mr. Zablowski?"

"That's me." He straightened up and looked at the badges in perplexity. "What in hell do the cops want with me?"

"Do you have an employee here, a young colored fellow?"

Zablowski wiped his hands on a towel, staring at them curiously. "Why, yeah, I do. Jay Walker. He spells me a few hours most days, why?"

"Do you have an address for him?"

"Has Jay done something? He seems like a nice enough guy." "Do you?"

"Well, I guess so. Somewhere. I got a phone number, I know." In the office, he rummaged, finally produced an address far out on Vermont. He was still standing there staring after them when they got back into the car.

"You feel like doing a little overtime, Joe?"

"To catch up to these boys, that's just what."

Maddox caught Sue just as she was leaving, and Feinman called his wife. They went down to The Grotto, and being off duty, had drinks before dinner. "Are we celebrating prematurely?" asked Feinman.

"I think we're due for some breaks."

If so, it wasn't immediately apparent. The address on Vermont was a barracks of a housing development, squalid and shabby even in the dark. They couldn't find a Walker among the mailboxes, and interrupted the superintendent at dinner to ask. "Oh, him; he lives in Forty-two B with Lila Mae Lincoln," he told them indifferently. They went up in an elevator that smelled of too many stinks to separate them.

And Jay Walker opened the door of Forty-two B to them: a tall, thin, very black man with a sharp nose and a bushy Afro hairdo. They looked at him, pleased, and showed him the badges, and he skittered back like a spooky horse. "What you want with me?"

"We think you were one of several men who burglarized a house on Micheltorena Street the other day," said Maddox. "Complete with moving van. At least you were seen there, in the van, and you're coming in to answer some questions. Now."

"Oh, my Lord God!" The exclamation was from the girl who'd just come up behind Walker, a thin black girl, perhaps twenty. "Now you see what it come to! I told you!"

"You shut up," said Walker. "I don't know what they're talkin' about."

He went on saying that, when he said anything at all. They might have to go the long way round here, get a search warrant for the place, look for the jump suit, find out about his known associates; but there was enough to hold him for twenty-four hours. They booked him into the Wilcox Street jail and went home.

The Tansy boy was still unconscious.

◆

Gloria Considine came in on Tuesday morning to look at mug shots, and D'Arcy took her downtown. He was feeling slightly more cheerful about his private life; he had a date set up with Joan Berry for Thursday night, and the end of the semester of her adult education course was coming up, and she wasn't sure that she'd enroll for the second one. She might be having some more free time.

Gloria pored over mug books for an interminable time, didn't pick out any photographs. When he suggested she might like to knock off, she said, "I want to help catch him if I can. I'm not tired, I don't mind. They say Ray's going to be all right eventually, but you know that man nearly killed him. Let me look some more."

◆

When Maddox and Feinman landed at the jail on Tuesday morning they found Lila Mae Lincoln there, sitting on the long bench at right angles to the desk, looking forlorn. She said, "You was the ones—last night. I come to see Jay, but they wouldn't let me in yet. I s'pose I better talk to you." They were all too pleased she wanted to. She trailed after them into one of the bare interrogation rooms and perched on the edge of the straight chair, holding her shabby black bag in both hands. She looked miserable. She wasn't a bad-looking girl, if too thin and shabbily dressed.

"I *told* him," she said. "We figured get married sometime, but he's outta work, only got that part-time job at the station, it don't pay much. I hafta pay the rent—I got steady work in the kitchen at a nursing home for old folks. This dude Jay knows, his name's Tony Ramirez, he says the place he works, they need another part-time guy, and it sounded good—only then it turned out to be thieving, and I *told* him get shut of it. Good money, he says, at least better, but I *told* him, I said You get outta that, you mess with something outside the law you gonna get burned soon or late, and then where are you? On the police books, and nobody give you a job. Now he's gonna find out." She took a breath and raised burning eyes to them. "But I'm not gonna see you take Jay for it and the rest of'em not get burned too."

"Good," said Maddox. "Do you know the rest of them?"

"Sure, their names. It's a place called Mundy's Secondhand Furniture and Antiques, on Western Avenue. Old man Mundy, he's the boss, and his two sons Bill and Ollie, and Tony Ramirez works there sometimes."

"And thanks very much," said Maddox. She just went on sitting there when they got up, holding the shabby bag, misery in her eyes.

"I *told* him," she said.

They put in an application for a search warrant; it would probably come through this afternoon. Meanwhile they took Rodriguez and went down to look at the place.

It was a triple store front, long unpainted, looking shabby and dirty. The sign over the door said *Thomas Mundy Secondhand and Antique Furniture.* There were crudely hand-lettered paper signs in the windows: BARGAINS—CHESTS $29.95—BEDS FROM $50—FINE SELECTION ANTIQUES.

They went in to a confusing mass of furniture stacked on all sides, crowding the big store up to a makeshift counter at the back, where a man sat on a stool working over a loose-leaf notebook. He hopped off the stool and came alertly to greet them. "What can I do for you, gents? Got a lot of good buys in right now." He was a tall, loose-limbed old man with a seamed brown face and a distinct New England accent.

"I would take a bet," said Maddox, "especially as you aren't paying out any overhead for stock these days." He brought out the badge.

Mundy's face went wooden. "I dunno what you mean."

"Oh, I think you do." Rodriguez and Feinman made for the rear door and came back with three men, two of them bearing a strong resemblance to Mundy, the third a rather handsome Latin type. "Just unloading the van," said Feinman. "I might guess, the tail end of the Leamans' belongings."

"Shortcut," said Maddox. "Pending that search warrant, Joe, let's get the Leamans down here to see if they can identify any of this."

"Dang cops," said Mundy. He went back and sat at the counter. Rodriguez rode herd on the other three, who just sat silent on an old couch at the back of the store. Feinman called the Leamans. Maddox looked around the place curiously. He didn't know much about antiques, but he noticed a walnut curio cabinet, intricately carved, against one wall, and not far from it an old rolltop desk. Mrs. Eady's?

The Leamans came, and excitedly wandered around, picking their furniture out of the hodgepodge. Some of it was still in the van behind the store. The Latin type suddenly burst out dramatically, "I have only done what I am told. How should I know they were stealing? Go and move furniture. How do I know he not buy?

I am no thief—" He went on until Rodriguez said something sharp and cold in Spanish, and he shut up, looking sullen.

"Well, that's quite enough for a charge," said Maddox. This was going to be the hell of a thing to sort out, and there would be a lot of red tape; fortunately, not so much for them as for the D.A.'s office. The Leamans were resigned to the fact that they might not get their furniture back right away.

They booked the Mundys and Tony Ramirez into jail, and took Thomas Mundy into an interrogation room. He just sat looking at them, a little furtively, from under woolly gray eyebrows like caterpillars. He just said, "Dang cops."

"Would you care to tell us how the bright idea occurred to you?" asked Maddox. Mundy just grunted. "Or would you be more interested in how we came to find out about you?"

The furtive eyes gleamed momentarily. "Danged if I see how anybody did."

Maddox told him. Mundy's knifelike mouth worked and his sallow cheeks suffused with a little color; he was, they suddenly realized, shaking with rage. "That dang stupid nigger! I shouldn't never've had no truck with him! I should've knew better! First he sticks me for that dang van, cost me big money, and then he gives the hull shebang away, just do a fool thing like that! Wearin' a name on his clothes! I should've knew he'd do some dang fool thing, stupid nigger. Give the hull show away."

"All right," said Feinman. "Now you've started, suppose you tell us all about it."

He was actually grinding his teeth. His face was wooden, but he was still filled with righteous wrath at the elementary stupidity which had given the game away, and his tongue was very slightly loosened.

"Dang truck," he said. "My old one died on me, and them things ain't cheap. That fool, he says furniture store up from the place he works was closing down, got a van for sale—cheap, he says, seven hundred bucks. Seven hundred! Better'n any other price I heard, I give him the money to get it. Dang thing just about runnin'—I'd took his word it was a good one. Not worth it. And the price you pay wholesale for stock, even unfinished stuff, it's sinful. Just sinful!"

"So you had the idea about how you could acquire stock without paying for it?" asked Feinman.

Mundy shot them a sly glance from under the eyebrows. "It's dog eat dog all the way, any kind of business. You got to keep an eye to the main chance."

"Just as a matter of curiosity," said Maddox, "when you started that project, just why the hell didn't you paint out Herschel's sign on the van?"

Mundy looked surprised at his ignorance. "D'you know what paint costs these days? Waste of good money. And then the dang thing lay down and died, not four months after I paid out that money—"

"That would be the day after you cleaned out that little house on Alexandria in Hollywood," said Maddox. Feinman sat forward where they faced Mundy across the little square table.

"I wondered about that," he said. "You were picking houses at random? Just neighborhoods where most people are away working, nobody likely to interfere? Why the hell did you—or your boys—pick that place? Or was it at random?"

Mundy licked his narrow lips. After a dragging moment he said reluctantly, in a surly tone, "I buy old silver pieces. Run an ad couple times a month, see what it brings in. That old lady, she called me about last August, about sellin' some silver, and I went up to look at it. She had some good antique pieces—I know somethin' about antiques. Just remembered it one day, and told the boys to hit there."

"And it was just unlucky the old lady happened to come home while they were busy," said Feinman. Mundy only growled.

Maddox sighed. The hell of a thing to sort out, trying to trace all the furniture, go over any account books he kept. It might be a rather complicated trial. "That walnut curio cabinet, was it part of the loot from that place?" Mundy shrugged and nodded. And what in the end would happen to the store and its contents was anybody's guess. But Maddox thought if he possibly could, he'd like to get hold of that curio cabinet for Sue; it was a handsome piece of furniture and she'd like having it.

They had contacted the other victims, asked them to come in this afternoon and try to identify anything still in the store. Feinman could sit on that.

They tried to get something to add up to statements from the other three, but even Ramirez had shut up and wasn't saying anything.

Maddox went back to the station, and before starting to write an initial report, called the hospital. The Tansy boy was still unconscious, but the doctor thought he was showing signs of coming out of it; the police would be kept informed.

They were now back to looking for the heisters, and had a new one: he'd held up a bar last night and taken a shot at the bartender for being a little slow in handing over. The bartender and a couple of customers had come in that morning to make statements; they had given a good description, and there was now a new list of likely men to go out and find, haul in to question.

Rowan brought one of them in about three o'clock, and Maddox joined him in the questioning; they didn't get anything conclusive and let him go. When Maddox came back to the office, Sue had gone out somewhere. Daisy, of course, was downtown in court at the Telfer trial; nobody else was in.

D'Arcy came back just then and said that Considine girl was a glutton for punishment. "She must have looked at every mug shot we've got in the books, but she didn't make any. I am beat. Sitting around like that's more tiring than all the legwork."

Sue bustled in and said, "Well, I don't know that we're in miles of catching up to him, Ivor, but the jewelry's turned up. A pawnbroker called a while ago and reported it, and I went over to see. The store's on Cahuenga, and he says he's pretty sure it was among some stuff he took in on Friday—he'd just looked over the latest hot list today. It's ours, all right—Dad's watch, and Mother's ring, and some costume stuff of Mother's."

"Did he give any description? Receipt get signed with any useful name?"

"After a fashion," said Sue. She produced a rather smudged carbon of a receipt. "The pawnbroker didn't remember anything about him. But of course he got him to sign the receipt. It says, as nearly as I can make out, H. Brackett, Eveningside Drive. Which is a new one on me. I thought—"

"Um, yes," said Maddox. He reached for the County Guide and thumbed through it. "An Eveningside Drive—the names these planners dream up for streets—in both Saugus and West Covina,

and somehow I doubt that our amateur burglar came all that way
to commit burglary and hock the loot. On the other hand, there is
a Morningside Court some five blocks from your mother's house.
Just for fun, let's see what might be in the phone book." He
looked, and at an address on Morningside Court was listed a
C. H. Brackett. "Yes," said Maddox. "They are mostly stupid to
start with, or on dope so often they get that way."

"The great sleuth," said Sue, but she looked excited. "Come
on, let's go look."

They took her car, in case they were lucky enough to be bringing him back with them.

It was a dreary little street with several old four-family places
dating from the twenties, flat-roofed, most of them needing paint.
The address was one of those; the name Brackett on the mailboxes indicated the left-hand lower unit. Maddox pushed the bell.
The door opened and a woman faced them, a short plump woman
with blonde hair fading to gray and a tired lined face. "Yes?" She
looked at the badge in Maddox's hand. "Oh," she said, and one
work-worn hand went to her mouth. "What do you want?"

"Mrs. Brackett?"

"Yes, I'm Caroline Brackett. I don't—"

"Do you live here alone?"

"Why, no—my son—my son Howie lives here. What do you
want with us?"

"Is he here now? We'd like to see him."

"What *for?* We're respectable people, I'm not on welfare, I
work at the London Grill—I always brought Howie up right, he—"

"If he's here we'd like to see him."

She said faintly, "He's—in his room—doing his homework or
something." She called, and stepped back; they took it as a tacit
invitation to go in. The living room was dark, unwelcoming, with
furniture sitting stiffly in corners, and too frilly ruffled drapes at
the one window.

He came into the room from the hall, and Maddox heard Sue
draw in a breath. He was a big, awkward lump of a boy, immature
in the face, probably seventeen or eighteen, but a hulk at least six
feet, two hundred pounds. He had long, stringy blond hair to his
shoulders. He stared at them, and at his mother. "Howie, he's a
policeman," she said. "He wants to talk to you."

Howie just looked stupefied, and then scared. "There are at least a couple of people," said Maddox, "who can identify you as the burglar who robbed and attacked them. Have you got anything to say, Howie?"

"Howie!" she shrieked. "Oh, no, he'd never do such a thing—Howie, you never—"

He just stood. He gave Maddox a sickly smile. Sue went to Mrs. Brackett to try and quiet her. "I—" he said. "I—didn't think anybody'd—ever find out. How—did you—find out?"

"Because like most crooks, you are stupid," said Maddox coldly. "Get a coat—we're taking you in."

Mrs. Brackett sat up on the chair where she'd sunk down moaning, and for a moment there was a kind of dignity in her tired face. "Why did you have to do this to me? Why?" she cried. "I tried so hard, bring you up decent—after your father walked out. I scrimped and saved and worked— Why did you do this to me?"

"Oh, Ma," he said. "Oh, gee, Ma. You got to have bread, take girls out—movies cost so much—you got to *have* things—and the lousy five bucks a week you give me—it wasn't enough, that's all. I never thought anybody'd know."

"There'll be another charge," said Maddox, "than burglary, you know. In at least two instances you committed assault on the householders. In one case, a serious assault. I suppose it never entered your mind that you might have killed somebody, as big as you are."

Bewilderment filled Howie's eyes. "Me?" he said. "Kill somebody?"

"Oh, get your coat. You're going to jail."

"It was all I could afford," said Mrs. Brackett dully. "He could've got a job after school, but he had to go out for the football practice."

The frustrating thing was, as it turned out, Howie was only seventeen, and of course it was his first count. The chances were that the court would put him on probation, no time at all. And the next time Howie wanted something without paying for it, he'd be all the surer he could get away with it. Someday he might end up killing somebody, quite without intention.

———◆———

On Wednesday morning the night-watch report listed another heist, and by the description it was the same boy who had taken a shot at the bartender. There'd also been another report of the nut firing at a couple in a parked car. Maddox considered ways and means to trap that one; one of these nights *he* was going to end up killing somebody.

He was frowning over that when a call came through, and Rodriguez took it. He slammed the phone down and said tersely, "The hospital. They think the Tansy boy's coming to."

They shot up there fast. In the corridor outside the room, Dr. Holt was waiting for them. He said, "Now, I understand you're very concerned to hear what he might say—if he's rational, seems to be making sense. But my first concern has to be for the boy. I don't want him confused with a lot of people around. All his reflexes are normal, and I've every hope that he'll recover quite well. His mother is in there with him and I want her to be the first person he sees."

"Yes, Doctor."

"You just keep out of the way."

They went in. Mrs. Tansy was sitting close up by the head of the bed, a nurse at the other side. The slight form of the boy, under the bedclothes, was moving restlessly; his head went from side to side, his arms twitched. His mother bent closer. "Sherman," she said quietly. And then, "Sherm, it's Mom. Can you hear me, Sherm?"

He quieted, and then his eyelids fluttered and he murmured, "Mom?"

"Yes, darling, I'm here. Everything's all right and you're safe. Everything's all right." The tears were running down her cheeks, but she kept her voice steady and reassuring. She had his hand in both hers, tightly.

He gave a long sigh. "Oh, Mom," he said. "Are we home?"

"No, darling, you're in a hospital. But you'll be going home soon."

He drew a long breath, and opened his eyes, and sought out her face above him. "Oh, Mom," he said, "don't cry."

"It's just because you're safe, Sherm. We thought you were lost, but everything's all right now."

He looked up at her a long moment. "Mom," he whispered, "it wasn't Rog Brent. It wasn't."

"Who, Sherm?"

"I thought it was—he looked just like him—and he said he was. But he wasn't. We went to the park where there wasn't anybody and he tied me up and put handkerchiefs in my mouth and I was on the floor of the car. Rog Brent wouldn't do that. And he took me—he took me to the library—"

She looked at the doctor a little wildly, but he gestured her to be quiet.

"I know it was the library, the one on Santa Monica where we go— I was trying to get loose, I'd got partly up on the seat and I saw the front—and then—and then he put me inside a great big cloth bag and took me in there— I *smelled* the library, all the books—"

"Oh, Sherm."

"I did! And he—and he— *Rog Brent*'d never do awful things like that—" The boy began to sob weakly, and the doctor went up to him.

Rodriguez tugged Maddox's arm, and they went out to the hall. "*¡Válgame Dios!*" said Rodriguez. He was looking awed.

"Who," asked Maddox, "is Rog Brent? It seems to ring a faint bell, but—"

"Oh, you Philistine!" said Rodriguez. "I know you're not sports-minded. He's the Dodgers' star pitcher, the latest team hero. My God, Ivor, what a gimmick! What a— Don't you see it? Well, it's not Brent, of course—for one thing, I don't think the team's here, they're in spring training somewhere—but what that says, this *hombre* looks like him. A ringer. And for God's sake, ever since he pulled the team out of a hole with his brilliant pitching last season, and he was plastered all over the sports pages then—my God, any baseball fan knows Rog Brent! Any boy in the greater Los Angeles area who's a baseball fan—and that's ninety-five percent of all little boys—knows the great Rog Brent!"

"What's he look like?" asked Maddox. They were on the way back to the elevator.

"Kind of a distinctive face, come to think. You wouldn't forget it—or miss it. He's big, he has a big nose and a long jaw, you could call it a horseface, with the kind of thick eyebrows that go straight across the bridge of his nose. My God, what a fantastic— If he is a ringer for Brent, Ivor, it's no wonder about the kids. He could crook his finger and any kid around here would run for him."

"And that's extremely interesting, all right," said Maddox, "but even more so is the library."

"Oh, yes," said Rodriguez. "The other half of it. The library— on a Sunday."

It was an old library, given a new face-lift recently but still an old building, with a flight of steep steps to the front door. They went in and caused a little flurry among the lady librarians, cops asking for the boss. The head librarian was a suitably scholarly-looking man named Nichols. He looked in astonishment at police invading his quiet office.

"What we'd like to know," said Maddox, "is just who possesses keys to this building."

Nichols adjusted his glasses. "Well, I do, of course. The two senior librarians, Mrs. Wengel and Miss Nugent. And our mainte-nance man. There is a spare set of keys in case any should get misplaced, and I keep those at home. May I ask—"

"The maintenance man," said Rodriguez and Maddox together, and Maddox went on, "What's his name?"

"Er—Arnold Lee."

"Has he worked here long?"

"Why, no—only a matter of a couple of months. The man we'd had for years, old Charlie Hunter, had a stroke—it was a shame, he'd been looking forward to retirement—quite helpless, I'm afraid, paralyzed and in a nursing home. But it made things difficult—of course it is a city job, and the city's never in any hurry to get things done, while we somewhat desperately needed— Lee was taken on, let me see, in November."

"Is he here now?"

"As a matter of fact, he called in and said he was ill. I don't—"

"Do you have an address for him?"

"Why, yes, but what—"

Before they left the library, however, they went down to the basement, where Nichols said the maintenance man had a room of his own, for his lunch and coffee breaks. It was a little cubbyhole of a place, but there was a chair, a table, a folding cot. They looked around, but didn't spot anything suggestive; quite possibly the lab would.

The address was an old apartment building on Virgil, and Lee's apartment was on the ground floor at the rear, twenty feet from the row of garages. That would have been very convenient. They went down the dark hall, and Maddox rapped sharply at the door. Nothing happened, and he tried it; it was unlocked. They went into a barely furnished living room and stood for a moment in silence, taking in a tableau almost too graphic.

The man on the couch in front of the window looked at least halfway drunk; he turned peevishly at the sound of the door opening. There was an empty wine bottle on the floor beside the couch and a half-full one beside it. There was a stack of magazines littering the floor all around the couch, and they all appeared to be hardcore pornography from the visible covers. Lying across a chair in another corner of the room was a large white canvas duffel bag.

"Who're you?" asked the man, turning on the couch to look at them blearily. He didn't seem much interested.

And Rodriguez said, "A ringer. By God, he's the dead image of Rog Brent."

The man squinted up, attracted by the name. "Yeah," he said. "'S right. Funniest damn thing—never been here b'fore, but I land here—wherever I go, kids—people— The little kids all crazy over me." He giggled. "Easy," he said. "So easy."

Maddox went into the bedroom, and he couldn't pry without a warrant, but he didn't have to. There on top of the dresser, precisely folded—the only neat thing in the place—were the missing clothes, the pants Harold Frost and Freddy Noonan had been wearing, the underclothes from Justin Lockwood. Funny, he hadn't kept any of Sherman Tansy's. Had he thought he'd killed Sherman? These men had quirks: maybe because he had taken Sherman to the library instead of bringing him here?

But it was quite enough. They couldn't talk to him officially while he was drunk. Rodriguez called up a squad car and the lab. They took him down to jail; he was still giggling and staring into space alternately. They printed him and booked him in.

Then they handed his prints to NCIC, and within ten minutes

got back some information. Maddox said this and that, looking at it. "Why cops get ulcers!" he said savagely.

The man they had just booked in for three sadistic sex killings and an attempted fourth was Arnold Lee Bates, twenty-nine, a native of Trenton, New Jersey. His trail started there, with counts of indecent exposure, child molestation; he had had charges in Philadelphia, New York, Pittsburgh—child molestation, forcible rape of male juvenile, sexual assault, enticement of minors. He had been charged with homicide twice, both sex killings of young boys, in Pittsburgh and Philadelphia. The first time he was adjudged insane and stashed away for two years, when the doctors had let him loose to do it again. The second time he got a ten-to-twenty and was paroled in four years. He had, in fact, got off parole four months ago in New Jersey, and had evidently made a beeline for a new stamping ground. Where he had discovered that he had a built-in spell to cast: the perfect gimmick for attracting small boys.

He had worked at libraries before, as a maintenance man.

"There's been some publicity on this," said Rodriguez, his mouth cynical. "Let's hope a few reporters ask the question loud and clear—why the hell was he loose?"

But at least they had him. For the time being. And neither of them would guess what the California courts might do with him. Another spell in the nuthouse, or a real sentence, and in either case maybe he'd be loose again within five years.

But that wasn't part of their job.

◆

At about five o'clock that afternoon, while Maddox was just finishing a rather lengthy final report on it for the D.A., a woman came into the office and marched up to him—he was the only one in—and said, "I'm told you want to see me. No notion why, but good citizen me, here I am. Bertha Erhardt."

"Oh," said Maddox. "Oh, yes, we've been trying to contact you, Mrs. Erhardt."

"So the girls in my salon said. I've been on a little vacation. Couldn't seem to shake the flu I had last month, I went over to Vegas a few days to take a rest." She didn't look as if there was ever anything wrong with her; she was a sturdy woman about thirty, with a round snub-nosed face, cheerful hazel eyes, a lot of very golden hair in a complicated style. She had on a smart black pantsuit. "Why were you looking for me, anyway? I been violating some new damn-fool Federal law?"

"Nothing like that," said Maddox, and told her about Erhardt. She stared at him, fascinated, and then she let out a lusty guffaw that nearly bounced the new typewriters off the new desks. "A hit man? Jim? That useless little twerp looking for a hit man to get *me*— Oh, my! Oh, my heavens above! That's the funniest thing I've heard in all my life!"

He had really made Bertha's day; when she went out she was still shaking with laughter.

◆

Ellis came back on Thursday, and they were glad to have him. There was a tangle of paperwork to get through on the Mundy case; people were still coming to the store looking for their furniture. They hadn't caught up to the heister yet. Sue had taken the day off to get her mother home from the hospital.

Gloria Considine came in that morning for a session with an artist and the Identikit, to try to get a good composite sketch of the rapist.

Feinman was at the furniture store, Rodriguez and Dabney out hunting the heister, and Rowan had just come in with a possible suspect when a sheriff's deputy called in. He had just spotted Jerome Simms' plate number in the lot of a restaurant in West Hollywood; did Hollywood want him to stake it awhile, or would they come get him? Maddox asked him to stake it out.

He and Rowan had just finished talking to the suspect, who had a tentative alibi, when the deputy came in with Simms and a pretty dark girl who was fighting-mad.

"Look, I don't know what you think you're doing, arresting perfectly innocent citizens—wanted for questioning, what does that mean?— Just having lunch at a respectable restaurant, and this big bully—"

"Now take it easy—is it Mrs. Simms?"

"Yes, it is Mrs. Simms! And just what this is all *about*—"

Maddox said, "Well, we have to talk to your husband. I'm sorry, but it's probably going to be a homicide charge. He's been definitely identified by eyewitness evidence. We'll want your current address, please."

"*Hom*— What on earth do you mean?" Her voice was suddenly pleading. Simms just stood there, a rather weakly handsome young man looking thoroughly miserable.

"You didn't know," said Maddox, "that he has a long record of robbery, and robbery with violence?"

She sat down very suddenly in Rodriguez' desk chair. "You mean *he's a crook?*"

Simms looked ready to cry. "Oh, Ella," he said.

Maddox was sorry for the girl. He managed to get an address out of her: an apartment on Hoover. Later on they got a search warrant for it, and under Simms' underclothes found a Smith and Wesson .32, which the lab would pinpoint as the gun which had killed Mapps.

It looked as if the honeymoon was over for young Mr. and Mrs. Simms.

◆

Alan Hancock looked at the single sheet of notepaper and said, "Well, you know, I think it's quite valid. It's perfectly true that a holograph will is legal in this state. More to the point"—he smiled somewhat cynically—"there aren't any relatives to enter claims, and I take it the property isn't worth much. The state isn't going to poke its nose in looking for technicalities to upset a homemade will unless there's loot to be had."

He looked at Sue and Maddox. "Look here," he said. "If you like, I'll shepherd it through for you. Matter of applying to probate court and paying a little bit of inheritance tax to the state. There shouldn't be any difficulty. It'll take a month or so."

◆

Mr. Parrott looked at the little house and said, "Thirty thousand."

"What?" said Sue and Maddox together.

"Oh, easy. The lot," said Parrott. "The house is nothing, of course. But it's downtown residential Hollywood. The lot's worth thirty—I might even get you thirty-five for it."

"Well, I'll be damned," said Maddox. "Though I should have known—all the new apartments going up."

"That's right. The lot's about fifty by a hundred and forty—you'd get twenty units on it easy, garages underneath. Little gold mine. We can ask thirty-eight five, and come down," said Parrott.

"You," said Maddox, "cast your bread on the waters, my love."

"I didn't mean to really," said Sue. There were tears in her eyes again.

"What about that place in Verdugo Woodlands?" asked Parrott.

"Well, you might offer them eighty-seven five," said Maddox. Parrott nodded. "Got a notion they'll take it. I'll advise'em to. They'll never get any better offer."

◆

Maddox hadn't been here before; he looked at the big two-story stucco house perched on the hillside with interest. Newly aware of real estate prices, he thought, At least a hundred and fifty thousand.

The door swung open and Herbert Sexton faced him. "I'll take just ten minutes of your time," said Maddox. Sexton stepped back silently, and Maddox went into a tiled entry hall, a big rectangular living room beyond, expensively furnished. He noticed the bar at the far end, the specially made unusual bar.

"You're staying on here?" he asked.

"Do sit down, Sergeant," said Sexton courteously. He looked just as polished, exuding the same air of frank charm, but he looked subtly older. He was rather carelessly dressed in old slacks, an open-necked shirt, a gray cardigan. "No. The house was left jointly to Louise's daughters, which was only fair. They would resent—after all, their old family home. I'll be moving on shortly. Probably north."

"To your old stamping grounds," said Maddox. "Where you arrange all your profitable land deals—when you're not being haled into court for fraud and misrepresentation."

Sexton faced him without a tremor. "Oh, you've learned about that. Business—" He shrugged. "There's jealousy and bitter feelings, unfortunately. Can I offer you a drink, Sergeant?"

"No, thanks. I just dropped by to tell you that we know you're getting away with it, Sexton. The police are usually a little smarter than the average citizen gives us credit for. You set up that accident, but there's just not quite enough evidence to nail you for it. I doubt very much that you planned to kill her"—Sexton's mouth twitched once—"but after she was dead, you covered it with the accident. Just don't think you were smart enough that we don't know it."

Sexton said remotely, "I really can't help what you might think, you know. Nor am I interested."

"I just thought I'd tell you," said Maddox evenly. "There'll be eyes on you, Sexton. If this has given you any, um, ideas for the future. We can make some pretty accurate guesses about that accident. You're just lucky that it'd be a waste of taxpayers' money to bring a charge." He hadn't sat down; he turned to the door. "Just watch yourself, Sexton."

Sexton gave him a sober look and shut the door without saying anything.

Maddox went down the narrow steep steps to the road and opened the door of the Maserati. It was just dark, and before him down the hill was spread the panorama of his town: the million brilliant colored lights spreading out in a glorious fan. The city at night, from this remote distance, looked clean and clear and beautiful. Only cops really knew the uglinesses underneath.

They hadn't caught up to the heister yet; Cooper was still finding Xeroxed dollars; the sketch of the rapist was being circulated. And there would be more new calls going down, tonight and tomorrow, in the jungle which was the city, on the endless job, and on and on.

He inhaled the cold night air. Aside from that, as far as his private life went—he got into the car and started the engine—everything was copacetic.